"If you've come to kill me, you'll have to use a gun."

When the full impact of the man's statement registered, Sara didn't know whether to laugh or run from the room. "What a horrible thing to say," she commented.

His ancient office chair squeaked as he slowly turned to face her. "Not to someone creeping around my house, it isn't."

"I wasn't creeping," Sara responded. "What would be the point of creeping after riding in that boat with the earsplitting motor? Don't tell me you didn't hear us arrive?"

"Of course I heard Winkelman's boat. I just figured Winkie had forgotten the toilet paper or something and was dropping it off. I sure never thought he was leaving behind a snooping female."

Her eyebrows shot up. "So now I'm creeping *and* snooping?"

He raised his hands as if he was stating the obvious. "Look," he said. "You came into *my* place without so much as a hoot or a holler and tiptoed up to *my* room like a typical nosy woman."

"Let's get one thing straight. This is *my* place and I'll walk around in it any way I please!"

That seemed to get him. His eyes registered the shock of bad news, then narrowed with irritation.

Sara couldn't help noticing that those eyes were a startling shade of gray.

Dear Reader,

I've spent most of my life fixing things. As a teacher,
I strove to improve young minds. When I became a
licensed auctioneer, and my husband and I bought an
auction house, my penchant for mending and refreshing
became more tangible. I polished silver until it gleamed,
and viewed every old piece of furniture and flea-market
find as a potential heirloom.

It was only natural that the heroine of my first contemporary
novel would be a fixer, too. But when Sara Crawford inherits
a run-down inn and a neglected vineyard on a Lake Erie
island and resolves to renovate, she doesn't know she'll
have to fix the island's four inhabitants, as well.

I hope you enjoy sharing Sara's determined and sometimes
humorous efforts to bring joy and purpose back to the lives
of the men of Thorne Island. And when her persistence
clashes with one sexy, stubborn man with a secret, she
learns that her own priorities could use a little revamping
themselves.

I'd love to hear from you. E-mail me at cynthoma@aol.com.
Visit my Web site at www.cynthiathomason.com, or write
me at P.O. Box 550068, Fort Lauderdale, Florida 33355.

Cynthia Thomason

The Men of Thorne Island
Cynthia Thomason

HARLEQUIN®

TORONTO • NEW YORK • LONDON
AMSTERDAM • PARIS • SYDNEY • HAMBURG
STOCKHOLM • ATHENS • TOKYO • MILAN • MADRID
PRAGUE • WARSAW • BUDAPEST • AUCKLAND

ISBN 0-373-71120-4

THE MEN OF THORNE ISLAND

Copyright © 2003 by Cynthia Thomason.

This edition published by arrangement with Harlequin Books S.A.

® and TM are trademarks of the publisher. Trademarks indicated with
® are registered in the United States Patent and Trademark Office, the
Canadian Trade Marks Office and in other countries.

Visit us at www.eHarlequin.com

Printed in U.S.A.

CHAPTER ONE

SARA CRAWFORD entered her office at precisely eight-thirty on Monday morning, walked halfway across the plum-colored carpet and stopped dead. "Whatever that is, it can't be good," she muttered. "Especially this close to tax deadline." The red-and-white Federal Express envelope on top of her desk had all the appeal of a hurricane warning flag on a Fort Lauderdale beach.

Tossing her purse and briefcase on a chair, she headed for the chrome credenza lining one wall. Before she could even think about tackling the contents of the package, she needed to deal with the coffee machine.

A crusty brown stain in the bottom of the glass pot did more to irritate her than her assistant being late again. Sara carried the pot into her bathroom, dribbled a few drops of detergent over the burned-on mess and filled the pot with steaming hot water.

Then she sat at her desk and picked up the cardboard envelope addressed to Sara Crawford, CPA. It wasn't particularly thick, so maybe it didn't contain a late-filing client's tax records. Nor was the return address familiar: Herbert Adams, Attorney, Cleveland, Ohio. Puzzled but relieved, she reached for her letter opener.

"Oh, hell! Look at the time."

Candy Applebaum's oath came from the reception room just before the administrative assistant stuck her head in Sara's office. Her red hair was piled on top of her head, secured by a bright orange elastic band that did nothing to prevent over-moussed strands from sticking out in all directions. "I'm so sorry I'm late, Sara," Candy said. "I almost made it on time, except I had one catastrophe after another this morning. My cat climbed on the table and swatted at the birdcage. The feed tray fell out of the rungs and all the bird seed went everywhere, and I had to…"

Sara smiled. "It's all right, Candy. I just got here myself."

Candy glanced at the credenza and grimaced. "I did it again, didn't I? Forgot to turn off the coffeepot. Was it really gross?"

"Well, it—"

"No problem. I'll take care of it." Candy headed for the bathroom, but stopped at Sara's desk and dropped a crumpled sack onto the cluttered surface. "Before I forget, this just came for you. Mr. Papalardo delivered it personally." She sighed as she went into the bathroom. "He's the sweetest man."

Sara set down the FedEx envelope and stared in horror at the brown paper bag. He'd done it again. After she'd warned him repeatedly, he pulled the same trick every year. She could just picture the world's "sweetest man" waiting on the sidewalk until she'd entered the building and then slinking inside. The security guard would greet him cheerfully. The janitor would wave hello. After all, everyone loved Tony Papalardo.

A dull ache centered itself behind Sara's eyes. She picked up the bag and turned it over, foolishly hoping it would be different this year. It wasn't. Bundles of paper loosely bound with rubber bands and paper clips scattered onto her desktop. Some scraps were actually identified with official Pappy's Pizzeria stationery. Most of them were barely legible receipts smudged with tomato sauce or memos scratched on chianti-stained napkins. Sara put her head between her hands.

"Something wrong, Sara?"

A rhetorical question. "Candy, do you think Mr. Papalardo has any idea that he's not my only client and today is April twelfth? Only three days to the deadline."

Glancing over her shoulder at the mess on Sara's desk, Candy said, "Oh, not again. Don't worry. I'll help you."

"Thanks." Sara glanced toward a pewter mirror across the room. She could almost visualize herself tugging every pin from her French twist and pulling out each strand of blond hair by the root. But she didn't have time. Instead, she picked up Tony Papalardo's paper bag and crushed it in her hands. "I'm going on vacation with my friends in five days, Candy," she said. "Nothing is going to stop me from getting on that plane to Aruba. I'm really leaving."

Candy grinned with delight. "Well, of course you are, Sara. And you'll have a wonderful time. Isn't that new guy you've been dating part of the group?"

Sara answered with caution, knowing where the question was leading. Candy was always trying to secure a happily-ever-after for her boss. "Yes, Donald is going, but don't jump to conclusions. We've only had four dates."

"Okay, but when you two stroll along those moonlit beaches, who knows what will happen?"

Sara shook her head and laughed. "You're incorrigible."

The phone rang in the outer office, and Candy scurried to answer it while Sara picked through the pile of pizzeria flotsam. She was interrupted when her intercom buzzed. "Yes, Candy."

"It's for you, Sara. A Mr. Herbert Adams from Cleveland. He said you'd be expecting his call."

Cleveland? Of course, the envelope. Sara reached for the FedEx package with one hand and grabbed the phone with the other. "Hello, Mr. Adams? This is Sara Crawford. I'm sorry. I haven't had a chance to open what you sent. I have it right here, though."

The voice on the other end was crisp and competent. "Miss Crawford, I was Millicent Thorne's attorney."

It took a moment for the name to register, but when it did, Sara smiled. She hadn't seen her mother's Aunt Millie for fifteen years, since the summer she'd turned fourteen—the summer her mother died. But she remembered the disciplined woman with her sensible shoes and pearl-buttoned cardigan sweaters. "Of course," she said. "How is Aunt Millie?"

There was a pause. "You don't know?"

"Know what?"

"Miss Thorne passed away five days ago."

Sara had only seen Millicent Thorne a half-dozen times in her life. Millie traveled a great deal, and Sara had been busy with school activities. Still, the news of her death sent a wave of sadness through her. Mr. Adams, a stranger, called to tell her that a member of her family had died, a woman she barely knew. There ought to be a sin covering this kind of situation. The sin of missed opportunities because at this moment Sara did indeed feel as if she'd let some part of her life slip away, and there was no way to get it back. "I'm sorry. I didn't know."

"I'm aware that you and Miss Thorne were never close."

"How did she die, Mr. Adams?"

"Peacefully in her sleep, and she wanted for nothing. Your aunt lived comfortably, thanks to a lawsuit she won a few years ago. Her last years were spent in relative luxury."

"I'm glad of that, at least."

"She had a sizable estate," Mr. Adams said, "and a will that clearly stipulated her wishes. She had a good many friends and helpful neighbors, whom she remembered in her will. And she remembered you, Miss Crawford."

"Me? Why me? I hardly knew her." Sara's headache intensified. "I can't accept an inheritance, Mr. Adams. If it's money, perhaps you could arrange for one of Miss Thorne's charities—"

"It's not money, Miss Crawford. It's Thorne-family property, and Miss Thorne very definitely wanted you to have it. She said she remembered you as a levelheaded girl. She thought you could manage it quite well."

Property? What did Sara know about managing property? Ever since she'd left her father's cozy bungalow in Brewster Falls, Ohio, she'd lived in college dormitories and rentals until settling a couple of years ago on the sixth floor of a Fort Lauderdale condominium. She'd given up fireplaces and front porches for the efficiency of a one-bedroom dwelling. She didn't have time to handle more than a few hundred square feet of ceramic tile. "Where is this property, Mr. Adams?" she asked.

"Open the envelope and see for yourself."

"Oh, of course." She cradled the phone between her cheek and shoulder and cut through the envelope flap. After removing the contents, she pushed aside a standard legal-looking document and reached for a colorful brochure. "Own a Piece of Paradise," was written across the top. There was a photograph of a lush green oblong of land in the center of a field of blue water. Underneath it said, "Beautiful, unspoiled Thorne Island."

"Thorne Island?" Sara said into the phone. "I've inherited an island?"

"Indeed you have, Miss Crawford. An island about five miles off the coast of Sandusky, Ohio, in Lake Erie."

Sara's jaw dropped. She grabbed the phone before it slipped from her shoulder. "I can't believe this, Mr. Adams. An island! I lived in Ohio most of my life, yet I've never heard of this place. The Bass Islands, yes. The resorts such as Put-in-Bay, of course. But Thorne Island? Where is it exactly?"

"Less than a mile from Put-in-Bay. The island played a role in the Battle of Lake Erie. I'm told Commodore Perry used it as a lookout. It's a small property, only forty acres total, but if the pictures in the brochure are any indication, it's quite lovely."

Sara opened the brochure. A quiver of delight replaced the shock as she gazed at the glossy photos of Thorne Island, *her* island. One picture showed a small harbor with a narrow dock jutting into the lake. Another was of a charming Colonial-style cottage surrounded by a picket fence. A wooden sign over a gate read Cozy Cove Inn.

The rest of the brochure was sales propaganda written by the Golden Isles Development Corporation. It consisted of glowing reports of the island's natural beauty, maps and details of how to reach it, various plots for sale and phone numbers of the development-company personnel.

"When was this brochure written, Mr. Adams?" Sara asked. "How long has the island been developed?"

"Actually it never was. I doubt there's been any change there since the original few buildings were constructed over a hundred years ago. I mentioned a lawsuit a few minutes ago. It was a class-action suit filed by owners of various Great Lakes island properties against the Golden Isles Development Corporation. Company executives purchased several islands under fraudulent circumstances. The corporation was exposed in the *Cleveland Plain Dealer* a number of years ago. Miss Thorne and her cosuitors reaped an impressive financial award in the judgment. And the chief executives of the corporation are, to my knowledge, still cooling their heels in jail."

"Wow. So does anyone live on the island now?"

"There were a few residents, people who paid rent to Miss Thorne, although no rental income has been deposited into Miss Thorne's account recently. I haven't kept up with the current population of the island. I found the brochure in Miss Thorne's papers and included it in your package so you would have some idea of the property."

"Do you know more about the island's history, Mr. Adams?"

"Miss Thorne once told me it was discovered by a missionary on an expedition paid for by the king of France. The island was originally called Bertrand Island after the missionary. Your aunt changed the name a few years before she died."

Sara couldn't help herself. She was falling in love with the old missionary's discovery. The peace and tranquillity of the island beckoned her like an oasis in the desert. Suddenly she knew she wouldn't be going to Aruba in five days, after all.

"I'll arrange to fly into Cleveland on Saturday," she said, rifling through the papers on her desk and finding the deed to her property. "Is there any reason I should see you before I go to the island?"

"Well, there is the matter of property taxes owed at the present time. I'd be glad to handle that for you if you like."

Property taxes? "How much is due?"

"I'm afraid Miss Thorne let this matter slide. With penalties and interest, there is a current balance of thirty-eight hundred dollars. Is that a problem?"

Thirty-eight hundred dollars! Sara pictured a huge wedge being lifted from the pie that was her savings account. Still, taxes had to be paid or penalties would escalate rapidly. And surely she would make up the deficit with the rental income. "No, it's not a problem, Mr. Adams. I'll send you a check."

"Very well, then. Enjoy your visit to your island, Miss Crawford, and good luck."

Sara hung up and buzzed her assistant. "Candy, please change my flight reservations. Arrange for an open-ended ticket to Cleveland for April seventeenth."

"Cleveland? You're going to Cleveland now?"

"That's right."

Predictably adaptable, Candy relinquished moonlit beaches and embraced the heartland. "Cool. I watch *Drew Carey* all the time. Cleveland rocks, you know."

"That's good to know," Sara said. She disconnected the intercom and punched in a number on her private line. A familiar voice answered after two rings. "Crawford's Texaco."

"Dad, hi."

"Sarabelle! What's new?"

"You wouldn't believe it if I told you, which I'm going to do in person. That's why I called, to let you know I'm planning to stop in Brewster Falls in a week or so."

"Hey, great! Best news I've had all day."

It was the reaction Sara expected. She leaned back in her chair, drew a deep breath and savored the sound of her father's voice.

THE FRIENDS with whom Sara had planned the Aruba trip were disappointed when she canceled—and baffled by her decision. She pictured Donald's expression from his tone of voice when she called him. "Why would anyone want to go to Lake Erie?" he asked. "Isn't it dead or something?"

"No, it isn't dead—not anymore." She told him about the anti-pollution groups that had worked diligently to clean up the water and explained that Lake Erie was now a safe playground for boating and swimming. Donald practically snored over the phone.

Sara ignored his reaction. Her growing enthusiasm for her trip more than compensated for her friends' pessimism, even though the five days before her flight were the most hectic of her life. She managed to complete all her tax returns, even Tony Papalardo's, while she tended to details necessary for an extended trip and packed a range of clothes to fit the capricious nature of a Lake Erie spring.

When she arrived at the Cleveland airport, she rented a car and headed west toward Sandusky. She planned to take a ferry to Put-in-Bay on South Bass Island—the largest of the Lake Erie islands. She didn't know how she would get to Thorne Island, but Herbert Adams had said it was only a mile farther, so she didn't anticipate a problem.

Leaving her car in the ferry lot, Sara boarded the large passenger boat midafternoon and arrived at South Bass less than an hour later. She was enchanted with the island's primary village, Put-in-Bay. Quaint, refurbished cottages lined the narrow streets. A small business district boasted ice-cream shops, cafés and specialty stores. Visitors could choose from several inviting hotels. The island's charm made Sara more anxious to see her own property. She inquired at the harbor about transportation to Thorne Island.

An employee of the ferry company gave her disappointing news. "There isn't any boat that goes to Thorne," he said. "Leastways, not a public one."

"Then how do people get there?" she asked.

"People don't," he said. "Not tourists, anyway, though Winkleman goes there two, three times a week."

"Wonderful. Where do I find Winkleman?"

"At the Happy Angler this time of day. You could set your watch by it."

Having gotten directions to the local tavern and a description of Winkleman, Sara located the captain she intended to hire. She walked into his boisterous circle of friends and tapped him on the shoulder. "Pardon me. Are you Mr. Winkleman?"

He set a mug of beer on the counter and leaned back on a well-used bar stool. "Guess I could be," he said.

"I'm looking for someone to take me to Thorne Island. I understand you go there."

Winkleman removed a sudsy mustache from his upper lip with his index finger and pushed an old naval cap back on a patch of thick gray hair. "Was just there yesterday. Don't plan to go again for two days."

A two-day layover—even in charming Put-in-Bay—was not part of Sara's plan. "I really need to go today, Mr. Winkleman. Is there anyone else who could take me?"

"Nobody else goes."

The sailor's succinct answer puzzled Sara. Why wasn't there regular service to Thorne Island? She recalled the photos of the pretty harbor and the delightful Cozy Cove Inn. Surely these attractions should lure tourists to the island. "I'll pay you of course," she said. "More than your regular fee, if that will help to persuade you."

He squinted at her from beneath scraggly charcoal eyebrows. "It'll cost you twenty bucks."

It sounded reasonable. "That's fine," she said. "I left my bags at the harbor office. Can we go now?"

"Gotta finish my beer first. Meet you there."

Fifteen minutes later Sara decided that maybe twenty dollars wasn't such a bargain, after all. The captain's boat smelled of fish, and twice during the short ride to Thorne Island, she had to pull her bags clear of a steadily increasing pool of water seeping into the stern.

Conversation with her captain was practically impossible because of the roar of the engine. She tried to ask him about the people who lived on the island. Again he said very little, commenting only that everyone there was a close buddy of his.

When a patch of green became recognizable as a shoreline, Winkleman slowed the boat. Sara tucked her wind-whipped hair into what was left of the French braid she'd fashioned that morning. Then she turned her attention to her island.

She thought she'd recognize the tidy little harbor from the brochure and looked for the bright yellow mooring ropes spanning the length of its pier. Instead, she saw a dilapidated wooden platform jutting into the water on precariously tilted posts. Winkleman maneuvered into position beside one of them.

"Is this the main dock?" she asked.

"This is the only dock," he said.

She climbed onto rickety boards that creaked under her feet. There was none of the usual activity one expected of a quaint village harbor. There were no shops or boats. The entire area consisted of a one-room clapboard bait house with broken windows.

"Oh, dear," Sara sighed. "I hadn't expected things to be quite this way."

Winkleman tossed her bags onto the dock and

grinned up at her. "Nice, ain't it? Some of these islands have begun to look pretty shabby. The fellows that live here keep Thorne up pretty good."

Her gaze wandered to the clumps of overgrown plants that skirted the shoreline. A narrow, dirt pathway through a thicket of brush and trees led somewhere. "There is a hotel on the island, isn't there?" she asked.

Winkleman appeared thoughtful. Finally a light dawned in his eyes. "Right. The Cozy Cove. It's just up that pathway."

Thank goodness. Sara's misgivings were replaced with a glimmer of hope. At least the delightful little bed-and-breakfast was real enough. So what if the dock needed some work? She could manage funds for a few minor repairs. She picked up her suitcases, anticipating her first evening on her island.

Winkleman untied his mooring line, took the twenty she offered and pushed away from the dock. "See ya."

Apprehension suddenly dampened Sara's enthusiasm. What if there was no phone on the island? In her rush to pack, she'd left her cell phone in Fort Lauderdale. And now her only link to the mainland was about to roar out of her life. "Wait! Mr. Winkleman, how can I reach you?"

He chugged back to her and took a ragged tablet from the console of his boat. "I'll be back in two days," he said while scribbling, "but here's my number if you need to call. Doubt you will, though. The boys take care of things. Ol' Brody has a cell phone. He'd probably let you use it."

She set down a suitcase and took the paper before it could blow out of his hand and into the water. Then she shoved it deep into the pocket of her purse. All at once, that phone number and a cell phone belonging to someone named Ol' Brody seemed absolutely vital to her existence. Winkleman was a hundred yards from the dock when she finally turned and headed up the pathway.

Following two twists in the lane, Sara came to a wood-sided building that appeared as weary as she suddenly felt. She leaned against the weathered picket fence surrounding the property and tried to associate the structure in front of her with the one in the brochure photo.

It was barely recognizable as the Cozy Cove Inn. Only a sign hanging by one rusty nail from a post at the front gate confirmed its identity. The front-porch roof sagged against the peeling white gingerbread molding of its supports.

Sara stepped onto the porch, dropped her bags by her feet and sank into a drooping wicker chair. She might have sat there indefinitely had she not noticed the baskets of blooming spring flowers hanging from the eaves. They were the only sign that someone still cared about the place.

She stood and paced the length of the veranda. Old wood planks groaned under her feet, but fortunately remained intact. With renewed optimism, she turned the knob on the door and entered *her* Cozy Cove Inn.

She stepped into a wide hallway furnished with only a guest-registration counter, a wall clock that had stopped at eight-twenty-two and a pair of Windsor chairs scarred with what high-priced decorators might call character.

To her left was a large parlor. It was impossible to determine the style or colors of anything in the room. Every piece of furniture had been covered by a sheet except one wing chair and a small table by the fireplace. The walls were adorned with peaceful country prints and shelves of hardback books.

Feeling more like an intruder than a proprietor, Sara slowly backed out of the room. Unease raised the hair on her neck. The inn appeared empty, yet Sara had the distinct sense that she was not alone.

She'd never believed in the supernatural, yet the presence of another soul in this house was as real to her at this moment as was the newel post at the bottom of the thick banister. She curved her fingers around the post and willed herself to go up the stairs.

A center hallway veered to the left and right of the second-floor landing. Doors stretched the length of the hall. All of them were closed except one at the very end. Weak sunlight mixed with an artificial glow poured into the passage. Sara approached cautiously, ready to bolt at the first sign of trouble. Logic told her that she wouldn't find any of course. Mr. Winkleman would have told her if there was something bizarre about the island. Surely he wouldn't have left her alone...

The first unnatural sounds of Thorne Island floated from the room to Sara's ears. It was a light tapping, almost like... Yes, that was it. Sara stood outside the open door listening to the harmless sound of someone pecking a computer keyboard.

She stepped over the threshold and had her first look at the other resident of the Cozy Cove Inn. It was a man and his back was to her. Dark, thick curls covered the collar of his knit shirt.

His hands halted above the keyboard. His back straightened and his voice, low and hoarse, reached her across the room. "If you're trying to scare me to death, it'll never work. So if you came to kill me, you'd best use a gun."

CHAPTER TWO

WHEN THE FULL IMPACT of the man's statement registered in Sara's brain, she didn't know whether to laugh or run from the room. She did neither, but instead spoke to the back of his head. "What a horrible thing to say."

His ancient office chair squeaked as he turned slowly toward her. "Not to someone creeping around your house, it isn't."

Though he faced her, he was still in the shadows. She couldn't detect any details of his features.

"Of course, I didn't know at first that you were a woman," he added.

Sara hated being at a disadvantage. The last amber rays of daylight speared through the louvered shutters at his back. He could see her clearly enough, but his form was nothing but an amorphous gray blob to her. "What difference does it make that I'm a woman?" she said. "I could still kill you."

He stretched one leg, then settled his ankle on the opposite knee, a casual pose for someone who just a moment before had thought he might be taking his last breath. "Yeah, but you won't. Women don't like to murder people after they've looked into their eyes."

"Then don't get too confident," Sara shot back, "because I haven't seen your eyes yet."

He deliberately moved his chair out of the shadow until sunlight fell across his upper body. "There, is that better?"

It was. The shapeless mass had transformed into an exceedingly acceptable-looking human. Except perhaps for his almost black hair, which was unstylishly long and untidy. It curled over his forehead to meet a slightly lighter pair of straight eyebrows. Much of the rest of an interesting face was hidden by at least two days' growth of beard. He was fairly young, near her own age, Sara assumed, prompting her to conclude that she wasn't looking at "Ol' Brody."

Once Sara had noted these details, the man's shirt commanded her attention. She'd given her father a similar one at least fifteen years ago when he took up golf, and her sense of humor had been quite different from what it was now. A beige knit background hugged the man's chest respectably, but it was the eighteen numbered golf flags fluttering around his torso that made Sara choke back her laughter.

Each flag had a different cartoon printed on its surface. Flag number sixteen, the one she could see most clearly, depicted a droopy-eyed fellow with an ice bag on his head and a thermometer sticking out of his mouth. The words "Feeling under par" were printed next to the caricature. Other clichéd golf references decorated the remaining flags. Sara covered her mouth with her hand, but wasn't successful in stopping a chuckle.

The man plucked a portion of the shirt away from his chest and stared down at it. "What? You don't like my shirt?"

"It would be all right if it were a cocktail napkin at the nineteenth hole."

"Hey, it's got a pocket. That's why I like it. Try to find shirts with pockets these days."

Sara's limited experience with shopping for men's clothes hadn't included an awareness of shirt pockets, so she just said, "I know, and it's a darned shame."

"It is if you smoke."

"Do you smoke?"

"Not anymore. But I like knowing I still have a pocket in case I start again. Basically I just hate it when manufacturers mess up a good thing after I get used to it."

The hint of a smug grin lifted the corners of his mouth. This man obviously liked to have the last word. And once he knew he wasn't about to be shot, there was no lack of confidence in his manner. "But we're off the subject here," he said. "What are you doing creeping around my place?"

"Oh, for heaven's sake. I wasn't creeping. What's the point of trying to remain unnoticed after riding in that boat with the earsplitting engine? Don't tell me you didn't hear us arrive."

"Of course I heard the boat. I just figured Winkie had forgotten the toilet paper or something and was dropping it off. I sure never thought that what he was leaving behind was a snooping female."

Her eyebrows shot up. "So now I'm snooping *and* creeping?"

He raised his hands palms up as if his point was obvious. "Look, you came into *my* place without so much as a hoot or a holler and tiptoed up to *my* room like a typical nosy woman on your little lady cat's feet…"

Suddenly his golf flags weren't amusing anymore. They were just stupid. And his hair wasn't untidy, it was unkempt. And his attitude belonged way back in an era before golf was even invented. Sara's index finger poked out at him as if it had a mind of its own, which it must have, since she hated for anyone to do that to her. "Now look," she said in a voice that quivered with underlying anger, "first of all, this is *my* place, and I'll walk around in it any way I please!"

That seemed to get to him. He gave her a dark look. "What do you mean, *your* place?"

"I mean this hotel is mine, this island is mine. In fact, every single place on this island—if there are any others—belongs to me." For emphasis, she yanked the deed out of her purse and held it up to the challenge in his eyes. "Would you care to inspect this document?"

He stood up from the chair, all lean six-feet-plus of him, and glared at the paper in her hand with eyes that she saw now were startlingly gray. "What's happened to Millie?" he demanded.

The mention of her aunt's name gave him some credibility. At least he wasn't a squatter. Sara softened her tone. "Millicent Thorne died last week."

He squeezed his eyes shut and pressed his middle finger to the bridge of his nose. "Damn it. Why didn't somebody tell me?"

His reaction caught her off guard. "You knew my aunt personally?"

"Millicent Thorne is…*was* your aunt?"

"Actually great-aunt, yes."

"Well, of course I knew her. I've been living on her island for the past six years."

"And not paying any rent for a good part of it, too."

His eyes, which had only just registered the shock of bad news, now narrowed with irritation. "Now, hold on a minute. I haven't missed a single month paying my rent. For your information, Millie stopped collecting my checks. She said she didn't need the money. Told me to hold on to them and send a bunch all at once when she asked for them."

"Why would she do that?"

He turned away from her and sat back down in his desk chair. "You'd have to ask Millie about that, which might be difficult at the moment, but I would suspect it had to do with a little something called trust."

"She trusted you?"

He opened a desk drawer and pulled out a short stack of checks held together with a paper clip. "She did, and for good reason." He thrust the checks at Sara, holding them at the level of her chest until she took them. "Those are my rent checks, every one of them for the last year, dated by the month. They're all there in chronological order. Go ahead, see for yourself."

She flipped through them. They were dated consecutively, made out to Millicent Thorne and signed "N. Bass." She looked up. "Bass? That's your name? After the island or the fish?"

"Pick one. It's only a name."

Sara returned her attention to the checks. Suddenly Mr. N. Bass's name wasn't important. The amount of the rent he paid each month was. "One hundred dollars?" she said. "You only paid my aunt one hundred dollars a month?"

He shrugged. "That's what she asked for."

The accountant's hackles on Sara's neck prickled.

"That's ridiculous. You live here practically like a king of your own private domain, in a cozy little inn, which, by the way, you've allowed to fall into pitiful disrepair, for the sum of one hundred dollars a month?"

He nodded. "I'm not complaining about the deal."

She thrust the checks and the deed into her shoulder bag. "Obviously not. Then I guess you won't mind if I raise your rent to help cover the cost of repairs around here."

He met her self-assurance with cool disdain. "Sorry. You can't do that."

"Why not?"

"Because I've got a twenty-five-year lease, with a clause prohibiting rent increases, and I've only lived here six of them."

Mr. N. Bass must have thought he was dealing with an idiot. "That's absurd," she said. "My aunt had an attorney, and even if you had tried to talk her into such a financially unsound arrangement, he would never have allowed—"

Mr. Bass leaned back in his chair and crossed his legs at the ankles. "You talking about Herb Adams?"

Herb? "You know Mr. Adams, too?"

"Sure. He was present when I signed the lease. He did, in fact, advise Millie against such generosity, but she insisted."

N. Bass had the nerve to follow that statement with a short burst of laughter. Sara quickly changed the shocked expression on her face to one of outrage. His cocky smile faded, but his attitude did not.

"Never mind asking a bunch of questions I have no intention of answering," he added. "I'll just tell you that Millie and I were friends. I helped her out once, and she repaid me.'' That odd little grin, which under other circumstances might have been interpreted as somewhat endearing, twisted his mouth again. ''Millicent was a fair woman. But then, you know that.''

Sara spied a chair a few feet from her. She stepped over to it and sank into its plump floral cushion. She had to think rationally. Sara prided herself on her ability to get to the fundamental truth of a situation. Finally she said, ''Mr. Bass, this all may be true...''

''It *is* true.''

''All right. I don't question your story, but the island belongs to me now, and any agreements you had with my aunt are no longer applicable. If I see fit to raise your rent, I am well within my right to do that.''

He clasped his hands in his lap and shook his head slowly. ''Nope. You're not. Millie assigned all lessee's rights to her tenants in the event a new landlord took over the property. I'll let you take a look at my lease. You might be able to fight it, but it would be expensive and time-consuming.''

''And with my luck someone actually would kill you before I won the case,'' Sara said. ''It wouldn't be any fun unless I had the satisfaction of seeing your expression when I beat you.''

A genuine grin split his face for the first time, and Sara found herself disliking him a little less. But if she had to accept this man's living arrangements on Thorne Island, then she and he were still a long way from bridging the gap from dislike to tolerance.

''Cheer up, Mrs....?''

''It's Miss. Miss Sara Crawford.''

He leaned forward and rested his elbows on his

knees. "There you see, things could be a lot worse between us."

"I don't see how."

"You could be married or ugly. And you're neither one of those things. I think we've got a future, Miss Crawford."

She gritted her teeth. "I think we've got a problem, Mr. Bass."

"Nick! Nickie! Everything all right up there?"

A low, booming voice rolled up the staircase and down the hall to Mr. Bass's room, and Sara nearly jumped out of her skin. "Who's that?"

"That's Dexter Sweet, former linebacker for the Cleveland Browns. He's a big man with thighs the size of tires, but don't let him scare you. The goodness in his soul could make nightingales sing. And that yelling thing he just did—*that's* how you enter someone's house."

"Oh, please, will you—"

"Everything's fine, Dex," Nick Bass called. "We've just got company."

An African-American male filled the doorway. Sara couldn't tell anything about his soul, but the rest of Nick's description was absolutely accurate, though he might have mentioned Dexter Sweet's height. It was just shy of a California redwood.

Dexter spared her a quick, astonished glance before settling a worried gaze on his friend. "I heard Captain Winkie's boat and thought something was wrong. He's not due back till day after tomorrow. Then I couldn't find Ryan, and Brody was still snoring when I looked in on him."

Nick extended his hand to indicate Sara. "Dex,

meet Miss Sara Crawford, our new landlady. Sara, this is Dexter Sweet.''

Amazingly, despite his size, there was something about the man's round boyish face that made his last name seem appropriate. She stood up, offered her hand and looked into Mr. Sweet's perplexed brown eyes. ''Did you say 'Captain Winkie'?''

He nodded.

She couldn't stop herself. Exhaustion and shock had taken their toll. Laughter bubbled from her throat and she could barely get her next words out. ''I'm standing here with Mr. Sweet and Mr. Bass, and we're all talking about Captain Winkie. Somehow I feel like I'm in the middle of a Saturday-morning cartoon.''

The two men exchanged a look that was part male commiseration and part she's-a-woman-that-explains-it. Sara wouldn't have been surprised if they both put a finger to the side of their heads and made circles.

''Tell me something, Mr. Sweet,'' she said through a continuing fit of laughter, ''do you pay rent on this island?''

''Yeah.'' He dragged the word out with caution. ''Been here almost six years now.''

''And how much do you pay?''

''A hundred a month.''

''Terrific. And are your checks stored in a drawer somewhere?''

''Yeah, Nick's.''

Nick Bass opened the desk drawer, withdrew a stack of checks similar to his own and brought them to her. Each one was dated and signed by Dexter Sweet.

It wasn't even enough to cover the back taxes, but

it was a start. "Thank you, gentlemen," Sara said. "Now I think I'll go find a room for myself. Do we have any fresh linens?"

"I'll let you use mine," Nick said. "The cupboard down the hall that they're sitting in is yours. But the spare sheets belong to me. Share and share alike I always say. Pick any room you like, Miss Crawford. Make yourself at home."

"I *am* at home, Mr. Bass."

A SHARP PAIN shot up Nick's leg. He limped back to the desk chair and sat down.

Dexter frowned at him. "Are you doing your exercises, Nick?"

"Sure, I'm doing them, just like you told me," he said without looking Dexter in the eye. "But I figure after six years a guy's just got to live with a little discomfort." He gave his friend a crooked smile. "It beats the alternative, anyway."

Dexter grunted his agreement and sat in the chair Sara had vacated. "What's going on here, Nick? Who is this Crawford woman?"

"I told you, Dex. She's our new landlady and Millicent Thorne's great-niece. Millie died last week and left the island to her. She showed me the deed, and it looks like everything's in order."

"What does that mean for all of us?"

"Actually, Dex, now that I've had a few minutes to think about it, Millie did us a favor."

"But Miss Thorne was the best landlady we could ever have had."

"True, but we knew she wouldn't live forever, and when you think about all the possible outcomes for Thorne Island, having Millie's niece as the owner seems like the best one. Sara Crawford will probably hang around for a couple of days, flex her landlady muscles a bit and then take off. You saw what she was like—nice clothes, educated manners, soft hands.'' His mind wandered to Sara's other obvious attributes, but he refrained from listing them. ''She won't have any interest in staying around here.''

Dexter nodded. ''Yeah, why would a woman like that want to hang around a bunch of independent cusses like us?''

''Exactly. I give Miss Crawford three days tops, then she'll be history.'' He grinned at his own private thought. ''Though I imagine she'll make us send in our rent checks on time.''

Dexter's answering grin curled into his cheeks. ''She makes a darned pretty chapter of Thorne Island history, though, doesn't she, Nick?''

Nick nodded slowly. ''Yep. She's not hard to look at.''

Dexter stood and headed for the door, but stopped before leaving the room. ''By the way, Nick, did she see what you had on the computer screen?''

''No. She wasn't the least interested. I use the name Nicolas Bass in the top margin, so she wouldn't have suspected anything, anyway. She doesn't seem like the type who'd be curious about the ramblings of a grumpy, thirty-eight-year-old hermit.''

JUGGLING BED LINENS and her suitcases, Sara chose a room at the opposite end of the hallway from Nick's. She flicked the light switch beside the door. A single bulb hanging from the ceiling crackled and spit, finally casting a sickly yellow light on more furnishings covered with sheets. Cringing at the potential cost of electrical repairs, Sara dropped her belongings onto the floor.

She snapped open one neatly folded sheet and fluttered it over a gray mattress. A fresh scent—familiar from Sara's childhood—filled the room. She hadn't smelled that clean aroma since the days her mother had folded the family's laundry from the backyard clothesline. Bass must dry his laundry in the open air, she thought. Probably because the inn didn't have a working electric dryer.

She doubted the island had many modern conveniences. In fact, considering the condition of the Cozy Cove, she'd been dumbfounded to see a computer in Nick Bass's room. She'd tried to read the screen, and once she'd recognized standard manuscript format, she'd been doubly curious. But she hadn't gotten close enough to actually read the words.

Strange, she thought now as she tucked a corner of the top sheet between the mattress and box spring, she wouldn't have been a bit surprised to see a racing form or even a video game on Mr. Bass's monitor. But a scholarly-looking bit of text—somehow that didn't fit the picture she'd formed of the man so far.

There's an old saying, Sara, she said to herself. *You can never tell a person by his dopey-looking golf shirt.* She was glad she had a full week to devote to this island project. It might take that long to understand her bizarre tenants, especially the aggravating—but oddly appealing—Mr. Bass.

CHAPTER THREE

THE ROOM Sara had selected turned out to be almost cheerful. She removed the sheet that had been thrown over a cedar wardrobe and found dainty floral stenciling on the doors. When she uncovered a pair of colonial arrow-back chairs flanking a fireplace, she discovered bright chintz cushions on the seats. She gave the shutters at the windows a thorough dusting, which gave new life to the well-polished slats.

Yes, she would be quite comfortable in this room, once she solved the immediate problem of food. Since the Cozy Cove obviously wasn't a working hotel, it probably didn't have a restaurant or the personnel to run it. A snack breakfast on the airplane and a nonfat yogurt cone in Put-in-Bay wasn't nearly enough to sustain Sara. Surely the inn had a kitchen. She went downstairs to raid the refrigerator.

Behind the registration counter and opposite the parlor, she located a spacious dining room with sheets hiding what appeared to be a long table and eight chairs. In the near darkness of dusk, she felt her way through that room to a kitchen beyond. She flipped the light switch by the entrance, and another single overhead bulb glared down on a red brick floor.

Sara made a quick inspection of the appliances and decided they had once been used to prepare meals for a large number of people. But they hadn't been operated in some time. She ran her hand across the porcelain top of a six-burner stove, and years of smeared grease stuck to her fingers. Hardened boil-over remains coated the sides of the oven. When she opened the door of an ancient refrigerator, she grimaced at the streaks of mildew.

The rest of the kitchen was in much the same condition. Pitted kettles hung from brass hooks in the ceiling or lay any which way on the rough wood of the countertop. An old oak worktable surrounded by four simple ladder-back chairs had an assortment of alien substances embedded in its scratched surface. Sara's stomach, which just moments before had growled to be fed, nearly revolted at the conditions under which its next meal would have to be prepared.

That was until Sara saw a little corner of the kitchen that made her heart—and stomach—rejoice. Sparkling under the unforgiving light, next to a modern apartment-size refrigerator, was a scrupulously clean area of counter. A gleaming-white two-burner stovetop and a microwave oven sat side by side on the varnished pine surface. A cabinet above this miraculously neat oasis held two spotless pans, a pair of matching skillets and assorted clean tableware. If these items existed in this chaos of dirt and grease, could decent food be far away?

She began a search for cans, bottles and jars, checking cabinets in the tidy corner of the kitchen.

"Can I help you, Miss Crawford?"

Like a child caught with her hand in the cookie jar, Sara slammed a lower cabinet door and stood up. "Mr. Bass, you don't have to sneak up on me."

Another of those smug grins tugged at his lips. "Now we're even, eh?"

He crossed the threshold into the kitchen and came toward her. A pair of brown chinos accentuated his long, lean legs and matched the sand traps on his shirt. Sara detected a slight limp in his gait, though it might have been caused by the uneven old brick flooring. She pulled her gaze away from him and continued her search for food. "I wasn't aware we were keeping score."

She sensed his amusement even though she couldn't see his face and hated the flush of embarrassment it brought to her face. "Oh, yes you were, Sara," he said. "You're just miffed because it's a tie."

"What nonsense," she responded, acutely aware that he'd called her by her first name. A chuckle rumbled from his throat and seemed to reverberate down her spine.

"What are you doing in my kitchen—oh, pardon me, *your* kitchen—going through *my* things?" he asked.

She banged another cupboard door closed. This one contained various cleaning supplies, and she tucked the information away for later use. "I'm looking for food. And while we're on the subject, may I say that under *your* supervision, *my* kitchen has fallen into a state that isn't fit for pigs."

"Then it's fortunate we don't have any pigs, or I don't know where they'd eat."

She scowled at him, though judging from his teasing grin, her glare had lost its effectiveness. She crossed her arms over her chest. "Mr. Bass, I need something to eat. You're not going to let me starve, are you?"

"You can buy food on the island."

"Thank goodness. Where?"

"At Brody's cottage. He's an ex-marine and he calls our supply store the commissary. He orders the groceries and we buy them from him. But he's not there now. He fishes every day at dusk. But no, I won't let you starve. In fact, you can even use my part of the kitchen, which I maintain for my own use."

She uncrossed her arms and managed a tight smile. "Thanks."

"What kind of soup do you like?"

Soup. She could almost feel a steaming mug of delicious broth between her hands, almost taste the savory herbs and spices. "That sounds wonderful," she said. "I like all kinds—broccoli and cheese, roasted chicken and wild rice, any of the new low-fat soups are delicious...."

"That's fine, but I meant, do you like Chicken Noodle or Tomato?"

"Those are my choices?"

"Brody volunteered to keep us supplied, but he isn't particularly imaginative."

"I see. Tomato, then."

Nick went to a tall pantry cabinet near the back door and produced the trademark red-and-white can, which he set on his clean counter. Then he went to his small refrigerator. "Now, what kind of meat for your sandwich?"

"Do we really need to go through this again?"

"No. We have salami."

He took bread and meat slices from the refrigerator. "And to drink?"

"You tell me."

"Actually I have six different brands of beer—"

She wasn't surprised.

"—and one Mountain Dew."

"Shall I fight you for the Mountain Dew?"

He took the can from the refrigerator and tossed it to her. "No. I'll let you win this one." He pointed to a stool next to the counter. "Have a seat. I'll even cook."

The entire meal process took less than thirty minutes from preparation to cleanup. And during that time the few sentences Sara and Nick spoke to each other involved passing the condiments and a smattering of comments about Millicent Thorne. Sara admitted that she hadn't known her great-aunt very well and even expressed her guilt about that situation.

"It's too bad," he said. "You would have liked her. In fact, I see similarities between the two of you."

Since he didn't elaborate, Sara decided to accept his statement as a compliment.

Once the dishes were put away, Nick went out the back door and stood on the stoop. "Will you be needing anything else from the refrigerator tonight?" he asked through the screen door.

"No, I don't think so. Why?"

"I always turn off the generator before I go to bed. Can't see wasting fuel. The food stays cold all night if the refrigerator door's not opened, and I'm an early riser."

He was turning off the generator? Sara's stomach did a somersault of alarm. "But does that mean the lights won't work?"

"Sure does. Take one of the lanterns from the parlor. They're not just decoration. There should be plenty of oil in the well. You'll find a flashlight in the pantry, too.''

Resigned to the conventions of Thorne Island, she got the flashlight and watched Bass step down from the back porch. His limp was more obvious now. In fact, a tightening of his facial muscles indicated that he was in pain. Since they'd just shared a few companionable moments, Sara felt comfortable enough to ask, ''Are you all right, Mr. Bass?''

He looked up at her from the yard. ''What do you mean?''

''Your limp. I couldn't help noticing.''

''And you want to know why I have it?''

''I don't mean to pry, but if you'd like to tell me…''

''A few years ago I was shot. The bullet entered at the base of my spine and pretty well screwed things up.''

The flashlight clattered to the floor. ''You were shot?''

''Yep. So when I told you earlier that if you meant to kill me, you'd better use a gun, I really wasn't relishing the idea all that much. Good night, Sara.''

That was obviously all the information she was going to get. She picked up the flashlight and spoke to his dark form as it blended with the angular shadows of the inn. ''Good night, Nick.''

THE NEXT MORNING Sara awoke to the sound of voices filtering through her second-story window. She got out of bed and opened the slats of her shutter just enough to peek outside. A cool breeze washed over her, and she breathed in the fresh, heady scent of the flowers in the porch baskets.

Four men stood in the overgrown front yard of the inn just beyond the edge of the porch eaves. Sara could see three of them clearly and just an arm and a foot of the fourth. She recognized Dexter Sweet, his huge arms bulging from the short sleeves of an athletic T-shirt. She heard the low timbre of Nick Bass's voice coming from under the porch. She didn't know the other two men, but assumed they were the pair Dexter had mentioned the day before—Brody and Ryan.

One man was short, thin, with brown, shoulder-length hair bound in a leather strap at his nape. The other was medium height, with a middle-aged paunch and slumping shoulders. "Ol' Brody," Sara concluded. He wore a canvas fishing hat with an ageless collection of rusty lures pinned to every square inch. Definitely the island's unimaginative grocer.

Sara tuned in to the conversation when Brody was speaking or, more appropriately, complaining. "Hell-fire! How long is she going to stay?"

Nick answered in a harsh whisper, but Sara couldn't make out the words.

The small man with the ponytail spoke next. He glanced up several times at the second story. Ducking out of sight, Sara was able to interpret his opinion from the tone of his voice. He didn't seem any more pleased about her arrival than Brody had.

When she risked a peek through the shutters again, she saw Brody nodding his head, causing the lures to bob up and down. "I agree with Ryan. I don't cotton to having a woman snooping around our island. Millie Thorne left us alone."

Dexter raised his hands as if to quiet the complaints of his friends. "Now don't go borrowing trouble,"

he said. "Like Nickie told me last night, she probably—"

Nick stopped Dexter's words with a sharp warning
and stepped away from the porch. He looked up at
Sara's window. She jerked back again. Then the men
moved down the crumbling walkway of the inn toward the path to the harbor.

Sara opened the door to her wardrobe, took out
underwear, a pair of jeans and a San Francisco T-shirt
and tossed them onto her bed. Then she slipped her
arms through the sleeves of her terry cloth robe and
tied it in front. Walking down the hall to the bathroom, she mumbled to herself, "Thanks for the welcoming committee, boys, and have a nice day!"

THE COZY COVE INN was an interesting blend of two
centuries. While the decorative moldings and wooden
ceiling planks in every room were clearly from the
1890s, the bath fixtures probably dated from the
1950s. Small black-and-white tiles lined the lavatory
walls and the small circular shower, and provided a
nice backdrop for white porcelain fixtures. The toilet
with its oddly squat shape worked sufficiently well,
but the night before, Sara had carefully checked the
oak seat for splinters before using it.

The inn had an adequate hot-water heater, though
insufficient pressure. It took Sara longer than normal
to rinse shampoo from her hair.

It was eight-thirty by the time she'd dressed, dried
her hair and secured it in a clip at her nape. Obviously
morning activities started early on Thorne Island.
With Nick gone, she'd have to scrounge around his
kitchen again in search of coffee. A trip to Brody's
grocery store and a thorough cleaning of her own area

of the big kitchen were first on her list after she had a jolt of caffeine. She didn't intend to "borrow" from Nick any more than she had to.

With sunlight streaming in the windows, the clean section of kitchen gleamed even more brightly than it had the night before. Unfortunately the grimy section looked even worse. But Sara's resolve was bolstered by the sight of the automatic drip coffeemaker on Nick's counter. Dark brew steamed from the glass pot, and a clean crockery mug and sugar packets sat next to it. Nick had obviously left the supplies where she would find them. Sara smiled to herself. If he didn't work so hard at being annoying, Sara could almost tolerate Nick for this one friendly gesture.

After her second cup, she took cleaning supplies from the cupboard and set to work on the stove. Layers of grime slowly dissolved under the onslaught of bleach and pine-scented solvent. An hour later she decided to tackle the brick floor and set about finding a mop and a bucket. She spied a wood-paneled door in the middle of an interior kitchen wall and thought it might be a cleaning closet. She grabbed the knob, but Nick's voice stopped her from turning it.

"I don't think you should go into the cellar," he warned through the back screen door. The hinges squeaked as he opened it and came inside. He wore a pair of cargo shorts that showed off muscular, tanned calves. A T-shirt with the faded logo of a Cleveland tavern on the front clung to his broad chest and disappeared into the waistband of the shorts. A Cleveland Indians ball cap sat low on his forehead, but she still had an all-too-intimate look at his silver-flecked eyes and freshly shaven face.

For a brief moment Sara found it difficult to

breathe. She covered the dysfunction with a hard swallow. Nick Bass had a certain indefinable appeal in the bright light of day, even if he was telling her she couldn't do something. "Why not?" she said. "What's down there?"

He settled onto the bar stool and shoved the hat back. "Spiders. Cobwebs. Some old barrels and a few dusty bottles of wine."

"I'm not too excited about the spiders, but I'd still like to go down."

"You can't see anything because the lightbulb burned out years ago."

"And you never replaced it?"

He shrugged. "I will…tomorrow."

A burned out lightbulb was hardly an insurmountable problem. "I'll use the flashlight," Sara said.

"Suit yourself, but if it's wine you're after, I've brought a few bottles upstairs already. You're welcome to sample those."

"Thank you. I may take you up on that offer, but if there's a real wine cellar down those steps, I want to see it."

He leaned back and studied her face, as if judging the level of her enthusiasm. "How would you feel about seeing six acres of real vineyard?"

Amusement underlined his offer and prevented Sara from taking him seriously. "And just where might this vineyard be?" she asked skeptically.

He hitched his thumb toward the back door. "Out there."

Amusement or not, he'd hooked her and was reeling her in. "Here? On the island?"

"You don't know much about your inheritance, do you?"

All commitment to cleaning fled from her mind. She ran to the door and looked out, but all she saw was a row of overgrown box hedges, wild winter cress and the yellow tops of dandelions. "I don't see any vineyard," she said.

He'd come up behind her and startled her by taking her elbow. "Then come with me, Miss Sara Crawford, because it's definitely out there."

Even with his limp, Nick easily navigated the un-pruned shrubs and prickly pears that poked their stubborn twigs between the flagstones in the pathway behind the Cozy Cove Inn. Sara had a more difficult time and was thankful when they emerged into an area only moderately suffering from nature gone wild. And as far as she could see, the gently rolling terrain before her was lined with rows of equally spaced posts and clinging twisted vines of various thicknesses. Definitely a vineyard!

She knew enough about cultivating grapes to be captivated by the prospect of owning a vineyard. She'd been fascinated by her tour of the California wine country the year before and had listened avidly to experts explaining the wine-making process. The dry acreage of Thorne Island was far different from the lush green carpet of Napa Valley, but it was obvious that there had once been a flourishing wine business on her island.

She wandered among the rows of thick trunks, stopping to examine the cordons and canes that split from mother plants and ran along wires from post to post. She used her thumbnail to scrape the bark off several plants, found green wood underneath and determined that the core trunks were very much alive. She called over her shoulder to Nick, who had stopped trying to keep up with her. "When was wine last made on this island?"

"I don't know," he said. "It's been six years at least. You won't even get one dried-up old raisin to harvest now." He spread his arms to encompass the whole six acres. "Look at this mess, Sara. For Pete's sake, I was kidding about this island having a real vineyard."

"Then the joke's on you, Bass," she hollered back. She plucked a cluster of shriveled fruit from a healthy shoot and ran back to him. "See this, Nick? Once upon a time these determined little 'raisins' probably made a fine chardonnay."

HIS LITTLE JOKE had backfired. Nick had figured if he took Sara out among the arid field that had once been a vineyard, she might see the futility of trying to make something of her flagging inheritance. Thorne Island's glory days were long over. She simply needed to recognize that and leave the island and its crusty inhabitants to themselves.

He took a beer and a sandwich to Brody's cottage and joined his companions for lunch. It killed him to have to admit the error in judgment he'd made this morning, especially since the other guys were counting on him to rid them of their interfering landlady.

At first he tried to put the blame on the little guy. "Hell, Ryan," he said, "this is all your doing. You just had to go out there and pluck and prune and probably baby-talk those plants into staying alive."

"I didn't know what I was doing," Ryan argued. "I was just passing time thinking it's a shame to let anything die in the winter frost. My clipping was just dumb luck."

Brody scowled at him and ran his hand over his thinning hair. "I told you to leave those plants alone. What do we care about growing a bunch of sissy grapes, anyway? We're fishermen and fortune hunters."

"Leave him alone, Brody," Dexter said. "I think his baskets hanging over at the inn look real pretty. If it weren't for Ryan here, we wouldn't have anything nice to look at."

Nick took a long swallow of beer. "It's not going to help if we argue among ourselves."

"Nick's right," Brody said. "It's that darned woman who's the enemy."

Nick held up his hand. "That's kind of a harsh way of putting it, Bro. It's not like she's entered our no-fly zone." He smiled at the image of Sara that suddenly came to mind. "You should have seen her this morning, running all around those dumb vines, scraping and plucking and cooing over them like a mother bird. She brought me a scrawny old cluster of dried-up fruit and presented it as proudly as if she'd grown it herself."

The image sent a quick spurt of warmth to Nick's groin, a reaction he hadn't had in a long time without seeing at least part of a naked breast. "It was kind of sweet, actually."

All three men stared at Nick as though he'd left his mind baking in the noon sun in the middle of the vineyard. He cleared his throat to knock Sara's face from his thoughts. "Still, though, we've got a problem."

Brody nodded. "That darned woman's messed up the chemistry around here. Pretty soon she'll be telling us to do a whole lot more than just pay the rent. That's the way women are.''

As the other men uttered similar groans of agreement, the door to Brody's cottage swung open, admitting the object of their despair. Sara stepped inside and smiled sweetly at each of them. ''Good afternoon, gentlemen,'' she said. ''I assume this is the commissary I've heard so much about.''

Nick gave hasty introductions.

''Mr. Brody,'' Sara said, ''I'd like to buy some food, and if it's all right with you, I need to use your cell phone.''

He squinted up at her, age lines crinkling the corners of his eyes. ''What do you want my phone for?''

''I understand Captain Winkleman will be back tomorrow. I'd like him to bring some fertilizer.''

Ryan jumped down from the up-ended barrel he was sitting on. ''There's a compost pile over by the old press house.''

Sara brightened as if the words *compost pile* were equal to *diamond bracelet*. ''There is?''

And if looks really could kill, Ryan would have been compost.

CHAPTER FOUR

AFTER SHE MADE her call to Captain Winkleman, Sara gave her grocery list to Brody. He quickly packaged her items and slid two bags across the counter toward her, jerking his hand back as if coming into direct contact with her would endanger his life. She muttered a succinct and insincere thank-you and left his cottage, making sure the screen door slammed loudly behind her.

"What a rude, ignorant, narrow-minded…" She let her voice trail off. There were simply too many adjectives that fit that anachronism with the tattered fishing hat. While she'd been in his presence, Brody had grumbled the whole time about women in general, and "one certain trespasser" specifically.

Nick Bass, thoroughly amused at her expense, watched the whole comedy of manners with a smirk on his face. At least Dexter Sweet had the decency to pick up a sports magazine and pretend he wasn't aware of his companion's rudeness. And poor little Ryan—he'd scuttled out the back way after his mention of the compost pile had turned the gathering quite hostile.

It was only a hundred yards on a narrow path through budding maple trees from Brody's small cottage to the Cozy Cove Inn. Aware that Nick was following her, Sara stomped her feet as loudly as her

Nikes allowed. She wanted the determination in her step to let him know she did not desire his company. When she reached the back door of the inn, she swung the screen open wide, stepped into the kitchen and let the door bang shut behind her.

"Damn it, woman!" he hollered. "You know I can't keep up when you walk this fast."

She slammed the bags on the clean counter, catching a glimpse of her catlike grin in the side of Nick's gleaming toaster. "I wasn't aware we were out on a stroll, Bass," she said when he came through the door.

He sat on a stool and whipped the Indians cap off his head. Dark curls tumbled onto his forehead. For the first time she noticed coarser strands of gray at his temples. They lent an air of dignity to a man who certainly didn't deserve it.

"That's not the only thing you're not aware of," he snapped.

She began yanking her purchases out of the sacks. "If you've come to spy on me, don't worry. I won't take much of your space."

"Yeah? Starting when?"

She slapped a package of bologna onto the counter, gripped the smooth pine edges and stared at him. "We're hardly overcrowded here, Bass. We're five people on forty acres. This isn't a ghetto."

He almost smiled, and since she was mad at him, she was glad he didn't.

"Look," he said, "if it makes you feel any better, I agree that Brody acted like an ass back there. But you've got to give him a break. He's hard to get along with even on his good days, and he started out grouchy this morning. At times like this, it's good to give him some space."

"I'd like to put him on a raft, tug him halfway to Canada and leave him in the middle of the lake. That ought to be enough space even for him."

Nick got off the stool, picked up the bologna and put it in the refrigerator. "Forget about Brody. I think Ryan's decided to give you a chance."

Sara refolded one of the bags and placed it in a lower cabinet. "At least he understands about the vineyard," she said. "But it won't be long before Brody turns him against me."

"Well, you did make him mad with all that special request nonsense."

"Oh, for heaven's sake." Sara handed Nick a jar of pickles and he slid it into the refrigerator. "Just because I don't want to eat Frosted Flakes or Captain Crunch."

Nick looked up at her, a mock-serious expression on his face. "Tony the Tiger and the captain are American icons."

She handed him a frozen dinner to put away. "And I don't mind microwave meals, but do I have to buy every one of them in 'hungry man' or 'family-size' portions?"

"When you're living with men, I guess you do. You're making life different around here already, Sara, and you've got to know that's not easy for any of us."

She scowled at him before she read the price sticker on a can of tomato soup. Then she read the sticker on a loaf of bread and a half carton of eggs. "All these groceries are from Kroger's," she said.

"So?"

"But the marked prices are the same as the ones Brody charged me. He didn't add anything to the Kroger price."

Nick didn't say anything. He indicated another question by raising his eyebrows.

"Well, if he gets the food from Kroger's…"

"Winkie fills the order at Kroger's, according to Brody's list, and delivers it to us," Nick corrected.

"Okay, but if Brody pays Winkie and doesn't increase the price to you guys, he's not making any money."

"He doesn't care about that."

Nick's offhand statement had just reduced years of accounting principles to insignificance. The idea of being in business, after all, was to make a profit. "He doesn't care about making money?"

"No. He's got tons of it already. And the thing about Brody is, he'll never take a dollar from anyone, but he'll never give one away, either. I guess that's how rich guys stay that way."

She pictured the scowling, ill-tempered old goat and almost laughed out loud. He wore that stupid hat with all the rusty lures. His shorts were held up with a tow rope. His canvas shoes had holes in the toes. He lived in a three-room cottage, which cost him a mere one hundred dollars a month, with a twelve-inch black-and-white TV for entertainment. "So Brody is rich?"

"As Midas."

"But how…?"

Nick read the label on a can of Vienna sausages and grimaced. "I don't know how you can eat these things," he said. "How'd Brody make his money?

He invented things. Then, for years he managed the factory that produced his inventions.''

Sara grabbed the can out of his hand and shoved it into the pantry. "What things did he invent?"

"If he wants you to know, he'll tell you."

That was a heck of an answer. "Well, at least he should see if there's a warehouse club around here, in Sandusky maybe, or—"

"Sara."

She clamped her mouth shut and stared at him.

"Leave it alone."

"But I could show him how volume buying..."

Nick stepped closer to her and put his hands on her shoulders. Suddenly the cotton fabric of her T-shirt felt warm, as if heated by the pressure of his palms.

For a moment he said nothing. He just kept a tight hold on her and stared into her eyes. "What do you do for a living?" he finally asked.

"I'm a tax accountant."

The temporary heat became a cold chill. Nick released her and took a step back. "That figures."

"What's wrong with being a tax accountant?"

"Nothing. It just figures. All that talk about volume buying. And the concern over the rent we pay. Your comment yesterday about Millie's 'unsound financial arrangement.' I should have guessed."

The hot blood of indignation surged through her veins. "What's wrong with caring about money? What's wrong with making it, tracking it, keeping it, for heaven's sake?"

"It's fine, Sara. Be the best accountant you can be. Just let Brody be the kind of grocer he wants to be." He turned away from her and headed for the door.

"I've got work to do," he said. "Maybe I'll see you later."

An unwelcome press of guilt weighed on Sara's shoulders, and she tried to shrug it off. Why should she feel guilty for making a few comments meant to help the man who'd treated her abominably just a few minutes ago? And yet she did feel guilty. It was ridiculous. All she was doing was offering a little common-sense advice that anyone with half a brain would recognize as logical and...

Sara's mind wouldn't let her continue her rationale. All at once every heightened sense was focused on the man walking out of the kitchen. All she could think about were his strong, broad shoulders and the graceful tapering of his hips under loose-fitting shorts. Such a man could banish all rational thought from any woman's mind. "Excuse me," she said.

He stopped in the doorway and looked back at her. "Yeah?"

"About that bottle of wine you promised me. If you bring it, I'd be willing to share my family-size lasagna tonight."

"I don't know," he said. "I've got a lot to do." He left her standing there with her temper skyrocketing and her ego plummeting.

She grabbed the cleaning supplies from the cupboard and began scrubbing and scouring everything in sight. And she pictured Nick Bass's face in every grimy surface.

BANNING CROUCHED in the dark hallway and pulled his service revolver from the shoulder holster. The smells of unwashed bodies and stale beer mingled with the scent of his own fear.

"Come on, come on," Nick grumbled to the screen. For the last thirty minutes—ever since he'd left Sara—he'd been staring at the words he'd entered into his computer and willing others to follow. These first lines of chapter five of *Dead Last* had come to him last night just after he'd gotten into bed and turned out his lantern. He'd struck a match and relit the wick so he could scribble the words down on a dog-eared tablet on his nightstand. He often did that—committed the words to paper so his next writing session would start fluidly.

He'd tried to come up with the next line in Detective Ivan Banning's crisis before extinguishing the light a second time, but nothing else had come to mind. Telling himself a literary lightning bolt would strike him the next morning, Nick had snuffed the lantern flame again and settled down to go to sleep.

Only sleep hadn't come, and Nick knew why. In the six years he'd lived in the Cozy Cove Inn, never once had a soft, willowy blonde lain between her own sheets—well, his sheets, really—just a few doors away from him.

Nick loved to write about guys whose lives were always in turmoil, men for whom the word *norm* was synonymous with boredom. But he didn't like it when his own situation threatened to follow that same path. He'd gotten used to the flawless, undiluted routine of life on Thorne Island, and Sara Crawford was like oil to the pure water of Nick's existence.

He didn't like thinking about her sleeping down the hall. He didn't like not sleeping because he was thinking about her. And he especially didn't like the hot, sweet jolt of energy that thinking about her brought to parts of his body that had become accustomed to their own special tempo of regularity.

And now there was this new dilemma. He couldn't figure out how in the world Banning was going to move from that smelly hallway into apartment number seven. Sure as black on a bat, Nick had writer's block. He rarely suffered from it, but the inability to put words to paper did afflict him every once in a while. Like when he remembered with spine-chilling clarity the cold, gray gutter slush of Prospect Avenue seeping into his clothes and turning red with his blood. Or when he recalled the hands of the medics working over his lump of a body, and the one cheerful guy telling him he would be all right. And Nick knowing full well he was lying.

Now those were *good* reasons to experience writer's block, but Sara Crawford? If he had to rate the significant moments of his life, he wouldn't put meeting her up there with nearly dying. Thinking about it rationally—and telling himself that thoughts about women could be handled this way—Nick knew why Sara's presence had affected him so adversely.

He'd touched her.

In the kitchen he'd put his hands on her shoulders and looked into those fresh-water-blue eyes and nearly forgotten what he was saying.

That had been a mistake. As long as he remained distant from her, he could be objective. But once he'd felt her soft flesh under his palms, once he'd been close enough to admire the determined thrust of her chin and the spark of indignation in her eyes, she'd become all too real. And that could mean trouble for him. Not the kind of trouble Detective Banning had to face in apartment number seven, but trouble nonetheless.

The last person Nick needed in his life was an accountant. He hadn't filed a tax return in six years, and he imagined the IRS frowned on people who just disappeared without a forwarding address. He didn't need a finicky bean counter looking into his private life, probing his secrets, turning him into a computer entry again.

All right, maybe he'd been a little rough on her when she'd asked him to share her stupid lasagna. He conceded that, but she'd get over it. Besides, why would a guy named Nicolas *Romano* whose paternal ancestors came from Napoli want to eat factory-produced lasagna, anyway?

He pushed away from the computer and stared out the window rather than face the barren monitor screen any longer. But then it was Sara's face that crept into his mind, and that didn't make him feel any better. He supposed it wouldn't hurt him to go down later and eat some of her dinner. It was the decent thing to do, and after all, she wasn't staying forever. Feeling a surge of pride at his unselfish decision, Nick risked glancing at his monitor again. He rested his hands lightly on the keyboard, then lifted one of them to plow his fingers through his hair.

Stubborn strands coiled onto his forehead. He needed a haircut. It had been more than a month since his last one. It was definitely time for Gina to come over from Put-in-Bay. Now there was a woman who didn't ask nosy questions. She just gave a damn good haircut to a man who needed some pampering once in a while. He'd be okay after he saw Gina and after he squared things with the accountant. Nick smiled in anticipation of having all his parts back in working order again. He liked an orderly life.

The knob turned slowly, guided by an unseen hand... The door to number seven eased open.

All right! Nick Bass and Ivan Banning were back in business.

AT SEVEN P.M. the first pungent aromas of garlic and tomato sauce wafted up the stairs. Factory-produced or not, the lasagna smelled darned inviting. Maybe Sara Crawford actually knew enough about cooking to add the right ingredients to a store-bought concoction to make it better.

Nick turned off his computer and headed for the bathroom down the hall. After a quick shower and shave, he pulled on a pair of jeans, a Cleveland Cavaliers T-shirt, his favorite worn Docksiders and made his way to the kitchen. He was going to enjoy seeing Sara's face when she realized he was taking her up on her invitation after all.

A single place setting, consisting of a plate, silverware and one wineglass, was on the kitchen table. Nick almost changed his mind about dinner. The thought of eating on the grime-imbedded dinette was certainly unappetizing. But when he noticed the overhead light reflecting off the polished surface of the table, he recognized that something was different in the Cozy Cove kitchen. It was clean.

Lasagna sat on top of the gleaming stove. Cheese bubbled around the edges of the pan and rippled golden brown on top. Canned sliced pears were in a bowl on the counter. And Sara, oblivious to his entrance, had her head in the refrigerator.

She was wearing a long dress made of some thin material with big splashy flowers all over. Since she was bent at the waist, the hem of the dress was raised well above her feet and showed off a pair of canvas sandals with ties going halfway up her calves. Her very shapely calves.

Nick's appetite for lasagna plunged. He would have been content to stare at Sara's backside for another few hours, but she stood up, denying him the privilege. She removed a bottle of White Thorne chardonnay from the refrigerator and set it on the counter. Obviously she'd been snooping again and discovered the secret cache he'd brought up from the cellar and stored at the bottom of the pantry. But it was technically *her* wine now, anyway.

Nick stepped all the way into the room. "Is it a good year?" he asked.

She turned abruptly, causing the flared hem of her dress to swish around her ankles. She'd caught most of her hair up in a white, shell-shaped thing. But straight honey-colored strands trailed down her neck. It looked as if she hadn't done anything to style it, but the effect was soft and feminine. The word *angelic* came to Nick's mind, though that was a word that rarely entered his vocabulary.

All similarity to a heavenly entity ended there because Sara's eyes sparked with animosity that made him stop a good ten feet from her. "What are you doing here?" she said.

"You invited me, remember?" He jerked his thumb at the lone place setting. "Though it looks like you forgot."

She turned away from him and carried the wine

bottle to the table. "I withdraw my invitation. You're free to go."

"I don't want to go."

"Well, I don't want you here."

What the devil was the matter with her now? He was doing the decent thing, coming down to eat her supper as she wanted and she'd done a complete one-eighty. Nick had no intention of leaving. He'd seen the lasagna, smelled it and had a good long look at the cook. Nope. The kitchen was right where he wanted to stay. He walked over to her, affected a grin that ought to win her over if only she'd look at him, and tapped her on her bare shoulder. "Let me guess," he said. "You're mad at me for some reason."

She didn't see the grin. She was too busy looking in a drawer, probably for a corkscrew. He debated whether or not to tell her it was in the pantry.

"I don't play guessing games, Bass," she said. "I'm only too happy to tell you that I am definitely mad at you."

"And the reason?" he persisted.

She slammed the drawer shut and spun around. Her expression registered such fury that he couldn't manage to put the grin back in place.

"The reason is that you are rude and inconsiderate—for starters."

He tried to look guilty. "That's true."

He'd opened the door to a personal attack, and she stormed in. "You have no regard for anyone's feelings. And your manners are atrocious."

"True again, but isn't that just sort of repeating the first reason?"

She crossed her arms under her breasts, pushing soft, womanly flesh above the scooped neckline of the dress. Nick cleared his throat and raised his eyes to return to the safer territory of her face. Her lips, which he'd just noticed were tinged a glossy pink, parted as she contemplated how to answer him. "Yes, I suppose it is," she conceded. "But you're extremely opinionated—and just plain weird."

He reached around her and picked up the bottle. "Okay, I'm those things, too. But I have knowledge that can add to the success of this meal, and I'm willing to share it with you for a plate of lasagna."

Her sandy-brown eyebrows arched as she huffed out an impatient breath. "And what might that be?"

"The whereabouts of the corkscrew."

He resisted the urge to look down at her pink-painted toes tapping a beat of impatience on the floor. He knew she was weighing her options. Should she allow an ill-mannered oaf to sit at her dinner table in return for her first taste of White Thorne nectar? It was a tough one.

"This is really ridiculous," she finally said in exasperation. "All right, sit down."

He headed for the table, but she grabbed his elbow. "*After* you get the corkscrew and open the wine."

THE WHITE THORNE CHARDONNAY, a 1991 vintage, was deliciously tangy with a rich, fruity base. And Nick Bass proved to be a tolerable dinner companion. In fact, when Sara asked questions about his life on Thorne Island, he actually answered some of them, though his answers were evasive.

"You haven't been here every day for six years, have you?" she asked. "You do leave the island once in a while."

"Just for hours at a time," he said. "I've been to

Put-in-Bay and Sandusky on personal business. But I probably wouldn't leave at all if I could train Winkie to clean my teeth.'' He winked, a simple gesture that somehow seemed ripe with teasing sexuality. ''There are some things a guy just can't do for himself, Sara.''

Then he changed the subject and talked about his Italian grandmother and how she made her own pasta and grew her own tomatoes and spices, and how the idea of expressing an opinion opposite her husband's was as alien to her as making spaghetti sauce from a can.

But buried somewhere in Nick's humorous exposition on the parameters for a successful relationship between the sexes was an underlying affection for—and pride in—his past. Sara ended up telling him about her life in Brewster Falls. Nick said he'd been there once. He liked the town, claiming it was typical Americana, in a good, town-square/band-shell kind of a way.

She talked about her father and how he'd done his best to raise his teenage daughter alone. And how he still worried about her and called two or three times a week just to talk and offer advice. And she admitted that leaving Brewster Falls after graduating from college had been a tough decision.

''So why did you go?'' Nick asked.

She explained about the charismatic recruiting executive from the Bosch and Lindstrom accounting firm who'd spoken to graduating seniors at Ohio State University. She submitted her résumé, and they'd hired her by phone a week later.

Nick leaned back in his chair and appraised her. ''So you must be a pretty darn good tax accountant then, right?''

She made the mistake of thinking he was sincerely interested in her skills and allowed her enthusiasm to guide the discussion in a new direction. "Well, yes, I am," she admitted. "And I see so much potential for this island."

His eyebrows came together to form a ripple of worry over the bridge of his nose.

Sara wasn't deterred. Nick and his buddies might as well know some of the details she'd been considering. "The buildings I've noticed on the island are basically sound," she said. "A few minor structural repairs, a little fixup here and there, a massive cleanup of course, and Thorne Island could be a delightful, exclusive hideaway."

"It already is a hideaway. For us." The sharp tone in his voice matched the dangerous narrowing of his eyes.

"I mean for vacationers," she persisted.

A vision of the improved island had already taken shape in her imagination, and she proceeded to tell him about it. "Nothing expensive of course. A place where families could come for a summer weekend. A nice beach, a modernized harbor, maybe a miniature golf course for children. And this inn—it wouldn't take much to bring it up to par."

A muscle worked in Nick's jaw as he inhaled a deep breath. He drew himself up until his back was as straight as the fence posts in front of the Cozy Cove must have been originally. Then he leaned forward. A threatening glare in his eyes silenced Sara.

"You're not seriously thinking of doing all this to Thorne Island, are you?" he demanded.

Her determination flared anew. "I've been having some thoughts along this line, yes. I can't see letting the island fall into ruin, especially when a profit can be realized once a formula for investing a guarded amount of capital is devised…"

She felt the buildup of his anger from across the table. He drummed his fingers, stopping after each four-tap for emphasis. "You can't do this, Sara," he said in a voice that trembled with underlying fury. "What about the people who live here and like it the way it is? What about Millie's promise to them?"

"I don't intend to fight your leases," she said. "All of you are free to stay as long as you like. I don't see what difference it will make to you if civilization slowly encroaches. I'm only trying to make things better—"

"That's bunk, Sara. You only care about making money."

She stood up from the table and slammed her chair under it. "So, we're back to that again. The sin of making money. I don't happen to think it is a sin, Nick. I think it's the smart thing to do. If you want to know what I think is a *real* sin, I'll tell you. It's four men hiding from life on an isolated island. You're like turtles drawn inside your shells for reasons that frankly scare me to death when I imagine what they might be."

He stood up and came around the table. Planting her feet solidly on the brick floor, Sara refused to let him intimidate her into backing away.

"You don't know anything about us," he said.

"Then tell me."

"I'm not telling you anything about these men, but I will tell you one thing—it's a piece of advice you'd do well to heed. This development thing, it's been tried before, and it didn't work."

"You mean the Golden Isles project?"

His eyes rounded and he drew in a sharp breath. He looked as if she'd physically struck him. "What do you know about that?"

"Only that what I'm proposing is nothing like what that company wanted to do. I'm not even considering selling plots of land."

Relief softened his features but apparently didn't lessen his anger. "Right. You only want to turn Thorne Island into a circus."

Sara shook her head in dismay. This man had the most irritating habit of exaggerating everything she said. "I do not. I only want to—"

"Leave the island alone, Sara. If you want to play accountant, go back to Florida and crunch numbers all you want. We like things the way they are."

She threw her hands in the air. "Oh, really? You like eating tomato soup and taking naps and watching your world crumble into decay?"

"And not obsessing about where our next dollar is coming from, yes!"

He wrapped his hands around her shoulders the way he'd done that afternoon, but this time his grip was forceful. Sara wasn't afraid. She stared into his pewter eyes and blasted him with the same words he'd said to her the day before. "If you're trying to scare me to death, it won't work." She let her lips curl into a satisfied grin. "I can outrun you, Bass."

His fingers flexed just before his hold on her moved to her upper arms and tightened. A tremor ran through his body and shuddered into hers. "God, you are one aggravating pencil pusher," he ground out.

She thrust her chin at him. "Why don't you tell me what's really bothering you, Bass?"

He sucked in a breath and held it, his gaze fixed intently on her face. "You want to know what's bothering me? Okay, I'll tell you. You're what's bothering me. You and your accounting principles, formulas and plans for modernizing things, and you…just you." He stopped talking, pulled her to him.

Before Sara could make an evasive move, his mouth was on hers. The kiss was hard and hungry, fired with frustration and the indefinable essence of powerful maleness. It tasted of Italian spices and tangy wine and filled her senses with something infinitely dangerous, undeniably provocative.

When he raised his head, she released a warm, drugged breath that ruffled the hair on his forehead. She swallowed hard. "Why did you do that?" she asked.

"Don't expect any explanation," he snapped at her. "Because I don't have one that would satisfy either one of us. Just think of it as my way of saying thanks for dinner." He strode from the kitchen without looking back.

A simple thank-you might have been more conventional, she thought. But it wouldn't have left such a lasting impression.

CHAPTER FIVE

"NICK, COME ON! For pity's sake, time's wasting!"

The urgent call from outside her window jolted Sara from a light sleep. She sat up in bed and focused on the sound.

"Let's go, Nickie!"

There was no mistaking that grumpy voice. Sara knew before she even reached the window that it was Brody issuing orders from in front of the inn.

"What is it with men?" she grumbled. "Is it some rite of manhood, this having to prove they can irritate the rest of society before the sun's even up?"

Next she heard Nick's irritated response coming from his window. "Keep your shirt on, Brody. For God's sake, you start this little exercise earlier every time!"

Sara peered out the window at the walkway below. *What the heck are they doing?* She couldn't see anything of Brody, since he was hidden under the metal canopy of a motorized golf cart. Just as she was getting the courage to widen the shutter opening for a better look, Brody poked his head out the side of the cart and risked a glance at her window.

Apparently satisfied when he didn't see her, he said in a coarse whisper, "You know how I feel about Digging Day, Nick. Dex and Ryan are already there."

Digging Day? What in the world was Brody talking

about? She waited until he was hidden under the cart canopy and then parted the slat again. At the back of the cart, where golf bags were usually stored, was an assortment of digging tools—shovels, spades, a couple of buckets. And flying whimsically over all of it was a yellow plastic flag of the sort kids attach to their bicycles.

"Well, isn't that cute?" Sara said to herself. "Brody must be afraid of being run over by all the traffic on Thorne Island!"

And yet the flag could prove useful. She could follow it and get to the bottom of this Digging Day thing. She was determined to learn as much as she could about the men of Thorne Island.

"Take your time, Bass," she muttered, allowing herself one last furtive peek out the window. Drat! He was already stepping off the porch. He backed up slowly toward the golf cart, his gaze intent on her window. Sara grinned to herself. At least he hadn't forgotten about her in his zeal to meet Brody. Even in the predawn light, his impressive figure sent tiny shockwaves of remembrance through Sara's system. She definitely hadn't forgotten his impulsive kiss the night before.

"Why don't you wake up the whole island, Brody?" Nick grumbled, crooking his thumb at Sara's window.

"She didn't hear me," Brody shot back. "I've never known a woman who didn't sleep past sunrise."

Sara darted to her wardrobe to pull out shorts and a T-shirt. "A lot you know, Mr. Brody. With your attitude, I'll bet your research sample has been pretty slim!"

Sara left the inn about two minutes after the golf cart carrying the two men pulled away. She followed the tire tracks until they disappeared around a corner of one of the narrow island paths, and then she cut through a wooded area to save time.

There was enough sun now for her to pick her way through the underbrush. Budding maple and oak trees were still in the early stages of new leaf growth, and parting the lowest branches, Sara spotted the bright yellow flag fluttering over the cart several hundred yards away.

The lush ground cover gave way to flowering plants, wild ferns and sumac the closer Sara got to the opposite side of the island. A cool mist rolled over the shore, bringing with it gentle swells to wash up on the rocky soil and retreat with a repetition that calmed the spirit.

Sara decided she would return to this part of the island some time when she wasn't on a mission. She would choose one of the tall, straight paper birches that lined the beach, spread out a blanket and spend several hours reading a good book. But she didn't have time to dwell on that now. The golf cart rounded a bend by a stand of sycamore trees. Two men emerged from the trees and met the cart when it stopped a few feet from the water. What an odd picture the imposing Dexter Sweet made as he walked beside the small, wiry Ryan.

Nick and Brody climbed out of the cart, and each man chose a tool from the bag-storage area. Sara crouched behind a patch of cattails and watched while the men set about doing exactly what the name of the day implied. They dug. Sand and rocks flew in the air with each upward swing of the shovels. When wa-

ter seeped into the widening hole, one or more of the
diggers jumped back and shouted a mild obscenity
about possible damage to his shoes.

Once in a while one of them would stop and fill a
mug from a thermos, prompting Sara to remember
that she hadn't yet had her coffee. After more than
half an hour, she grew impatient waiting for something to happen.

Fifteen minutes later the men had produced a sizable hole. Results of their labor sat piled up around
them in uniform pyramids of dirt, rocks and sand.
Apparently the group decided the hole was large
enough for their purpose, whatever that was. They
stopped digging and stared at the ground.

Finally Brody removed his hat and wiped his brow.
He spoke the only full sentence Sara had been able
to distinguish from any of them since they'd started
their chore. "Nope, nothing here," he said. "Might
as well get the rods."

With that proclamation, the men walked back to
the trees and returned with fishing equipment. They
removed necessary supplies from tackle boxes and
prepared their lines. The hole, at least for the moment,
was forgotten.

"This is ridiculous!" Sara said, swatting for the
umpteenth time at a persistent mosquito that obviously didn't know the sun was now fully risen. "I'm
not going to stay here and watch these guys fish!"

She headed back toward the inn. Her expedition
had left her more puzzled than ever. What were they
looking for? A body? No, surely not. Nevertheless
Sara's mind conjured up images of bleached white
bones and grinning skulls. She envisioned the men of
Thorne Island as part of some evil conspiracy. The

Erie Islands had a long and colorful history. Perhaps the diggers knew of a heinous murder that had taken place, and they were determined to unearth the grisly evidence of the crime.

By the time she reached the inn, Sara had convinced herself that such a scenario was unlikely. Dexter Sweet, whose goodness overshadowed his size and strength, and who, according to Nick, prompted the nightingales to sing, was not likely to disturb the remains of the dead. Neither was gentle Ryan who cared about flowers and a dying vineyard. And Nick Bass, antisocial hermit and mysterious gunshot victim? Well, anything was possible with him. Then there was Brody. A chill ran down Sara's spine. She could almost picture him enjoying digging up bones.

Deciding she'd had all she could take of macabre thoughts for one day, she put the matter out of her mind. She entered the inn by the front door, then walked into the parlor and surveyed the nondescript lumps of furniture covered by yards of white cloth—harmless chairs, sofas and tables made to look like ghostly specters.

''Enough of this!'' Sara announced to the gloomy room. She yanked back the draperies and opened all the windows. Then she ripped the cover from the lump nearest her to expose a beautiful balloon-backed Victorian chair. Its brocade seat was worn, but its curved mahogany arms could be brought back to their previous splendor with a little polish and some energetic rubbing.

Sara decided upon her project for the rest of the morning. She hoped Bass had left the coffeepot on in the kitchen. She'd have a cup first, then gather up supplies to dust and sweep. She would coax life back into the parlor of the Cozy Cove Inn.

NICK AND DEXTER walked back to the inn after fishing for two hours. Brody had offered to drive them in the cart one at a time, but Nick refused, and not just because Dex had told him the walk would be good for him. The truth was, he'd had about all of Brody he could handle for one day. Also, Nick was getting tired of Brody's damn Digging Day. Ritual was one thing, but there was no reason this particular ritual couldn't be carried out at a decent hour. Plus, the guy could really be a cantankerous old coot. Sara was right about that, though Nick would never admit it to her.

Nick thought about Brody's son, Carl Junior, who hadn't seen his father in years. The two men had fought over money long ago, but Nick called Junior every few months to give him an update on Brody's well-being. He'd been making the calls for years, hoping someday the two Brody men would put an end to their feud. But that wasn't likely to happen very soon. In fact, Brody would have a fit if he knew Nick kept in contact with Junior. But how long could one man hold a grudge? Forever, it seemed, if his name was Carlton Brody, owner of Good Company Hygiene Products.

Nick almost laughed out loud as he approached the steps to the Cozy Cove veranda. To think that slovenly Brody had made his millions by making other people deodorants and bath oils! Yep, someday Nick was going to call Carl Junior and tell him to get over here. It was time to put that family back together.

Dexter stopped at the bottom of the stairs. "Don't you want to come in?" Nick asked. "I'll buy you a cup of coffee."

"No thanks," Dexter said. "I'm working on a couple of end-run plays I think might click. Wanna get them down on paper. But I'll come back later if you want help with your exercises."

Nick waved him away. "Nah, I'll do them myself." Seeing the skepticism in Dexter's eyes, he added, "Really. I promise. You don't need to play nursemaid, Dex."

The men parted at the porch, and Dexter headed toward his two-room cabin down the lane from Brody's place. The small accommodations suited the large man just fine, or so he said. Just enough room to catch the sports events on his big-screen TV and analyze the heck out of them when they were over. All the guys had chipped in on the satellite dish, but it was Dexter who dictated what channels they could watch.

They really were an odd bunch, the men of Thorne Island, Nick decided as he stepped into the inn. But they were his family now, and he accepted them with all their faults. But that didn't mean he wouldn't try to make them see the error of their ways once in a while.

Nick stopped in the lobby and sniffed the air. What was that smell? Lemon and ammonia. It was strong but not unpleasant. And it sure as hell wasn't a scent common to the Cozy Cove. The source came to his mind immediately. Sara Crawford was playing at housekeeping again.

He stepped into the parlor and was bombarded with floral fabrics, needlepoint tapestries and gleaming mahogany. All the furniture he'd covered so carefully years before now basked in the sunlight coming through washed windowpanes.

And Sara Crawford, her pleasing little butt covered by a skimpy pair of cutoffs and her hair wrapped in a bandanna, was crouched over the hearth sweeping old ashes into a dustpan.

"Good morning, Bass," she said without looking at him.

He stood, legs slightly apart, fists on his hips. It was a strong, manly stance, he thought, but it had little effect on a woman who didn't bother noticing. So Nick dropped his hands and took two steps closer to her. "Just what the hell do you think you're doing, Sara?"

She looked up at him. Smudges of soot streaked her face and a gleam of perspiration dotted her upper lip. Strands of blond hair trailed over a shoulder not covered by her knit tank top. God, she looked adorable. Nick had to remind himself that was not the issue.

She set the dustpan on the brick hearth. "Really, Bass, your powers of observation are limited at best. You just asked a woman holding a whisk broom and a pan of ashes what she was doing."

"That's not what I meant and you know it." He waved his arms to indicate the entire room. "I'm talking about all this…this…"

"Cheerfulness?" she suggested with an infuriatingly smug grin.

"Interference! You're doing it again."

"Doing what?"

"Changing things. You're leaving in a couple of days—"

"I never said that."

"Okay, a couple of days, a week, whatever. Anyway, you'll be gone, and I'll have to go around and cover all this stuff up again."

She feigned innocence. "Why would you do that?"

"We don't use this room, Sara. Sometimes in the winter I come down and sit by the fire in this chair." He walked over and slapped his hand on the back of one of the two pieces of furniture that hadn't been covered. Dust rose in the air. "This is the only chair that is used in this room—ever."

She stood up and adjusted the tank top so it covered the tantalizing band of skin revealed at her midsection. Nick felt deprived.

"Until now," she said. "For your information, I intend to come into this parlor and move from chair to chair and then start all over again. I intend to sit in every blessed seat in the room until I leave Thorne Island." She marched over to a window and pulled the heavy drapes even farther apart. "And I will do it in brilliant sunlight!"

She was daring him. Did she think he was a vampire and she could kill him with sunshine? "You are one stubborn, bossy lady, you know that, Crawford?"

She muttered something he couldn't quite make

out, but he thought he detected the word *ghoul* somewhere in her sentence. "What did you say?"

She didn't back down. Instead, she approached him with a swagger in her step. "I said, 'At least I'm not a ghoul out digging graves.'"

Oh, so that was it. He should have added *nosy* and *sneaky* to her list of attributes. "I get it," he said, reaching for her. When he grabbed her hand, she flinched, but it only made him hold on tighter. He ran a finger up her arm, stopping at intervals. "I see you have several mosquito bites. And now I know how you got them."

"So what?" She pulled her hand free. "It was your buddy who hollered under my window like a foghorn this morning. Besides, it's a good thing I did follow you. I need to know what manner of degenerates I'm dealing with on this island."

"Yeah? And what manner are we?"

She scratched absently at one of her bites. "Unfortunately I don't know…yet."

"Did you actually think we were digging up a grave?"

"Well—"

"Sara, at the risk of having Brody flail me with his hat full of tetanus-infected lures, I'll tell you what we were doing. We were digging for hidden treasure, like we've done every Monday morning when the ground isn't frozen for the last six years."

Her jaw dropped, and she stared up at him. There was no mistaking the sudden interest in her eyes. "There's hidden treasure on this island?"

"Frankly I don't think there's so much as a single *sou,* but Brody does, so we look."

"Why does he think there's treasure buried here?"

"It's some loony bit of folklore about the first French fur trappers who came to the island. They were with this missionary named Father Bertrand. He had a small fortune in coins and jewels entrusted to him by the French monarch, and he was supposed to barter with the Indians for land that might be valuable to the French crown. According to Brody, who studies things like this, the fortune was never spent, but left here on the island. The story has passed down through generations since the eighteenth century. But like I said, I don't believe—"

"Wow." A veiled wonder had suddenly appeared over the bright blue of Sara's eyes. "You must believe it, Bass. Otherwise why would you help Brody find it?"

Don't women get anything? "Because he wants me to," Nick said simply. "It's what he does."

Sara's perplexed look told him she still didn't get it. "But do you keep records? Maps? Logs of your diggings?"

Just like an accountant! "No."

"How do you know you're not digging in a place you've dug before?"

"I suppose we could be. Who knows? We always fill the holes before we leave."

She sank onto the sofa and placed her sooty cheeks in her palms. "This is incredible, Bass. I don't understand you men at all."

That was the first thing she'd said that he could agree with.

"You spend your time on what you believe is a totally fruitless endeavor," she went on, "and you don't even do it with a modicum of precision or planning." She gave him a look that was part bewilderment and part sympathy. "You're all spinning your wheels, Bass. You're not getting anywhere."

He shrugged. "That's about the size of it. But, hey, it's Brody's thing. I just go along for the ride. But don't you get my point?"

She gave a rather unfeminine belly laugh. "You mean to tell me there's a point to this?"

"Of course. I told you about the treasure to illustrate a very important one." He thumped his chest with two fingers. "This is what we're all about. We're men doing our own thing on Thorne Island. You can't come a-callin' for a few days and change things all around. You may be a great kisser, Sara Crawford, but—"

Blue fire danced in her eyes. "Don't you dare bring that up. You had no right to kiss me last night."

"Really? I'm sorry you feel that way because I was thinking about doing it again."

She thrust out her hands, palms up as if to fend off an attack. "Don't even think about it, Bass."

"Why? Because you're not thinking about it, Sara?"

"Of course I'm not thinking about it."

He gave her a skeptical look so she'd know he didn't believe her.

"Stop looking at me like that!"

Nick just smiled as he grabbed her hand and tugged her off the sofa. "Come on up to my room."

"I will not! I just told you—"

"Don't get your hackles up, accountant. I don't want to take a lap around the track with any lady who's been cozying up to a fire grate." God, he was a liar!

"Then why are we going to your room?"

Was it his imagination, or did she almost sound disappointed?

"Because I've got a bottle of calamine lotion in my closet. I'm going to paint your arms with pink polka dots."

CHAPTER SIX

AROUND NOON Sara pulled on a Sloppy Joe's T-shirt with Ernest Hemingway's picture on front and hurried downstairs. She'd grab a quick lunch and be ready for Captain Winkleman when he arrived early that afternoon. She couldn't resist looking in the parlor and admiring the furnishings she'd polished and dusted. Even the rugs looked fresher, though all she'd found to use on them was an old Bissell sweeper.

It was a pleasure to go into the kitchen, as well. When Winkleman brought the food she'd ordered, she would put it into the main refrigerator, now shiny and smelling of lemon. Meanwhile she was still using Nick's. She opened the door, reached in for the salami and noticed the fading pink dots on her arms.

At first she'd resisted Nick's attempts to relieve her itching, but he'd insisted. He'd made her sit on his bed while he found the bottle of calamine lotion and cotton balls. Then he'd deliberately, and with unsettling care, dabbed the thick lotion on each of her bites.

Thinking about it now, Sara smiled and rubbed the pad of her index finger over the crusty circles of calamine. Then she washed her hands and did something she probably wouldn't have done if Nick hadn't let her glimpse his gentle side. She made two sandwiches, one for herself and one for him. She secured his in plastic wrap and put it into his refrigerator.

He'd already gone back to his computer and might not think of food for a while.

She'd just tossed the crumbs of her own sandwich into the backyard for the robins when she heard the unmistakable roar of Winkleman's boat. She left the inn and headed for the harbor to retrieve her food and the fertilizer she'd ordered, and also to arrange for the captain to take her to Put-in-Bay. If she was going to stay on Thorne Island an extra week—as she'd decided that morning—she needed to purchase a cell phone so she could keep in touch with Candy and the office. Plus, she wanted to see her father and buy supplies to make her stay more comfortable. And she had to do something about the rental car parked in the lot in Sandusky.

Sara's decision to extend her stay had been a logical one, especially after she'd come to the rather astounding realization that she was enjoying herself. And this, despite the attitudes of her island neighbors. The feeling had come from deep inside as if it had been buried under layers of all the things that had defined her life the past few years—calculators, appointments and spreadsheets.

But a new Sara Crawford was emerging. One who looked forward to the challenge of fixing up the inn. Improving the conditions on Thorne Island wasn't just a wise financial decision. It actually fulfilled a need in her she probably never would have known about if she hadn't come to the island.

She loved how—through her efforts alone—shine had replaced grime in the kitchen. She'd returned the pitted and tarnished fixtures on the bathroom sink to their original sparkle. And she'd changed the cold, spectral parlor into a retreat of comfort and understated beauty.

She considered asking Winkleman to take her back with him today, but there were considerations on the island more pressing than her chores on the mainland. If Winkie had brought the fertilizer she ordered, she needed to identify the most promising vines behind the inn, remove the weeds from around the bases of the trunks and spread a mixture of fertilizer and compost into the soil. April was a crucial month in wine production, and if well fed and tended, the vines could produce ripe grapes as early as the end of August.

There was so much to do! As she approached the harbor, Sara thought about all the improvements she wanted to make. She couldn't wait to spruce up the inn with fresh paint and wallpaper and fertilize the neglected gardens. Absorbed in picturing the results of her labors, she came upon the clearing at the dock and her enthusiasm plunged like a January thermometer. Had she really ordered all that fertilizer?

Dexter, Brody and Nick were already there, looking down at six thirty-pound bags of Sow and Grow, a fertilizer made of organic materials and old-fashioned manure. Sara wrinkled her nose when she caught a whiff of the sacks.

Nick grinned at her and tipped a box of groceries he'd just unloaded from the boat so she could see the contents. "Look what I got from Captain Winkie, Sara," he said with a teasing smugness. "I know it's only frozen dinners, bologna and beer—" he nodded toward the manure "—but it looks pretty good next to what you got."

"Very funny, Bass. Actually, our orders are quite

similar when you consider what they're made of."
She stopped a few feet from the fertilizer and
frowned. How was she going to cart these bags back
to the vineyard?

Captain Winkleman held up a sack of groceries. "I
didn't forget you, Sara. I've got the things you
wanted."

She reached for the sack while Winkie enumerated
the contents.

"I brought your yogurt and whole-wheat bread and
thin sliced turkey just like you asked. Had some trouble with no-fat mayo. Hope what I got is okay."

Ignoring the sour expressions on the men's faces,
Sara cradled her food protectively. "I'm sure everything's fine," she said. "Thank you very much."

Brody started back to the pathway with Dexter on
his heels. "Come on, boys. Let's get this stuff to the
commissary." He leveled a smirk at Sara over his
shoulder. "Miss Crawford, I expect you'll want to
keep your grub with you so it won't be contaminated
by real food."

"That's fine with me. Besides I wouldn't want my
yogurt to tempt you in the middle of the night." A
solution to her transportation problem suddenly came
to mind and she interrupted Brody's retort mid mumble. "Oh, Mr. Brody, before you go, could I borrow
your golf cart for a few minutes? I need to move these
bags of fertilizer to the vineyard."

Without pausing, he tossed a succinct answer back
to her. "Battery's dead. Won't be charged until morning."

Sara's temper simmered on the verge of boiling.
She'd always been able to tell when someone was

lying. Brody and Dexter disappeared into the trees, but Nick stayed behind, his arms laden with groceries.

"Look, Sara, if you can wait till I take these things to Brody's…"

Wonder of wonders, Nick Bass was actually going to offer to help. She was about to express her appreciation when a cry from the pathway diverted her attention.

"Where in hell are you going with that thing?" Brody hollered.

"I'm helping Sara," Ryan replied. The defiant words were immediately followed by the appearance of a dilapidated but functional wheelbarrow with Ryan gripping the wooden handles. He crisscrossed the dock with awkward determination and set the wobbly cart next to the bags. "I figured you could use this," he said proudly.

Sara could have kissed him. Instead, she beamed at him and said, "How nice of you."

Nick released a cynical grumble. "There you see, Sara, chivalry is not dead on Thorne Island."

"You're right. It isn't. I just figured you boys must have buried it so deep in one of your holes, you'd never find it."

Nick shook his head and started after his companions. "Don't worry, Ryan," he said with obvious sarcasm. "We'll carry your supplies to Brody's."

"Thanks, Nick," Ryan answered with innocent appreciation.

Captain Winkleman slapped the edge of the dock. "Well, now that everything's settled, I'll be on my way."

Sara put up her hand to stop him from revving his noisy engine to life. "Wait, Captain. I need to ask you a favor. Could you come back tomorrow morning? I've decided to go to the mainland.''

He touched the brim of his soiled nautical cap. "No problem. I have to come back to bring something for Nick. It'll still cost you a twenty spot, though. Can't run this baby on goodwill.''

Sara almost reminded him that he'd just admitted he was coming anyway but thought better of it. "Fine," she said.

Nick stopped in the pathway and strained to hear the conversation at the harbor. Did Sara just say she was going to the mainland?

What the hell did she mean? That she was going for good? Surely not. She'd just ordered all that fertilizer. But if she was, Brody was to blame. The grouchy old fool's refusal to let Sara borrow the cart must have been the last straw. You'd think that rusted old contraption was a vintage Rolls-Royce the way Brody was acting. *Dead battery my ass!* Nick thought. He'd seen Brody run that cart all over the island for hours and still brag that it could go another round.

Nick couldn't blame Sara if she did up and leave. Some men were downright pigheaded when it came to women. Nick sure hoped he didn't turn out like Brody, bitter and cold.

He paused before going up the short set of stairs into Brody's cottage. What was he thinking? Of course Sara had to go. He'd known that from the start. In fact, he'd politely pointed out her interference a time or two himself. She had a life in Florida, and he had a life on Thorne Island—a calm, regimented life where he could set his own hours, seek his own companionship and pursue his writing without anyone telling him what to do.

So why was he feeling anything but calm at this moment? Why was he stewing about Sara Crawford's going back to Fort Lauderdale where she belonged? He ought to go into Brody's place, slap the old guy on the back and thank him for sending her away. But he didn't feel a bit like doing that. In fact, he could picture his hands around Brody's throat a lot more easily than he could see himself slapping his back.

Nick shook his head and climbed the steps. "Get a hold of yourself, Romano," he grumbled. "You're letting a cute butt and a pair of blue eyes get to you." He paused before opening the door. *And a damn fine figure, too.* Nick recalled the black-and-white image of Ernest Hemingway clinging to Sara's breasts. Damn! Now he was actually jealous of a guy's face on a T-shirt, and a dead guy at that!

The image exploded from Nick's mind like it'd been blasted with a stick of dynamite—Brody's voice had that effect. "Come on, Nick, bring that stuff over here to the fridge before it's not fit to eat!"

NICK TRIED TO WRITE. For three hours he tried to become Ivan Banning and follow clues to the drug pushers. He'd known it would be a difficult task after he'd found the sandwich wrapped in plastic in the refrigerator. It even had his name taped to the top.

The last time anyone made a sandwich for him he was still in middle school, and the burden had been placed on Paloma, his mother's Peruvian housekeeper. Paloma was nice enough, but she'd always ruined his lunch by sticking carrots or celery into the bag. Sara had left a chocolate bar. Granted, it was low-fat and tasted like cardboard, but it was still a heck of a lot better than carrots.

After three hours of typing a sentence or two every fifteen minutes, Nick gave in to his curiosity about what was happening in the vineyard. He went to a bedroom with a window facing north, where he could see Sara and Ryan working like little grape elves a hundred yards away. Then he went back to his monitor, deleted everything he'd written so far and shut down the computer. It was no use trying to write. He went to the kitchen, out the back door and headed for the vineyard.

Ryan was gone, but Sara was still there. She'd made the rusted spigot on the side of the old press house work, and she was bent over splashing water on her arms. Nick watched her, thinking that this simple act of a woman cleaning her arms might very well be the most sensual, intimate thing he'd ever seen. His insides coiled like a spring.

She stood, balancing herself with one hand on the rough stone exterior of the press house, and rotated a bare foot under the running water. That was when she saw him. And Nick Bass, alias Nicolas Romano, who never thought for a moment that she would be glad to see him, felt her welcoming gaze pour through him like warm honey.

She waved him over. "Nick, come here. You have to see."

He joined her as she turned off the water and playfully flicked a couple of drops into his face. "Promise me you won't be cynical."

He pretended to be insulted—in fact, he was a little. "Who, me? cynical? Can't remember when I ever was."

She snickered while sliding her feet into plastic sandals. Then she walked down a row of vines until she came to the one she wanted to show him. Reaching through the new growth of wide green leaves, she brought out a mysterious cluster of tiny objects that she cradled in her palm. "They're alive, Nick," she whispered reverently. "See for yourself."

Nick stared down at minuscule green pellets clinging to a thin thread and determined that they were indeed grapes and showed a lot more promise than that shriveled-up piece of refuse Sara had shown him yesterday. And one day, with a little luck and a dash of Sara's determination, they might just defy the odds and end up pleasing somebody's palate.

"Well, I'll be," he said. "Nobody's paid any attention to these plants for years that I know of. Even Ryan only clipped away randomly."

She gently returned the tender cluster to its nest of leaves. "There aren't many healthy vines," she admitted. "But there might be enough to have some kind of harvest, maybe by late summer." She pointed down the row to patches of dark, moist earth. "Ryan and I turned the dirt and fertilized around the bases of the most promising ones."

Late summer. She's talking about harvesting grapes in late summer.

"Of course Ryan will have to take care of the vines. I won't be here, but it will be enough to know that we succeeded."

So she was leaving, after all. The practical side of Nick experienced a flood of relief. This was best for the men of Thorne Island, wasn't it? But the emotional side, the one he'd never been well acquainted with, gripped like a vise around his heart and made his next breath hitch in his throat.

"He may not want to do the work when I'm gone," she said, turning away from Nick and facing the rows of vines.

"Who, Ryan?"

She nodded. "It's hard when you don't have a partner to share the responsibility. And of course it will be especially difficult if the rest of you make fun of him."

"We wouldn't do that."

She rolled her eyes. "Well, at least try not to. Ryan is a sensitive guy, you know."

He nodded slowly, trying not to smile. "Oh, I know. We're all careful not to bruise the little guy's feelings."

She pivoted and narrowed her eyes at him. "Funny. Now, would you do me a favor while we still have a little daylight?"

"What's that?"

"Get me the key to the press house. I'm dying to see inside. Since you're the village banker, I figure you've got the keys to the kingdom, as well."

"I'm your man." He walked back to the house for the keys, telling himself he had his emotions in check. Sara was going away. Everything would be back to normal in a couple of days. In fact, maybe she'd decided not to turn Thorne Island into a summer playground. Maybe the grapes had satisfied her homemaker's need to repair and improve.

Okay. Ryan could piddle around in the dirt a little and trim a few vines. And the rest of them could go on with their lives just as they had before Sara Crawford showed up. And that was what he wanted, right?

"Damn straight," he said to himself. "Just me and the guys like it's been for six years. Pure, unspoiled contentment." So why did he feel so discontented?

SARA LEANED against the exterior wall of the press house and watched Nick stride through the brush toward her. His limp was barely noticeable today. A large, round key ring swung from his hand and jingled almost ominously in the cool air. Waning sunlight cast his body in shadows. He might have been a medieval jailer traipsing through the bailey on his way to the castle tower—except for his navy-blue cargo shorts and the gray golf shirt with faded splashes of magnolias surrounding the words "Augusta, Georgia." That attire was strictly Nick's.

A scowl settled on Sara's face. Confidence and strength seemed to ooze from every pore of this man. Too bad he'd gone out of his way to be critical and uncooperative. In fact, the pale pink splotches of calamine lotion on her arms were all that hinted of a gentler side to Nick Bass.

"We'd better hurry," he said, coming up to her. "It'll be dark soon, and I'm not sure you'll like this place then." He wiggled his fingers in a spiderlike motion.

Ignoring his attempt to frighten her, she led the way to the heavy oak door at the front of the building. "When's the last time you were in here?" she asked.

"I don't know. Three years ago, maybe. I was looking for some electrical tape and a pair of wire cutters."

"Making a bomb, were you?"

He frowned at her while inserting a key into the rusty lock. "No. Sorry to disappoint you. I was repairing the cord to my computer. You probably expected something more sinister, more ghoulish from me.''

Nick had to press against the door with his shoulder to make the swollen wood cooperate. Finally the huge iron hinges squeaked in defeat and the door swung inward wide enough to allow Sara and Nick entrance.

Sara went first, and felt immediately thrust back to another century. She paused, allowing her eyes to adjust to the near-darkness. The last rays of sunlight filtered through narrow, grimy windows along the ceiling and revealed the stark, stone walls. She took a few tentative steps.

The room smelled of the hundred years of patience and craftsmanship that had come before her—a sweet, fruity aroma mingled with the scent of old wood and the dank, musty smell of neglect. A three-foot-high circular vat, held together with pitted metal bands, occupied the center of the room. It recalled the days when grapes were crushed with hands and feet. Sara had never seen an authentic crushing vat before. Smaller tubs surrounded it, providing a place for the crushers to wash their feet before entering the vat.

The rest of the room was testimony to the winemaking process. Vitreous crocks stood on one side, while basket presses occupied the other. Thick pads of gauze were stacked on high shelves next to bottles with faded labels identifying yeast, sulfite solution, sucrose and various chemicals designed to alter the acidity of the wine.

Sara circled the room, running her fingers over the various textures of the alien but enticing environment—the smooth, porous surface of the crocks, the brittle, sharp planks of the press baskets, the cool iron of their handles.

"It's all so wonderful, isn't it?" she said, not expecting Nick to appreciate the significance of the moment.

He didn't disappoint her. "If you like the smell of mold and mildew and looking at a lot of old stuff, it is."

She turned toward him, surprised to find him so close behind her. Their footsteps had been silent on the old wood floor. "Tell me about the wine makers," she said.

He shrugged. "Not much to tell. All I know I learned from Millie. She bought the island sometime in the eighties from the Krauses, who originally came from Germany in the 1800s, settled here and made wine for few generations like a lot of people did on these islands."

"When did they stop?"

"Years ago. I think it was the fourth generation of Krauses in America who gave it up. Millie hired people to run the vineyard until the early nineties, but I guess it was too expensive to continue."

"What became of the Krauses?"

"I heard they moved to Detroit."

"I think it would be hard to leave all this." Sara looked away and saw for the first time narrow stairs descending to a lower level. "What's in the basement?" she asked, going closer.

"That's the fermenting room," Nick said, staying close to her. "It has low ceilings, and from what I remember, is darned cold. There's just a lot of old bottles and barrels down there."

"I want to see."

He reached out for her when her foot found the first step. "No, Sara, don't. It's too dark. You won't be able to see anything. You might hurt yourself."

Curiosity and stubbornness pushed all logic from her mind. Sara groped her way along a limestone wall while her feet navigated the next dark stair.

The third step was broken.

Sara's hand slipped from the moist stone she'd been holding and she lost her footing. She likely would have tumbled the whole way down if Nick hadn't suddenly wrapped a powerful arm around her waist and hauled her back up against his chest. She closed her eyes and clung tightly to his arm.

The full realization of what almost happened left her dizzy and trembling with fear and mortification. "Oh, God, I'm sorry Nick," she said when her breathing returned to normal.

He slowly backed them away from the steps. "Don't you ever take advice, Sara?" he asked not unkindly.

She turned to look at him. He didn't slacken his hold, and she was grateful. She was still shaky, but a sense of security was seeping into her, and she didn't want him to let go. His gaze met hers, and her heart responded with a quick, heightened rhythm. She was no longer frightened of falling, so there had to be another reason for this reaction.

His gaze, as ashen as the scented shadows surrounding them, settled on her lips. She lay her palm on his chest, covering one of the magnolias. Her fingertips grazed the opening of the shirt, sliding in to settle on a mat of coarse hair. "I do take advice…sometimes," she said.

His fingers curled under her chin. He lifted her

face, drawing her mouth closer to his. "You should take it more often, Sara."

"Why do you care, Nick? You don't seem to care much about anything."

"And you care too much."

He shook his head. The movement was almost imperceptible. "It's taken me years to get this way, sweetheart, and I don't like the idea of someone who doesn't even know me trying to change the way I am and the way I live."

She jerked her face away, but he cupped the back of her head, keeping her close. "I'm not trying to change anything," she said.

"You're trying to change everything, and you know it. Now here's another piece of advice. Stop talking."

His mouth covered hers and he pulled her close. Darkness enveloped them. Old things creaked around them. Live things skittered along the walls. The sweetness in the air made Sara dizzy. The lingering kiss made it all go away. The world was connected at one place, one glorious center where their lips met and held.

When he pulled away, Sara could still feel the pressure of his mouth. She still felt the moisture from his lips. "Nick—"

He held up one finger. "Don't say anything, Sara. Don't try to make me talk about this. It was a kiss, that's all. A going-away kiss, at that. Take it as your goodbye from Nick Bass."

Quite unexpectedly she wanted to laugh. He looked so serious. "But I'm not going away," she said.

"What? I heard you tell Winkie—"

"—to pick me up and take me to Put-in-Bay for

the ferry. I've got some errands to run on the mainland, and I'm going to Brewster Falls to see my dad. But I'll be back the next day."

He dropped his hands and backed away as if her head had sprouted snakes. "Hell, Sara, you're making me crazy!"

He pivoted away from her with almost military precision and strode to the door without looking back.

She called after him, "Thanks for giving me all the credit, Nick. But I think you were crazy long before I got here."

CHAPTER SEVEN

IT WAS BARELY eight-thirty when Sara heard Winkleman's boat and once again noted that rising with the sun seemed to be a mark of manhood for the men of Thorne Island. She'd observed Nick's desk light glowing from his room for more than an hour already and suspected he was working on his computer at whatever mysterious task occupied his daylight hours.

Sara tucked her extensive shopping list into the side pouch of her overnight bag. If Winkleman was ready to leave right away, she'd easily catch the ten-o'clock ferry from Put-in-Bay to Sandusky. The boat's engine was silent when Sara zipped her bag closed, indicating Winkie was at the dock. She pulled on a white zip sweatshirt and sneakers and gathered her hair into a ponytail. Her last trip with the captain taught her that it was a waste of time to worry about appearance for the ride across the lake.

Hoisting the bag off her bed, Sara left her room, closed the door behind her and headed for the stairs. "See you tomorrow, Bass," she called to the partially open door at the opposite end of the hall.

"If I don't decide to take a hike," he hollered back.

"Hah! As if you would actually leave."

She was still smiling when she reached the lobby and headed for the exit.

The screen door swung open before she reached it.

Sara's expression changed to astonishment as a dark-haired, olive-skinned woman with a shiny gold satchel slung over her shoulder sauntered in with a casual "Hi" and a demeanor that indicated she was not at all surprised to see Sara.

It wasn't polite to stare, but Sara couldn't help herself. The woman seemed to fill the lobby with color and energy. She wore tight-fitting black leggings and a sleeveless tunic top that covered her torso in alternating pink, teal and black stripes. Short, dark curls escaped from the hot-pink scarf wound round her head. The scarf matched her lip color perfectly. Artfully applied makeup made it impossible to determine her age.

The mystery woman must have come in Winkleman's boat. Forcing herself to remember her manners and the fact that she was now mistress of the Cozy Cove Inn, Sara found her voice. "Welcome to the Cozy Cove," she said. "Can I help you?"

"Nope. Thanks, anyway." The woman cracked a piece of chewing gum with a skill Sara had tried to master in middle school. "I know where I'm goin'." She pushed her glittering vinyl satchel to her back for better balance and headed for the stairs.

"Are you staying the night?" Sara asked.

The woman stopped with one foot on the first step and turned around. "Sure. I always do." Then she pointed a sculpted pink-and-silver nail at Sara. "You must be wonderin' who I am, right?"

That was an understatement. The woman's declaration that she was staying overnight, her beeline for the stairs and the overstuffed satchel had led Sara to a rather unsettling conclusion that involved Nick Bass. "Well, I don't mean to pry..."

The woman returned to Sara with her hand out-stretched. "I'm Gina. Gina Sacco. I've been givin' the boys haircuts for years. That's what I do. I'm a hairdresser."

Sara pumped the offered hand as relief engulfed her. "I'm Sara Crawford. I've only been here a few days and I'm just learning what goes on. So you're a hairdresser. Of course that explains...your visit."

She drew a deep breath and assumed her role of innkeeper. "Do you have a regular room? I don't re-call that we have one made up right now. Just mine at the end of the hall." She pointed in the direction of her closed door. "You're welcome to stay there tonight. I'm going back to Put-in-Bay with Captain Winkleman."

"I know. Winkie told me about you. Thanks for the offer of the room, but I won't be needin' it." Gina's gaze darted upstairs to the opposite end of the hallway where the artificial light from a computer spilled out the door. "I'll just stay where I usually do." She gave Sara a knowing grin, accompanied by another crack of gum.

"Oh, well. I see..." Sara grasped the handle of her overnight bag so tightly her fingernails dug painfully into her palm. Her cheeks flushing, she backed out of the inn. Gina stayed in Nick's room! Sara's heart pounded in her chest and echoed in her ears. She barely heard Gina's cheerful call. "Have a good time in town. Nice meetin' ya."

As Sara hurried down the path to the harbor, she tried unsuccessfully to erase persistent images of what tonight would bring to Thorne Island.

SARA WISHED more than ever that the noisy engine on Winkleman's boat would drop a few decibels. At least then she could attempt a conversation with the captain and could avoid the scene at the inn replaying over and over in her mind. When they reached Put-in-Bay and Winkleman headed for the Happy Angler, Sara still wasn't able to dismiss thoughts of Gina and Nick. Ten minutes later she was one of only five passengers on the ferry to Sandusky, and the other four seemed content to keep to themselves.

With the entire world apparently intent on silent withdrawal, Sara had only one person to whom she could talk about her emotional turmoil—herself. *Well, what did you expect, Sara Crawford?* she demanded to know. *Did you think Nick Bass was a monk?*

She already knew that wasn't so. A man who kissed the way he did—so impulsively and thoroughly—celibate for the past six years? Not likely. Not a man like Bass.

A man like Bass. The phrase rolled over in her mind like the chorus of a familiar song. Just what kind of man was he? What motivated Nick Bass, who sat for hours at his computer? And what was the story behind the gunshot wound to his spine? Was honor involved? Or deceit? Loyalty or treachery? Love or hate?

Sara picked up her bag and stepped onto the dock. The only significant question was why it was so important for her to know what kind of man Nick was. Why was she searching for answers about such a complicated, difficult individual? She had an entire island to think about. "Forget about Nick Bass," she said aloud, giving herself a mental shake.

She walked past the ferry ticket office toward the parking lot where she'd left her rental car. When she spied the blue Chevy Cavalier with its Alamo sticker, she fished for the keys in her jeans pocket. Maybe it was a good thing she had this time away from the island. She needed to get her priorities in order. She planned to turn Thorne Island into a profitable venture that she could manage from her condo in Fort Lauderdale. Nick Bass could stay or go. It shouldn't matter to her what he did—or who he slept with. She would proceed with her renovations despite him and his band of lost boys.

Feeling proud of her resolve, Sara suddenly stopped walking and let out an exasperated breath. She'd walked right past the blue Cavalier and out of the parking lot. So much for her pep talk. If she wasn't careful, thoughts of Nick would have her walking in a daze all the way to Brewster Falls.

"Nick Bass," she grumbled, retracing her steps. "Now who's driving who crazy?"

Moments later Sara tossed her bag into the back seat of the Chevy, started the engine and headed toward Brewster Falls, an hour's drive from Sandusky. She very much needed to see her father, to experience his cool, logical approach to everything and his tender protective concern. All the errands she needed to run could be accomplished in her hometown.

An hour later she pulled off the freeway and onto a two-lane county road that led to Brewster Falls. At the base of Dewer's Hill, Sara saw the large wooden sign that had welcomed people to the town for as long as she could remember. The insignias of the Lions and Rotary clubs were still proudly displayed on the sign, along with a broad selection of places of worship. Even the numbers on the removable placard showing the town's population had varied by only a couple of dozen over the years.

Sara yielded to oncoming cars before entering the light flow of traffic on the road that surrounded the center of town. In the middle of the shaded, grassy area interspersed with brick walkways was the band shell where local musicians showed off their talent on warm summer evenings. Brewster Falls—a band-shell kind of town. That was what Nick had called it. And it was also the town that had nurtured her through her childhood years and still called her back from a steel-and-glass Fort Lauderdale high-rise.

Sara pulled into the lot of Ben Crawford's Texaco, one of the few full-service gas stations still around. Earl Pasco, who'd worked at the station since it opened, dropped the hood of a customer's car, shielded his eyes and stared at the blue Cavalier. When recognition dawned, a wide grin split his leathered face. "Well I'll be. Howdy, Sara!"

"Hi, Earl."

"Your daddy know you're here?"

"Not yet. But he knows I'm coming." Sara nodded toward the service bays. "Is he inside?"

At that moment Ben Crawford, tall, robust and solid as the rocks along the Brewster River banks, came out of the middle bay and wiped his hands on an old rag. "Whoa, will you look who's here!" He didn't wait for Sara to get out of the car on her own. He opened the door and practically hauled her out and into a hug that had always been strong enough to squeeze the problems out of Sara's life.

"You're a sight for sore eyes, Sarabelle," he said, stepping back and giving her a thorough appraisal.

"You, too, Dad."

"Now tell me all about this business deal you're into. I've been curious as can be since you called yesterday."

"It's a long story, Dad. But an interesting one."

"Then I guess you'd better tell it over a couple of tall, cool ones."

Sara grinned. That was what her father always called the vanilla colas at the drugstore soda fountain. He called over his shoulder to his mechanic, "Earl, you replace the distributor on Lou's pick up. I'm going down to Percy's Drugs with Sara."

NEVER ONE TO SETTLE for just a vanilla cola, Ben lifted a hefty spoonful of his hot fudge sundae to his mouth and grinned like a kid who'd just hit a grand slam. "Oh, that's good," he said, licking the spoon.

Ben studied Sara for a moment, then said, "Now, let's get to the heart of the matter, Sarabelle. What's going on? Why do you need all these things on your shopping list?"

She'd been bursting to tell him the news, and once the practical matters were out of the way, she was free to confide in him. "Dad, do you remember Mom's aunt, Millicent Thorne?"

"Millie? Why sure. What about her?"

"First, there's some bad news. Millie died a few weeks ago."

Sadness veiled Ben's eyes. He was obviously shaken by the news. "Jeez, Sara, that's a damn shame," he said. "I didn't know. I haven't seen her for a few years. She drove all the way up here from Columbus one time. She was a corker, that Millie Thorne."

"Why did she come to see you?"

"I didn't tell you when it happened?"

Sara shook her head.

"It must have slipped my mind. It was really something at the time. You see, Millie owned this island in Lake Erie, a little place, not much to it, but she bought and paid for it, and it was all hers."

"I know all about that island, Dad."

Ben sat back in his chair, the hot fudge sundae forgotten for the moment. "You do? You know about the trouble, too?"

"What trouble?"

"From the development company. Millie came up here to see me because this slick guy from some developer..."

"The Golden Isles Development Corporation?" Sara offered.

Ben snapped his fingers. "Right. That's what it was called. How'd you know?"

Sara waved away his question, anxious to hear more. "Go on, Dad. I don't know the whole story."

"Okay. This guy talked Millie into selling the island to his company, saying that Lake Erie was so badly polluted it was in her best interest to sell out while she could still get a few bucks for the property. He showed her geological surveys, marine samples, other stuff that proved the lake was dead as a doornail. The reports were all phony, by the way. Then he told her he was only interested in the material things he could get off the island—some wine-making equipment, antiques, that sort of thing."

Sara nodded. "In other words, he was priming her to take a low offer."

"Exactly right. He was a con man, Sara, no doubt about it. Even years ago when this happened, Lake

Erie was already on the mend. But Millie didn't know that. She sold out. Then she was contacted by some folks who'd had land on some of the other small islands in the Great Lakes. Seems they'd been swindled by this same guy. His stories varied a little from property to property, but basically he got folks to sell for very little money."

"What did he plan to do with the properties, Dad? Do you know?"

"Divide them up into resort lots and make a bundle selling them off. But Millie and these other folks banded together and started a class-action suit against the company."

"Good for them," Sara said. "So why did Millie come to you?"

"She said her group needed more ammunition against this corporation, that the lawsuit was flagging and their chances in court didn't look too good. She said she remembered me as being a kind of savvy guy, and she thought I could suggest a way to bring the company down."

"And did you?"

He grinned. "Matter of fact, I did. I suggested she call an investigative reporter from the *Cleveland Plain Dealer* and tell him what was going on. Those fellows can dig up dirt from a cement parking lot. And that's exactly what she did. The paper sent a guy down here, and he was sharp. If he asked one question that day, he asked a hundred."

"So your plan worked?"

"I guess so. The reporter was definitely interested. He left here cackling over what a story this was going to be. He told Millie not to worry her little head over

it. He'd expose this corporation and get her money
back.''

"And did he?'' Sara remembered the attorney, Mr.
Adams, telling her that her aunt had won a lawsuit,
so she already suspected what her father's answer
would be.

"That and a lot more. She called to tell me the
good news some months later. Thanked me and offered me a big pile of her settlement, which I turned
down of course. Doesn't that beat all, Sarabelle? Millicent Thorne who never paid me any mind at all,
trying to get me to take her money?''

It certainly seemed as if Aunt Millie repaid debts
of kindness. She must have been a fair-minded
woman. "If she tried to give you money, I wonder
what she did for that reporter?'' Sara asked.

Ben laughed. "I wouldn't be surprised if she gave
him the whole damn island in her will, the way she
was crowing over the outcome.''

"You'd be wrong, Dad. She left the island to me.''

Ben's eyes widened in shock. "You? Why'd she
leave it to you?''

"I don't know. The attorney said it was because
she remembered me as a levelheaded girl. But now I
think it was her way of paying you back. Thanking
you through me.''

He nodded slowly. The idea obviously made sense
to him. "So that's why you're here. To check the
place out.''

"I already have,'' she said. "And it's wonderful.
A little seedy here and there, but lots of possibilities.''

"And that's why you need a vacuum cleaner.''

Sara laughed. "That's just the beginning. I'm going back to the island tomorrow, Dad. I'm hoping to

stay another couple of weeks. There's so much I want to do.''

Ben's brows came together in a worried knot. "I don't know if I like you being there all by yourself, Sara."

"I'm not alone, Dad. There are four people on the island."

His face eased into a sort of smile. "Oh, that's okay, then. A family?"

This could be a problem. "Not exactly."

"Two couples?"

This could definitely be a problem. "Four singles, actually."

"There are four women living on Millie's island?"

"No."

He pointed his finger at her and shook it at her nose. So that was where she got that awful habit. "Now look here, Sara, my daughter's not staying on an island with four *men*."

It was definitely time for her to stand up for herself. "Yes, Dad, she is," she said. "But you don't have to worry. The men are harmless. They really are. They're quite wonderful, in fact. Sweet and help-ful..." Was God going to make her choke on these lies?

At least the finger lowered. "They don't go for girls, then?"

"Dad! I don't know about that." More lies. Nick Bass definitely went for girls. One particular girl pushed her pink-striped image into Sara's mind and cracked her gum in Sara's ear. "All I know is they've been very nice and polite to me. I'm perfectly safe there."

Physically safe, that was true. The only danger Sara

had experienced on the island was almost falling down the press-house stairs, and that was a result of her own stupidity. But she wouldn't have bet a quarter on the stability of her mental state at this moment.

Her father looked only half-convinced. "Are you telling me the truth, Sara Crawford?"

She reached under her chair and crossed her fingers, a practice from her childhood, and said, "Of course, Dad. The absolute truth."

"I'd feel a whole lot better if I could go back with you, but the garage is too busy what with folks late getting snow tires off and needing coolant, things like that. But if there's anything else I can do to help…"

"There is," she said, thinking of her canary-yellow 1979 Volkswagen beetle that no doubt still occupied a special place in the family garage. "How's the bee?"

"Tip-top shape as always," he said with pride. "I even repainted the little black stripes along the sides this winter."

"Great. Dad, if one of the guys from the garage can follow me up to the airport tomorrow, I want to drop off my rental car and drive the bee back to Sandusky. I think they'll let me take her on the ferry, and I'll figure some way to get her to the island. I could really use her there."

"Consider it done, Sarabelle—on one condition."

"What's that?"

"As long as you're getting that cell phone…"

She reached across the table to cover his hand. "I'll call you often, Dad. I promise."

CHAPTER EIGHT

NICK PICKED dark hairs off his hands and tried not to squirm. Gina had been fluffing and snipping and drying for what seemed like hours, though his watch indicated it had only been thirty minutes. "Aren't you done yet, G?" he asked.

She aimed the blow-dryer at his face, and he jerked away from the hot air. "What's your hurry, sweetie?" she said. "It's not like you got someplace to go." She forced the wiry curls at his temple into submission with a blast of heat. "Okay, I guess I'm done. I gotta tell you, Nickie, I've cut the hair of five-year-olds who were better behaved than you were today." She rested her chin on the top of his head and looked at their images in the bathroom mirror. "Didn't your mama teach you any manners?"

"Not a one," he teased. "She knew it was pointless."

Gina reached around him for the hand mirror she'd set on the vanity. Her pink neck scarf shifted, giving him a tantalizing view of her most inviting body parts. Nick caught a whiff of her musky fragrance and anticipated his customary reaction.

Nothing.

She held the mirror at the back of his head. "There. What do you think?"

"It's great. Thanks."

She cracked her gum and plopped a fist on the perky jut of her hip. "I'd appreciate the compliment a whole lot more if you'd actually looked in the mirror."

He appeased her with one quick glance. "It looks good, G. Really."

She cocked her head to the side, reminding Nick of an attentive poodle with a hot-pink collar. "What's with you today, Nickie? You got problems? Are you leaving the island, is that it? You act scared outta your wits."

Nick Romano had only been truly scared once in his life, so he knew fear and how his body reacted to it. This was different. Not fear exactly, but not far off, either. "Come on, Gina, don't try to second-guess my moods."

"Are you runnin' out of money?" she asked. "You told me when you first got here—when was it? six years ago?—that you'd stay on Thorne Island till you ran out of money or died." She ran a slim, pink-tipped hand down his arm and gave him one of her sexy grins. "Since it's obvious you're still alive, then it must be money."

"It's not money. Nothing's wrong. Really."

"Honestly?" She drew out the word, letting her fingers walk back up his arm.

He turned in his chair, reached for the tight, round bottom covered in black stretch material and gave it a squeeze. "Does this feel like something's wrong, G?"

She slithered away from him to deposit her gum in the garbage pail. When she came back, she dropped into his lap and kicked her feet as if she was dipping them into a cold stream. Her pink sandals hit the floor.

"This feels like something's right, Nickie." She pulled his head down for a long, wet kiss.

His radar was definitely working. "Woman on board" was blinking inside his head in bright green digital letters. His mind was sending signals to all parts of his body. So why was there no response? His messages hit dead air where nerves and muscles should have picked up the command and run with it.

Gina drew away from him and stood up. "Come on, Nickie," she said. "We're *peasanos.*"

"Sure, G."

"Italians are supposed to speak the hot-blooded language of lovers, right?"

He nodded. "Yeah, I guess that's what they say."

"But right now when I look at you, I'm not seein' anything but some boring subtitles."

"Look, Gina—"

"If you're gonna apologize, forget it," she said. "I think I know what's wrong. I have a hunch the girl you really want in your lap went the other direction on Winkie's boat this morning."

Deny it, Romano. Tell Gina she's wrong. Tell her nothing could be farther from the truth. Nick opened his mouth, but no words came out. He was an idiot. That was the only explanation. Here was Gina Sacco, willing, luscious as a piece of ripe fruit, *and* Italian. What did he want, for Pete's sake?

Never in his wildest dreams could he have pictured himself turning down a sure thing like Gina to moon over a woman like Sara Crawford. Pushy, domineering, milk-fed Sara Crawford. And yet just thinking about her had his heart beating double time.

Gina planted a chaste kiss on his cheek before slipping her feet into her sandals. "I can see you're off somewhere without me, Nickie,'' she said. ''I'll just go on over to Dexter's. I think the Indians have a game today.''

Nick watched her go, knowing he could have stopped her with a word. But the only words that came from his mouth were the ones he uttered when she was down the stairs and out the front door. ''You ought to have your head examined, Romano.''

THE NEXT AFTERNOON Nick looked at his watch, stood up from his desk chair and went to the bedroom window that faced toward Put-in-Bay. Through the tree branches that thickened more each day with new growth, he saw a sliver of blue water. Where was she? It was nearly four o'clock. If Winkie didn't have her back soon, it would be too dark to start out from Put-in-Bay. He thought back to yesterday morning when Sara had called down the hallway. ''See you tomorrow, Bass.'' Yes, that's what she'd said. ''See you *tomorrow*.''

Thinking he heard the faint sound of a boat, Nick cupped his ear and leaned over the windowsill. It didn't sound like Winkie's old tub, but it was worth investigating. He left his room, went down the stairs and onto the front porch. Gina was there, sitting in one of the wicker chairs, an entertainment magazine open on her lap.

She raised her head when he came out, but it seemed as if she were looking through him rather than at him. It was the first time he'd seen her since she'd left the inn the day before, though the other guys had kept him informed of her whereabouts. ''I'm filling out a questionnaire,'' she said. ''Who do you think has the sexiest eyes? Kevin Costner, Mel Gibson or that *X-Files* guy?''

''Look, Gina, I'm sorry…''

She flashed him a warning glance. '''I'm sorry' isn't one of the choices, Nickie.''

''Okay, Costner, then.''

She smiled at him as she made a check mark. He was forgiven.

Nick picked up her gold vinyl satchel from the porch floor. ''There's a boat coming, G,'' he said. ''Maybe it's Winkie.''

She closed the magazine, tucked it under her arm and fell into step beside him as they approached the harbor.

The noise Nick had heard was definitely a boat engine, but it wasn't Winkleman's. Nick shielded his eyes against sunlight reflected off the water and the blue-and-white paint of a pontoon boat still at least half a mile away.

''Who's that?'' Gina asked.

''One of those flat party boats tourists rent.'' It moved like a clumsy cow, lumbering through the water at no more than six or seven miles an hour. ''It won't come here.''

Gina frowned up at him. ''Not if it's a *party* boat it won't.''

Nick started to turn away when an unusual object caught his eye. He touched Gina's shoulder and pointed to the pontoon boat. ''Do you see that? There's a big yellow *something* smack in the middle of the boat. What do you suppose it is?''

Gina fished a glasses case out of her bag and settled a pair of tortoiseshell spectacles on her nose. After a close look she said, ''I think it's a barbecue grill.''

He sputtered his disbelief in a burst of laughter. "A yellow grill?"

"Sure, why not? Yellow's a condiment color. I think it's kinda cool."

He shrugged. "I'm going back. You coming?"

"Nah. I'll wait here. Winkie'll be along soon."

Nick returned to the inn, took a beer from his refrigerator and went upstairs. Staring at the computer screen, he vowed that Sara Crawford's comings and goings wouldn't cause him one more moment's concern. She'd either come back or she wouldn't. Either way, life on Thorne Island would continue.

He'd only managed to compose one decent sentence when Brody's voice carried up the inn staircase as if he was speaking through a bullhorn. "Damn it! What the hell's that woman doing now?"

Figuring Gina must have jumped off the dock to swim back to Put-in-Bay, Nick slowly got up and ambled to the top of the stairs. "Whatever Gina's done, you handle it, Brody," he said.

"I'm not talking about Gina," Brody growled. "That other woman. Our friggin' landlady. That's who I'm talking about!"

"Sara?" Nick's body was suddenly charged with renewed energy. He bounded down the stairs as fast as his limp would allow. "Where is she?"

Brody burst through the screen door. "Come see for yourself. I can't even describe this one."

Despite Brody's head start, Nick passed him on the path to the harbor. And what he saw when he got there made him gasp. The large boat passed the dock and slowly eased to the shoreline. Winkleman operated the controls, and Sara Crawford fluttered about the deck like an excited mother hen. Her "baby," as yellow as a newborn chick, was a brightly painted Volkswagen beetle.

Once he recovered from the shock of seeing an automobile float to Thorne Island, and after he'd convinced himself that Sara really had come back, Nick allowed pure masculine exhilaration to take over. If most men were truthful, the blood that flowed through their veins was fifty percent gasoline, and at this moment, Nick's pumped like premium high test.

"Damn," he muttered, shaking his head in admiration. "I haven't seen one of those old bugs in this good a shape in years."

Winkleman shut off the engine, tossed a rope to shore and called out, "Grab the line, will you, Nick?"

He did, and pulled the boat as close as the water depth would allow. Winkie jumped off and waded to shore. Together they managed to pull the vessel another few feet closer.

Winkie walked back and opened a wide gate in the railing that surrounded the boat deck. "Okay, Sara," he said, "can you scoot the ramps over here?"

She pushed first one, then another red metal ramp to the edge of the boat. Catching on to the procedure, Nick grabbed one and Winkie took the other. They set their ends in the sandy soil. Damn, if Sara Crawford wasn't going to drive that VW off the boat and onto Thorne Island!

An impatient shout came from behind him. "What is the matter with you two? Haven't you heard a word I've said?"

It was Brody, and no, Nick hadn't heard a word. He'd picked up some incoherent ranting, but Nick's senses were tuned into what was happening in front of him. Once the ramp was firmly imbedded on shore,

Nick turned to his irate friend. "Relax, Brody," he said. "It's just a little VW."

"A little VW?" the older man echoed. "It's an invasion of our peace and quiet. What the hell do we need that thing for? We've got the golf cart."

Sara answered his bluster from the railing of the pontoon boat. "*I* need this thing, Mr. Brody. Precisely for the reason you just mentioned—*you* have the golf cart."

Brody pinned Sara with his angriest glare. "What do you mean by that?"

"Well, you know, Bro," Nick said, "if you'd let her use the damn golf cart in the first place…"

Darts shot from Brody's eyes. "Whose side are you on, Nick?"

Right then Nick was on the side of a guy who hadn't driven an automobile in six years and whose palm suddenly itched to wrap itself around the cool rubber knob of a five-speed gearshift. Granted, Thorne Island wasn't the Indianapolis Speedway, but Nick figured this little beetle could handle the narrow paths and sharp turns with heart-thumping precision. Damn, had he really missed driving that much?

"I'm not on anybody's side, Brody," he lied, forcing his mind back to reality. "I'm just facing the facts. Sara does own this island, and she can run around on it any way she likes."

Sara opened the driver's door of the car and slid behind the wheel. "Thank you, Mr. Bass," she said. "Now, gentlemen, if you'll please get out of the way…"

Gina, who'd been watching the proceedings with amused interest, jabbed Brody in the ribs. "I think it's the cutest thing I've ever seen," she said. "It looks like a big ol' bumblebee."

Brody scowled at her. "Women!" He shook his head, admitting temporary defeat, and retreated up the pathway to his cottage. Nick heard him grumble before he was out of sight, "Don't even like my damn haircut, either."

The Volkswagen sputtered to life with Sara at the controls. Then, like a lawn mower on steroids, it lunged toward the ramps. Winkie waved frantically, directing Sara first to the right, then the left, then to the right again. Nick watched as finally—after much maneuvering—the front tires of the little car actually settled dead center on their targets. And Sara rolled onto shore.

"See, I told you there wouldn't be any trouble getting this vehicle over here." Winkie's words belied the perspiration rolling down his face. "Now let's get the rest of your gear unloaded so Gina and I can leave. I've got to get this barge back before dark."

Sara and Winkie—with some help from Nick—carried the cargo off the pontoon boat. Soon boxes, sacks and crates packed with dozens of items that probably had no use on Thorne Island sat in complete disarray on the shore.

"You didn't get all of *this* into *that,* did you?" Nick said, pointing first to the pile and then to the car.

"No, of course not," Sara answered. "I had a van follow me to the ferry."

Nick could only shake his head. But he kept his eye on the prize. The prize, he tried to tell himself, was a spin in the beetle, *not* a roll with its owner.

WITH EVERYONE BUT Brody helping, all of Sara's purchases made it from the shore to the inn. Sara had never been more pleased with her little car than the day she introduced it to the residents of Thorne Island. In Brewster Falls, the VW had been a familiar sight, buzzing through the parking lot at the grocery store, or sitting at the curb outside Percy's Drugstore. But on Thorne Island the car was a phenomenon.

Ryan and Dexter showed keen interest in it, but Sara knew at once that Nick was practically drooling to get behind the wheel. She didn't offer him the keys. Instead, she gave in to the purely selfish satisfaction of depriving him. Especially after the night he'd had with his ''hairdresser.''

Once Ryan and Dexter left for their own cottages, she expected Nick to go off, as well. He didn't. He plopped down in a chair on the porch and thumped one of the boxes with the toe of his Docksider. ''What is all this stuff?''

She opened a box, looked inside and determined the articles were targeted for the bathroom. ''Just some things I picked up for the inn.''

He craned his neck to see over the tops of several bags. ''It looks like you bought out the store.''

She smiled. ''Actually the manager did come out of his office with a bottle of champagne to thank me for shopping there.''

''Sure he did.'' Nick snickered. ''So why did you buy so much?''

''Because, Bass, if guests are going to be staying here, they'll need nicer amenities than plastic dishes and threadbare towels that have probably been used to clean fishing gear.''

She expected a typical Bass outburst, but he only shrugged.

She carried a box into the kitchen and returned for more. Nick had gotten up from the chair and was leaning over the porch railing, looking up at the eaves. "I don't know, Sara," he said. "I'd say this old place has a long way to go before people can stay here. There are Sandusky city codes to think about."

Aha, so he'd come up with what he believed was a surefire argument against turning the Cozy Cove into a profit-making venture. No wonder he'd acted so nonchalantly. He reached up and pulled a sliver of wood from the fascia board. "Dry rot," he said, holding the wood out to her like a gift. "Yep, it'll be some time before this place meets even the lowest standards required to accept paying guests. You would be personally liable if anything went wrong."

The time had come. She might as well tell him about the appointments she'd had that afternoon in Sandusky. She took the piece of wood from his hand and tossed it over the railing. Then glancing back at him, she said, "Oh, I don't know about that."

His eyes widened just slightly, enough for her to see a quick flash of something like panic in their stormy depths. He was worried. "What do you mean?" he asked.

She couldn't stop a grin of triumph. "You gentlemen can expect some company on the island starting day after tomorrow."

"Company? Are you crazy? You can't bring people over here to stay at the Cozy Cove! The wiring is fifty years old at least. Some of the porch boards are nearly rotted through. A kid could go right over the edge of the dock. The authorities would close you down and slap a fine on you so fast—''

''The people I'm expecting aren't guests, Bass,'' she said calmly. ''They weren't *invited*. They were *hired*. They're fully licensed, bonded and insured.''

There was no mistaking the squall brewing in Nick's eyes now. Again, Sara waited for the tirade she expected to erupt from his mouth, but for several seconds his jaw remained tightly clenched. He took a determined step toward her, and one of those loose floorboards he'd just mentioned sagged under his weight.

Sara held up her hand to stop his approach. ''Now, Nick, calm down.'' She said the words as soothingly as her suddenly alert instincts would allow. ''Do I have to remind you that I have every right to make changes on *my* island?''

The air around him seemed to vibrate. The board under his foot creaked threateningly. ''Let me get this straight, Miss Tax Accountant,'' he said. ''In two days we can expect to see our island, the place we've lived for six years, invaded by electricians, carpenters...'' He stalled, apparently at a loss for words to enumerate what other menacing demons might cross his precious boundaries.

She couldn't resist helping him out. ''And painters, wallpaper hangers... Nick, no one is going to ask you to leave your home.'' She rolled her eyes. ''I couldn't even if I wanted to, since you negotiated those terms with my aunt.''

He snorted his annoyance and rocked back on his heels. The board moaned in protest. ''It won't be our place any longer, don't you realize that? Strangers will be wandering around talking about sing-alongs and barbecues and suntan lotion. It'll be oh-so-nice and homey, and color-coordinated, for God's sake!''

She waved her hand in the air. ''Nick, you worry too much.''

''You're killing us, Sara. Little by little you're stifling the breath right out of our lungs.'' He lifted one foot to take a step closer, leaving the bulk of his weight on his other foot and the loose board.

The old plank cracked down the middle. Nick's foot and a good amount of rotted wood plummeted to the ground two feet below the porch. He yelped in shock and pain as his gaze shot to the side of him that was buried from the mid thigh down. ''Damn it!''

Sara lunged for him. ''Now you've done it!'' She positioned her shoulder under his arm, and he leaned his weight on her. Slipping her other arm around his waist, she held him and tugged until he twisted his foot free and stepped back onto the porch.

''Nick, if you want my advice...'' Sara began.

''I don't—not that it'll matter.''

''What's going to kill you is having this place fall down around you. You're lucky you haven't been electrocuted or conked on the head by part of the roof.''

He leaned more heavily on her. He was obviously in pain, but at least some of his color had returned. ''What are you all afraid of, anyway?'' she asked. ''Why does civilization scare the daylights out of you guys?''

''How do you know it scares us?'' He interspersed the words with short gasps. ''Maybe we just don't like it much.''

''Nonsense. You told me yourself that you haven't been more than a few miles from this island in years.

And it's my guess that none of you men would leave at all unless it was an absolute necessity. That's fear, plain and simple.''

He settled an arm around her waist so that they ended up in a sort of awkward embrace. "Look, we just happen to like it here, all right? The real issue is all these little fix-ups you're planning. I'm warning you, Sara, when the others hear about it, there's going to be trouble.''

She smiled up at him. "I welcome the challenge.''

He released a long, normal breath. He even managed a halfhearted grin. "Maybe you do. But remember, I'm the only one who thinks you're cute enough to put up with.''

He brought her around so she was standing straight in front of him. His eyes had mellowed to a soft ash-gray, the same shade as the early-evening shadows bathing the inn porch. His hair, neat and trim and touchable, just covered his ears and brushed his collar. Jeez, he looked good. Sara had to give Gina Sacco credit for the good haircut. And some higher power credit for the rest of this man.

"You see, Sara," he said, "I'm the only guy on Thorne who's willing to cut you some slack. The other guys—''

His words were drowned out by some blasted primal instinct that hummed through her senses. Good God, she was going to kiss him. He'd just been bullying her, and still she was drawn to that slow-moving mouth until his words didn't matter. They were barely words any longer. It was just his voice, his eyes, his hands on her arms.

Finally, some of what he said broke through. "...I

don't know how I'm going to keep them from coming down hard on you…"

Shut up, Nick. Pull me just a couple inches closer. That's all it would take.

"…especially since you know that I think what you're doing is wrong. If you want *my* advice, I'd suggest you take a big step backward…"

She blinked hard, breaking the hypnotic contact that had clouded her senses. He'd just given her the best advice of her life! No matter how this man tweaked every impulse in her body, fired every cell into tingling awareness, he was opposed to everything she wanted to do.

Enough! She was going to turn this disaster of an inn into the most charming place anywhere in northern Ohio. And she was going to love doing it! Didn't he understand that she needed to do this? Didn't he care? No, of course not. That much was clear, so she did as he said. She took a big step backward until several feet separated them.

"I'm not going to change my mind, Nick. Those men are coming on Friday. I'm going to start patching up holes around this place, and no one is going to stop me."

She picked up a box of new bath towels and stormed into the inn.

CHAPTER NINE

NICK ROLLED OVER in bed, squinted one eye at the clock on his nightstand and sucked in a breath of pain. Seven-thirty. Normally he'd have been up for at least a half hour. Morning was his most productive time of the day, except for Mondays when he devoted the best hours to Brody's treasure hunt.

He'd been awake for hours, staring at the moonlit water stains spreading across his ceiling. All the while he'd contemplated the logic of Sara Crawford's fix-up scheme. So what if every good rainfall left its mark on the roof of the Cozy Cove? Nick had been up in the rafters himself a time or two, and they still looked sturdy enough. As sturdy as the planks on the front porch had seemed—until yesterday.

Drat the rotted wood! Nick slowly moved his legs to the side of the mattress. Pain shot up his right thigh and settled in the small of his back. He rubbed his ankle, wincing when his fingers connected with the black-and-blue spots. Gingerly he lowered his right foot to the floor. The pain ebbed a little. He'd have to walk it off or Dexter would double the exercise sessions. Nick didn't know which was worse—having Dexter mother him or suffering the pain in silence.

He stood up and felt his right knee start to give way. *Oh, no you don't,* he scolded the obstinate joint as he locked it in place. *We're walking. At least to the bathroom.* He rolled his shoulders. Tight muscles began to loosen.

Nick massaged the base of his spine, finding the hardened knot of scar tissue that marked the entrance of the bullet. The old wound had puckered down to an area no larger than the size of a quarter. Small, considering the size of the man, but it was enough to have changed his life.

"Enough moping, Romano," he said, and limped to the door. He didn't relish running into Sara, not in the state he was in. He glanced down the hall. Her door was still closed. Not surprising, since he'd heard her puttering around the second floor of the inn till past midnight. She'd made these chirpy little comments to herself every few minutes as she unpacked her boxes. *That's a perfect match. How adorable.* She'd said a bunch of other things that separated men from women.

Nick ambled down the hall, avoiding rolls of wallpaper against the baseboards and country prints stacked randomly against the walls. Waiting till the painters did their thing, he supposed. When he entered the bathroom, he was bombarded with shades of gray and peach that splashed across curtains and towels. Curtains! What did they need curtains for on a second-story window? There was even a soap dish filled with little peach-colored shell soaps next to his razor.

"What the hell?" He stepped onto a thick area rug with a seagull in the middle of a charcoal background. The room even smelled like peaches. Despite his gloomy disposition, he sniffed the air appreciatively. This part wasn't so bad. Then he spied a gray acrylic magazine holder with several glossy selections poking out the top. "Just what we need, a reason to loaf around in the toilet!"

He managed to return to his room without incident. After pulling on a pair of corduroy shorts and a faded Akron University T-shirt, he made his way downstairs and into the kitchen. This room was as full of surprises as the bathroom. Shiny copper-bottomed pots and pans sat on the countertops. A tablecloth printed with little blue flowers covered the scrub table where he'd eaten lasagna with Sara. He didn't dare open the utensil drawers and look inside for fear he wouldn't know the names of half the stuff she'd probably put in them. And more curtains!

"She must think the world is full of Peeping Toms," he remarked to himself as he plugged in the coffeepot. Or maybe she liked to run around in her skivvies. That thought brought a smile to his lips.

He took his coffee out to the back porch and sat on the top step. The rain had stopped, leaving a fresh, loamy scent in the air. Fat drops still fell with soft plops from the oak trees at the back of the inn. Spring was nice, Nick decided. The best time to live on Thorne Island, since the summers were too humid and winters were so cold he couldn't loosen up in the mornings.

He liked it here for the most part. Sara had her nerve suggesting that he was afraid of something and was using the island as a refuge. Nothing could be farther from the truth—at least for him. Maybe not for the other guys, though. Ryan had only been to Put-in-Bay three times since he got here, and that was because he'd had such terrible toothaches he would have gone to the moon to get relief. But the little guy had good reason to be scared of his own shadow. He hated crowds and feeling closed in. Being locked up in the state penitentiary for eighteen months did that to a person. Yeah, Nick supposed Ryan could be afraid of going back into the real world.

And Dexter…it was possible that fear ruled his motives, too. The ex-football star hated the thought of being recognized. And hell, he would be, too. The one time he'd gone to Sandusky to buy clothes at the Big and Tall men's store, some well-meaning but ignorant person recognized him and brought up the less-than-admirable end to his career. There was a time when Dexter Sweet's face had been as familiar to Cleveland Browns fans as Jim Brown's. And then the franchise folded in 1996 and no other team would give Dex a chance. Too Old. Washed Up. Those had been the headlines in the sports pages.

"What a waste," Nick said, remembering the silent, beaten man he'd brought to the island several years ago. Dex was getting better, though. Still, he was scared. Sara was right about him, too.

And now that he thought about it, Brody was probably scared of his son. If he'd only forgive Junior's past mistakes and talk to him, as Nick did every so often, he'd understand that Carl truly cared about Brody despite the older man's lousy attitude. Brody had called Carl Junior a "money-grubbing son of a bitch" many times. Nick didn't know if that was true, but after all this time he figured the name-calling was just a cover-up. Brody was afraid to face Junior and have it out with him once and for all. Maybe he was afraid his son wouldn't like him. It wasn't all that easy to like Brody. Nick had to work at it every day.

Nick upended his coffee mug to get the last of the liquid, which suddenly tasted like motor oil. "Hell," he said to himself, "that pushy tax accountant might be right about these guys."

He shook off a wave of apprehension. "I suppose she might have been right about me, too, a while ago. But not now." He had to admit that after the shooting, he'd decided that no story was worth his life, no matter how great it was. He'd come to Millie's island to get away from everything while he healed and decided what he wanted to do with the rest of his life. He still hadn't made his decision, so staying here was the logical thing to do.

Over the years he'd gone to Sandusky for various appointments. He'd always come back to Thorne Island the same day, but not because he was scared. He returned to the island because he liked it here. No other reason. Sara was wrong about him. Satisfied with himself, Nick picked up his cup and went back into the kitchen to have a bowl of Frosted Flakes and a cherry Pop-Tart.

A half hour later, when he climbed the stairs to go back to his room, he couldn't resist a look at the other end of the hallway. Sara's door was half-open. He walked toward it, stopping just beyond the bathroom when he heard her voice. It sounded different this morning. She wasn't talking to herself like she had the night before. This time she was speaking to *someone*. Who the hell could it be? Ryan? Dex? Nick tried to imagine a liaison between Sara and either of his two friends. "Nah," he said, shaking his head. "It'd never happen."

Then, in an instant of unanticipated relief, Nick realized he was listening to a one-sided conversation. Sara was talking on the phone. He knew he should walk away. She had a right to her privacy like everyone else. But he flattened his back against the wall and inched toward her room and the sound of her voice.

SARA BLEW a stubborn strand of hair off her forehead and tapped a pencil on the case of her new laptop computer. She'd called her office and spoken to the receptionist and the night cleaning lady, who was just leaving. Now if she could just connect with Candy! Why was it taking so long for her assistant to pick up? She'd promised to be on time the week Sara was away, and it was now eight thirty-five.

Ten rings. Sara was reaching for the end button on her cell phone when a breathless voice came from the small speaker grid. She returned the phone to her ear.

"H-hello! I mean, good morning. Miss Crawford's office. Candy Applebaum speaking. May I help you?"

"Candy? It's me."

"Oh, Sara, how are you? I miss you."

"I'm fine. I miss you, too. How are you getting along with the boss?"

"Oh, great. Mr. Bosch has birds, too. Did you know? We've been swapping budgie stories."

"Great." Sara couldn't help smiling. "Candy, I have something to tell you. If there aren't any major problems, I'm planning to stay here a while longer."

"You must be having a good time. I just knew you would. Maybe I'll go to Cleveland myself some-time."

"It's not really Cleveland. I'm on an island—"

Candy's voice rose to an excited pitch. "Oh, you won't believe what's been going on this week!"

Sara froze. "What?"

"Mr. Papalardo was so grateful for the way you handled his tax return—you know, getting it in on time—"

"He should be grateful," Sara interjected.

"Well, anyway, he's called up every day this week to ask what kind of pizza you want delivered—free! I told him to load it up with everything, but heavy on the anchovies. I said you loved anchovies."

Sara smiled into the phone. "Candy, I hate anchovies."

"I know, but you're not here."

"True. So you've had pizza every day?"

"Yeah, and I've gained four pounds. I look grotesque."

Sara muffled her laughter. *Grotesque* was hardly the word she'd use to describe rail-thin Candy Applebaum, even after she'd consumed three loaded pizzas. "Tell you what, Candy, today tell Mr. Papalardo that all I want is a tossed salad with low-fat Italian dressing."

There was a long pause before Candy chirped back, "He'd never believe that. You've had me call him every day to tell him how much you loved the pizza."

Sara laughed out loud. "Candy, I really do miss you." And it was true. "Take down this phone number. It's my new cell phone." She recited the numbers. "Call me anytime if you have questions. I don't want Mr. Bosch to get upset. And tell him I have business in Ohio that's keeping me longer than I expected, but that I'm checking in regularly."

"Business? Aren't you having any fun at all?" Candy sounded genuinely distressed at the possibility.

If you only knew, Sara thought. *I'm having the time of my life. I'm bringing beauty to what was drab and*

*life to what was dying. And meeting one of the biggest
challenges of my life by doing it all in spite of a bunch
of cantankerous, obstinate men. And one mysterious,
argumentative, incredibly sexy man who pushes buttons I never knew I had.*

"I wouldn't say I'm not having any fun," Sara
answered cautiously. "Candy, I have to tell you, I
met this—"

"Oh, sorry, Sara," Candy whispered. "Mr. Bosch
is coming into the office. Can I call you back?"

"Sure. It wasn't important. I'll talk to you later."
Sara ended the call and went to her wardrobe to get
socks and sneakers. By the time she'd laced her shoes,
her common sense was in gear once more. *Are you
nuts, Crawford?* she asked herself. *What in the world
were you going to tell Candy? That you've met a man
whose sensitivity and manners are strictly in the debit
column, but that you can't stop thinking about him,
anyway?*

Relieved that she hadn't blurted out the details of
a situation she didn't understand herself, Sara headed
down the hall to the bathroom. Just as she reached
the door, it swung open and Nick Bass stood on the
threshold. He leaned against the door frame, crossed
his arms and gave her a huge grin. "Good morning,
Crawford," he said. "Beautiful day, isn't it?"

"I suppose," she said. "Despite being wet and
soggy."

"True, but I've decided not to sue you for that
loose porch board, so that should put a little sunshine
in your life."

"You're all heart, Bass." She looked away from
the teasing glint in his eyes. She certainly didn't need
to find anything attractive about Nick this morning.

"So, you done in there?" she asked, returning her gaze to his face since there didn't seem to be a safe place to settle it.

He scratched the side of his head as if pondering her question. "I don't know. All that great reading material and soft, fuzzy places to put my feet, I'm tempted to stay all day."

"Well, forget it because you can't." She tried to shoulder her way past him, but it was like trying to knock a granite statue off its base.

He squared his shoulders, filling the entrance. "So, who were you talking to in your room, Sara? You have company in there?"

"Certainly not! I was simply letting my assistant know she could reach me on my cell phone. Unlike some people, I don't entertain in my bedroom." He squirmed just slightly at her implied accusation. "Besides, what were you doing listening to my conversation?"

"Were you trying to keep it private?"

"Of course."

"Then from now on, shut your door. We're the only two people who live in this palace. What affects you affects me." He jerked his thumb at the interior of the redecorated bathroom. "What you change affects me." He pointed to the supplies filling the hall. "Who you hire affects me. In fact, every damn thing you're doing affects the hell out of me. You can't blame me for listening in to see what other tricks you've got up your sleeve."

This man could have goaded Mother Teresa into a boxing ring. And yet, the more he annoyed her, the more Sara's other instincts raced into overdrive. His hair was still sleep-tousled and just needed a trail of fingers to smooth it into submission. His T-shirt fit his chest like a second skin, and his mouth... Even while he delivered his lecture of self-defense, his lips twitched in amusement. Sara knew only two ways to wipe a smug expression off a person's mouth. One was to slug it off, and the other...well, she couldn't let herself think about that one.

"Fine," she said. "You've made your point. I'll keep my door closed when I'm on the phone from now on."

He stepped aside and with a gallant sweep of his arm, invited her to enter the bathroom.

"Thank you," she said, and walked past him.

Nick headed down the hall, but before Sara closed the bathroom door, he called back to her. "Tell Candy to lay off the pizza. And by the way, the night before last—I slept alone."

RYAN ENTERED the front door of the commissary, wiped moist soil from his hands and took the beer Nick offered him. "What's up?" he asked.

"We're all here," Brody said. "What's the big emergency?"

Dexter took a long swallow of diet soda and leaned against the refrigerator. "Talk fast, okay? ESPN is running a special on the history of the Cy Young Award, and it starts in fifteen minutes."

"And I've got work to do in the vineyard," Ryan said. "This morning's rain made the soil perfect for adding more fertilizer. The roots will soak it right in."

Brody pointed his cell phone at each man. "And I've got to call in an order to Winkie or we'll all starve to death."

"Yeah, yeah," Nick said impatiently. "You're all

busy as little beavers, I can tell. But believe me, when you hear what I have to say, you'll understand why you had to give up a few minutes of precious time to listen.''

Ryan chewed on his lower lip. ''You're beginning to worry me, Nick.''

''I know, and maybe you should be worried. Here's the story. Our new landlady—''

Brody's fist came down on his counter. ''Damn it! I should have known that interfering female was behind this meeting!''

Nick cleared his throat and continued, ''Our landlady is determined to fix up the Cozy Cove and all of Thorne Island.''

''What the hell for?'' Brody demanded. ''She's not staying, is she?''

''She's staying another week for sure. Maybe longer. She's got it into her head that she can turn the island into some kind of summer resort.''

Brody moaned and put his head in his hands. ''Damn!''

''You mean we're going to have people swarming all over the place?'' Dexter asked.

Ryan grimaced. ''How many people? Can she do this?''

''Of course she can!'' Brody thundered. ''That woman's got a mean streak in her.''

Nick put a hand up to silence Brody, as if anything could. ''Yes, Ryan, she can do anything she wants. The island's hers, every tree, bush and grape.''

''She's out to ruin us,'' Brody said, a note of bitter finality to his words.

''No, I don't think she is,'' Nick countered. ''She's made it clear that none of us has to leave. But there may come a time when guests start arriving at the Cozy Cove.''

Hope flickered in Dexter's dark eyes. ''But it might not happen for a long time?''

''That remains to be seen. The immediate situation we have to face is that Sara has contracted people to come to the island and make repairs to the inn. They arrive tomorrow.''

''Tomorrow!'' A chorus of shouts filled the little room.

''That's right. Painters, carpenters, an electrician— along with supplies Sara ordered on the mainland.''

''I can't believe this is happening,'' Dexter said. ''What if one of them recognizes me? What'll I say?''

Nick walked over and patted him on the shoulder. ''You'll say, 'Hi, how ya doing. The name's Dexter Sweet.' And you'll be proud of it.''

Dexter shook his head as if he didn't believe a word of it.

''I don't want any people around here,'' Ryan said. ''I can trust you guys. And I'd just decided that maybe I could trust Sara. Now she brings a whole slew of strangers to the island.''

''Don't borrow trouble, Ry,'' Nick said. ''Not everybody in the world is out to frame you.''

Brody pounded his fist on the countertop again. ''Will you listen to yourself, Nick? You're siding with this woman and her half-baked scheme to turn our island into a Club Med! I don't blame these boys for getting upset. I'm mad as hell myself!''

''So what else is new? You're always mad.'' Nick walked to the door to get away from the grumbling so he could think. There had to be some way—apart from tarring and feathering their landlady—to deal with the situation. The subtle beginnings of a solution came to him, and he concentrated on making the details take shape. Getting this bunch of men to go for it might be as hard as getting them to vote for the abolishment of fishing on Thorne Island, but it was the only way out he could think of. At least it would buy them some time.

He turned around and faced his friends. "I've got an idea," he said.

"Well, spit it out," Brody demanded.

"We could offer to do the work ourselves."

Three incredulous stares met his declaration. And one dropped jaw—Brody's.

"Now just think about it for a minute," Nick urged calmly. "If we do the work, there won't be any reason to bring outsiders to the island. Our generosity will take the wind right out of Sara's sails, and might score some points in our favor."

The first spark of encouragement came with a slight nodding of Ryan's head. "Yeah, that's true," he said. "I could do a lot of the carpentry. I've had enough experience around stables repairing rotted and cribbed wood."

"Sure you have," Nick said. "Fixing up the porch and the eaves would be a snap for you."

"Well, heck," Dexter said, "anybody can paint. I'm sure I could do that."

Brody grunted his disagreement. "That's just great. I'll have Winkie bring me a video camera so I can record your impersonations of Martha Stewart. It'll make for a good laugh. What about the roof and electrical work? Which one of you do-gooders is qualified for that?"

Nick raised his hand. "Actually, Bro, I know a

little about this fix-up stuff. My mother lived in an old mansion in Akron, remember? I was a kid with nothing to do but watch the repairmen and learn.'' He let a sly grin curl half his mouth. "And as for the electrical work, that's right up your alley, friend.''

Brody gaped in shock. "Me? What I know about wiring you could put in a thimble and still have room for a bath.''

Nick wagged a finger at him. "You forget, Brody, that I know what you did before you started making people smell good. If I looked through your desk drawer right now, I might still be able to find the paper that certifies you as an electrician.''

Ryan and Dex both hooted at the expression on Brody's face.

"So, do we talk to Sara about the deal or not?'' Nick asked.

"She'll never go for it,'' Brody said in a last-ditch attempt to sway the vote.

"She's an accountant, Bro. She knows she'll save a bundle if we do the work.''

Dexter strode to the middle of the room. "If it'll keep intruders off the island for a little while, I say we do it.''

"Me, too,'' Ryan seconded.

All three men stared at Brody. "Ah, the hell with all of you,'' he grumbled. "I'm not about to stand alone. Count me in, but I don't like it. And—'' he glared at Nick "—I'm not talking to her.''

"Actually, Brody, I think that will work in our favor,'' Nick said. "I'll let her know right now.'' Looking at Ryan, he asked, "Is she in the vineyard?''

"Was when I left.''

Nick started to leave, but stopped at the door.

"You know, this might not be so bad. When you think about it, we are in kind of a rut around here. At least a little honest labor will be a change of pace."

"Speak for yourself," Brody shot back. "And before you run off, let's get this grocery list done." He pulled a sheet of paper from under the counter and began checking off items. "Frosted Flakes all right?" he asked.

Ryan and Dexter mumbled a weak agreement.

"No!" Nick said. "They're not all right. That's just what I mean about being in a rut. I want something different." The other men again stared at him as if he'd lost his mind. "What other cereals are there?" he asked.

Ryan cleared his throat. "I used to like Sugar Crisp."

Nick snapped his fingers. "That's it then. Sugar Crisp. Write that down, Brody. And while you're at it, order some vegetables. I'm tired of beef and potatoes all the time."

Brody's shock was expressed in incomprehensible mumbles.

"Quit griping, Bro," Nick said. "Ordering food's the easy thing. I've got to find our landlady and convince her of our sincere desire to help. Now that's a challenge!"

CHAPTER TEN

SARA REACHED into the wheelbarrow, scooped out another handful of gravel and spread it around the base of the vine at her knees. Her morning's work in the vineyard had convinced her of one thing. The tour guide on her Napa Valley trip who'd said breaking soil by hand was an easy job had obviously never done it. Sara's back ached from kneeling on the sloping hillside. Her wrist hurt from turning and twisting the trowel in the dirt, and her gloves were so caked with clay she doubted she'd ever get them clean. Yet all she needed to do was reach up and gently nestle a light-green cluster of baby grapes in her palm and all her efforts were worth it. Soon her vines would be thriving.

"Most people try to get rocks out of the soil, Crawford. Here you are putting them in."

At the sound of Nick's voice, Sara sat up with a start and stared into teasing gray eyes. "Shows what you know, Bass. The stones are for drainage. If vine roots get too much water, they rot." Responding to his less than enthusiastic shrug, she returned to her work and asked, "Where's Ryan? What have you done with him?"

"I don't think I like that accusatory tone," he answered, and took a step closer to her.

Sara slapped at his shin with the trowel.

Nick hopped back and rubbed his leg. "Ouch! What did you do that for?"

"You were about to step on my mixture. Shoes are very bad for the soil, bad for the grapes." She glanced accusingly at his feet. "Especially shoes the size of yours."

"Well, pardon me," he said as he stared at Sara's grubby bare feet. "I didn't know you were a horticultural authority."

"Well, I am. So are you going to answer my question?"

"I'm in so much pain, I forgot you asked one."

She speared the trowel into the dirt and stared up at him. "What have you done with Ryan? He's got the pruning shears and I need them."

"Oh, him. I locked him in the press house. I did it for you. I didn't like the tread on his sneakers."

"Very funny."

Nick reached into his back pocket and pulled out a pair of pruning shears. "Are these the ones you're looking for?"

"That's them." Sara took the shears and snipped several leggy canes near the base of the vine. "Has Ryan quit for the day?"

"No, he'll be back. We both agreed it would be better for his emotional well-being if he stayed away while I came to talk to you. If there's anything he hates more than strangers, it's confrontation."

Sara stood up and faced him. She knew exactly what he was referring to. "Nick, I told you, I'm going through with these improvements to the inn."

"I know. You made that clear." He jerked his thumb over his shoulder, pointing to an old bench at the base of the slope. "Can we sit there?"

"I suppose." She removed her gloves, set them in the wheelbarrow and wiped her hands on her cutoffs. Then she walked ahead of him to the bench and sat, angling her body so she could see his face clearly. "Okay, I'm sitting."

He settled beside her and released a long breath. "I told the guys about your plans today."

"And?"

"And they didn't take it well. Look, Sara, I'm willing to meet you halfway on one point. What you said the other night about us living here because we're afraid of something, afraid to go back to the mainstream…that might be true for the other guys, and you're setting off alarm bells in their heads."

"But no alarm bells in yours?"

He shook his head. "No. I'm not afraid. I told you that. But Ryan and Dex. Even Brody. They've got issues."

"No kidding." She hooked her elbow on the back of the bench. "I'm sorry about that, Nick. But I don't see how hiding out here forever will help them deal with their problems. And I don't see how my plans will disrupt their lives. I'm not suggesting that any of you leave. The changes I'm making won't affect the cottages where your buddies live.

"I'm not a tyrant, Nick," she added. "I've inherited this piece of property and I want to fix it up."

He rested his arm near hers on the back of the bench. "It's not that you're a tyrant, Sara. But those contractors coming tomorrow are strangers the guys aren't ready to deal with. Not yet."

"Not after six years?"

He shook his head.

"Well, Nick, the contractors have got to come. I

can hardly repair a roof myself or update the electrical system. And the painting and wallpapering alone—''

He laid his hand on her arm. ''I know. And I've come up with a plan.''

''A Nick Bass plan,'' she said skeptically. ''Why am I worried?''

''It's the perfect solution, Sara.'' His wide grin suggested that what he was about to say would change the face of the universe, not just the fixtures of Thorne Island. ''Let us do the work.''

A sputter of disbelief burst from Sara's lips. Was Nick really suggesting that the same men who celebrate the nonsensical ritual of Digging Day do the work of licensed contractors? A bubbling laughter started deep in her chest and worked its way up her throat. ''Nick, just exactly who do you mean by 'us'?''

His grin faltered a bit. ''You know who I mean. Me, Brody, Dex and Ryan. We can do all those little jobs you want done.''

''You mean to tell me that a slovenly millionaire, an ex-football player, a guy who plants flowers and you, who from all appearances has no talent at all—''

''Hey, that's not fair.''

''Sorry. Who appears to do absolutely nothing. You four can fix up the Cozy Cove and the dock?''

''Yep. That's what I'm telling you. We talked it over, took stock of our talents, which, despite your opinion, are many, and we're offering our services.''

He waited expectantly, reminding Sara of a little boy who's been told to stay in his bedroom on Christmas morning until Mommy gets the camera. Sara had to tell herself he was a grown man and should be able to handle a little disappointment. "Sorry, Bass, I don't think so," she said.

He jerked away from her, almost tumbling off the end of the bench. "What? Why not?"

"Well, for starters, how do I know you can do the work?"

"Don't worry about that. We can do it," he said with almost enough assurance to sway her. Almost. "Besides, if the code inspectors don't pass our work, then you can hire the big guns."

"Frankly, Bass, I don't see any reason I should take the chance. The licensed contractors are a sure thing. They have experience, references..."

"...kids to feed, bills to pay," he added with a self-satisfied smirk. "Look at it this way, Madam Accountant. We're not going to charge you for our services. You furnish the supplies, and bingo, the Cozy Cove ends up as inviting as a New England country inn."

Bingo? He thinks this is as easy as saying bingo?

"Count *those* beans and see what you come up with, lady," he said.

Sara lifted the hair from her neck and let the breeze cool her skin and divert her attention from the unexpected but suddenly shattering appeal of Nick's confidence. He needed a dose of reality now. Despite what she believed—that the men of Thorne Island would be lucky to pound a nail into a two-by-four without damaging their thumbs—she knew that Nick thought they could.

"I know this offer is just a delaying tactic, Nick," she said. "But your pals have to realize that their isolation can't last forever. Even if I agree to this, someday—"

He cupped a finger under her chin and lifted her face. "But not tomorrow, Sara," he said solemnly. "Not tomorrow. Let us do this. We'll do a good job. And you're asking too much if you think these guys can adjust to a crowd coming to Thorne Island so soon after they've had to deal with your arrival."

Every logical fiber of Sara's being was shouting at her to say no. A few contractors hardly constituted a crowd! But this sincerity coming from Nick was impossible to ignore. All at once he seemed vulnerable. His finger was still under her chin, but it felt as if he'd wrapped it around her heart. She released a long sigh, which ended in the surprising words, "All right. We'll give it a try."

His grin returned. "Atta girl, Sara," he said. "You're my kind of woman."

She shook her head. "Please, Bass, don't say that. You'll have me trying to drive the beetle off the edge of the dock to get away from here."

"It's that scary a thought?"

"Being your kind of woman? Yes. And we both know nothing could be further from the truth."

He inched a little closer to her and settled his fingertips on her shoulder. "That's for sure. You're not my type at all."

"Thank God," she snapped back, fighting a sudden twinge of disappointment.

His hand moved to the sensitive skin at her nape. His fingers trailed through her hair. And her toes curled involuntarily into the loose soil at her feet.

"I like redheads," he said. His other hand cupped the side of her face, and he lightly caressed her temple with his thumb. "And there's definitely too much up here," he said, stopping to tap her cranium. "I like a woman with a lot of extra room in her brain that she's not all that anxious to fill up with thoughts and ideas."

His hand crept slowly, sensually, down her arm while her heart skittered to an offbeat tempo. He flattened his palm just under her rib cage. "And this well-toned body of yours, while nice, isn't my thing. I like a woman who appreciates good Italian cooking and doesn't count calories."

His thumb rode up to caress the side of her breast. As he neared the nipple, a coil of warmth started in her abdomen and flowed through her bloodstream to meet his touch. Her mind demanded that she stop him, but her body had ideas of its own.

He pulled her closer still, until his mouth hovered over hers. His hand boldly covered her breast over the cotton fabric of her blouse. He kissed her cheeks lightly, the sensation like new spring grass on tingling skin. "No, Sara Crawford, you're not my type at all," he whispered into her ear. "But damn, sweetheart, you'll do."

"Nick…" Her feeble words of protest died against the lips that covered hers and were apparently determined to stop the formation of rational thought. A cloud covered the sun, cloaking the sky until they were bathed in a cool, gray ripple of earth-scented air. A breeze blew down from the hillside and slid like silk around Sara's limbs.

Nick's tongue probed at her mouth, and she opened it to let him in. She closed her eyes and relished the darkness that let her experience the wonder of his explorations. The top button of her blouse slid free, and his hand was inside, seeking. His voice floated above her from what seemed an ethereal place. "Oh, yes, Sara, you'll do just fine."

And then another sound—harsh, grating—split the damp, misty air. It came from a distant point and grew closer, louder. Nick pulled away, but kept one arm around her. "What the…?"

Sara blinked her eyes open. She patted her body, searching. "It's my phone."

He expelled a breath. "Jeez, Sara, let it ring. We're in the middle of a vineyard. What normal person would even get a call out here?"

She pulled the phone from her back pocket. "I can't just let it ring. It might be Candy." It took a moment to identify the voice. "D-Donald?"

Nick stood up from the bench and walked a few paces away. She tried giving him one of those can-you-believe-this looks that women sometimes use to get out of embarrassing situations. Although why she should be embarrassed she couldn't say. She and Donald were hardly more than friends, and besides, he was supposed to be in Aruba.

"Hold on a moment please, Donald," she said, and covering the receiver, looked at Nick. "It's this guy I'm kind of seeing," she whispered, realizing in the next instant how ridiculous that must sound to the person who'd been firing her senses with his mouth and hands a moment before.

Nick nodded sagely. "Then I guess I should leave you two alone."

"Well, yes. I think under the circumstances…"

"Right." Nick started up the path to the inn. "Nice talking with you."

Sara took a deep breath while she buttoned her

blouse. Then she said into the phone, "Donald, how are you?"

"Missing you," he said. "And I've decided to forgive you for backing out of the trip. By the way, Aruba's great. Clear blue water. White sandy beaches. Tanned natives." He snickered. "That reminds me. How's everything in that Lake Erie paradise of yours?"

Sara tried to hide her resentment of his sarcasm behind a lengthy explanation she knew would bore him to death. "Oh, fine. It's work, work, work, you know. A million things to do." As she filled him in on her activities, her gaze connected guiltily with Nick's when he shot her a glance over his shoulder. Then with a sigh of relief, she watched him turn away and cut through the hedges to the inn.

A SUDDEN SEVERE RAINSTORM sent Sara into the inn shortly after she disconnected with Donald. She still didn't understand why he'd called. Possibly to make her feel guilty or perhaps even jealous. He hadn't accomplished either. She patted her hair and skin dry with a towel and made herself a cup of tea. Enjoying the coziness of her warm, dry kitchen, she sat at the table and thought about the timing of Donald's call.

She ought to be grateful he'd gotten her number from Candy and phoned when he had. Who knew where the incident on the vineyard bench would have ended up? Nick Bass was definitely affecting her, and Sara couldn't come up with an antidote. She couldn't even explain what she and Nick had been doing just moments before, but she had to admit that she'd both feared and wanted more.

Sara shook her head. She had to finish the repairs

on the island as quickly as possibly and get Nick Bass out of her thoughts. It was true that Thorne Island was a challenge that excited her, but her *real* life was still in Florida, not here where no one liked or even wanted her. Her livelihood depended on the accounting firm of Bosch and Lindstrom, and only a fool would contemplate giving up a lucrative practice to try to make a go of a run-down inn and a struggling vineyard in the middle of nowhere. And Sara was no fool.

The rain had stopped and she walked out the back door and sat on the top porch step. Water seeped through her cutoffs, but she didn't care. It was hard to remember her Florida reality in the rain-washed air of Thorne Island. It was as if the rain had cleansed away thoughts of grumpy old men and obligations a thousand miles away. Even the dandelions—stubborn weeds and the curse of every gardener—shone with a brilliance that matched the sun.

Flowers. She would plant flowers around the inn before she left. Tall, elegant, colorful blooms, which would sway in the gentle breezes of Thorne Island.

There was nothing like the stillness in the air after a spring rain to nurture such satisfying thoughts. Suddenly each glorious sound of Thorne Island seemed magnified. The song of a robin, the cheerful chirrup of a cricket. The strains of James Taylor singing "You've got a friend."

James Taylor? Sara hadn't heard anything by Taylor in years, though his words and his voice were timeless. She stood up, dusted off her cutoffs and went into the inn. Then she climbed the stairs, following the music.

NICK SAW SARA'S REFLECTION in his rain-streaked bedroom window. She stood in the doorway uncertainly, as if afraid to enter but unwilling to walk away. He turned slowly to look at her. Her clothes were wet, making her seem smaller, more compact. Vulnerable.

"Nice music," she said.

He nodded toward his stereo. "James Taylor. You like him?"

"Uh-huh."

Nick waved her in. "Have a look." He crossed to the stereo in a corner of the room and lowered the volume. "I've got other albums by him."

"Albums?" She knelt in front of the low shelf and looked at his collection. "Well, I'll be. These are record albums."

"Yep. And that's a state-of-the-art turntable."

She grinned up at him. "'State of the art' and 'turntable.' Isn't that an oxymoron, like 'the convenience of eight-track tapes'?"

"Not if you like true, undiluted composition the way Taylor meant it to sound."

She flipped through his albums, reading off the names of the artists. "John Denver, Paul Anka, Waylon Jennings, Pete Fountain. My goodness, the many moods of Nick Bass."

"Is there anyone you'd like to hear?" he asked.

"No, not right now."

He raised his brows as if to say, "Then why are you here?"

"I want to talk about what happened in the vineyard," she said. "It was a little awkward."

Nick leaned against an old dresser and folded his arms. "Oh, yeah? Just because I was lip-locked with Donald's girlfriend when he ding-a-lings into her back pocket? The only thing awkward I see about that is he got closer to the body parts I was aiming for than I did, and he was a thousand miles away.''

She stood up and planted her fists on her hips, just as he knew she would. ''Don't be crude. For the record, he's not my boyfriend, and besides, neither of us planned that little episode. It just happened.''

He waggled an eyebrow at her. ''How do you know it wasn't planned? It's not like it hasn't happened before.''

Her cheeks, framed by damp strands of wispy hair, turned a telltale crimson. ''Well, it shouldn't have happened at all,'' she said. ''We're complete opposites, for heaven's sake. We've done nothing but snipe at each other ever since I arrived.''

''Nothing?'' He rubbed his jaw with an index finger. ''So why did it happen, Sara?''

''It was a lapse in judgment. I know I'm somewhat responsible. I'm not proud of myself.''

Nick knew he shouldn't tease, but he couldn't help himself. He'd deduced right away that Sara and this Donald guy weren't the real thing. Someone like Sara would never mess around on a serious relationship. And what had happened in the vineyard went a step beyond messing around to Nick's way of thinking. He attempted to appear pensive. ''Let me understand. You mean you're not head over heels for me, Crawford?''

She snorted. ''Absolutely not. In the vineyard we made a business deal, one that if it succeeds—and I have my doubts about that—will be beneficial for all of us.''

''So?''

''For that reason, you and I will have to maintain

an association. There's work to be done, Bass. I don't want what happened between us to affect the repairs on Thorne Island."

He nodded. "Of course not."

She paced away from him. "If there *is* some sort of weird, unexplained chemistry between us, we'll simply keep our distance from each other."

"For as long as the repairs take?" he asked.

"Yes."

He stepped in front of her, stopping her in her tracks. "So I'll have to wait till the renovations are done before I can kiss you senseless?"

"Don't put words in my mouth," she warned.

"I wasn't thinking of words..."

Just like a Sunday-school teacher exasperated with the kid who refuses to learn the simplest lesson, Sara lifted both hands and shook her head. She looked defeated. Nick took pity on her. "It's okay, Crawford. I'll be a good boy. If you don't want any extracurricular activities, I'll behave myself. But," he couldn't resist adding, "it won't be easy. It's all I can do not to jump your bones right now."

"Then I'm glad you fell through the porch. It put your jumping days on hold for a while."

CHAPTER ELEVEN

SARA WENT DOWNSTAIRS for coffee the next morning at seven-thirty. As usual, Nick had beaten her there. The pot already simmered with his rich brew, and her cup sat next to it.

Taking her coffee and an old ladder-back chair to the big kitchen window, she sat down to enjoy a day promising bright sun and warm temperatures. A perfect start to her projects. She hooked her toes around the chair legs and took the first sip from her mug.

"So, boss, what do you think I'd be good at?"

Sara jumped at the familiar voice coming from the back porch. How did he always manage to surprise her?

"Probably not replacing the eaves," he continued. "If I got a splinter, I'd have to put up with Mother Dexter and that sewing needle he uses to dig them out."

Sara stood and walked to the screen door. She stared at the back of Nick's head. The baseball cap was on backward, and she smiled at the team's grinning trademark face. "I don't think you'll be good at much of anything, Bass," she said. "I'll just let you putter around so you'll feel like one of the boys."

"What about painting?" he said, still looking out at the yard.

"Takes too much patience. You don't have any."

"Electrical?"

"Have you ever smelled charred skin? It's not pleasant."

He turned slowly, meeting her gaze with a serious narrowing of his eyes. "You know what I'm especially good at, Sara?"

Yes, she did, but now wasn't the time to bring it up. "No. What's that?"

"Thinking."

"Thinking?"

"You know, problem solving. I like to tackle problems before they get a toehold. Anticipate the roadblocks and head them off."

Sara knew this conversation was leading her somewhere as surely as if he'd snapped a leash around her neck. She decided to play along. "What problems do you think we might have?" she asked, taking a sip of coffee.

He stood up and faced her through the screen door. "The first one is the transportation of materials. You've got a boatload of supplies coming from the mainland, right? Paint, paste, nails, tools, lumber, wire…"

"Everything but qualified help," she said.

He ignored the gibe. "Have you thought about how you're going to move these materials from the dock to the inn?"

She knew exactly where he was going. "Of course I have," she answered. "Why do you think I brought the car back? It'll take a few trips, but I can get everything here in the bee. I'll load up the trunk and the back seat…"

The muscles in his face tensed with impatience the

longer she talked. Finally he cut her off midsentence. "Let me drive it, Sara."

She pretended not to have heard. "What? What's that?"

"I want to drive the damn car, Sara."

With the exception of one other activity she could think of, this was probably the most fun she'd had with Nick since the day she met him. "I'll have to think about it, Bass. You've been on this island for so long I don't know if you even have a valid driver's license."

His eyebrows drew together in an obstinate scowl. "I promise to avoid the cops."

"Well, I might consider it...on one condition."

His enthusiasm deflated like a week-old party balloon. "What's that?"

"I want information. And I'll trade you these—" she pulled the car keys out of her pocket and dangled them in front of the screen door "—for it."

"Heck, that's easy," he said. "I've already told you a little about the island's history. And about the Kraus family and their wine making. What else do you want to know?"

"I don't want that kind of info, Bass."

"Then what?"

She opened the door and waved him inside. Making him wait, she refilled her coffee mug, sat down at the table and said, "Tell me about Ryan. Why is he here? And why is he so timid at the prospect of being around other people?"

"Aw, come on, Sara, I can't talk about him. It's privileged information."

"Strictest confidence, Bass, I promise." She meant it, and knew he'd believe her.

"Still…"

She jangled the keys one time and then clamped her fist around them. "No story. No keys."

He looked up at the ceiling, then back down at her. She could tell the end was beginning to justify the means. "Why Ryan?" he asked. "Why not one of the others?"

"Because I've sort of got the others figured out. Brody's story is obvious. He's here because nobody else will have him. And you other three are just weird enough to overlook his faults and maybe even envy him for them."

Nick rolled his eyes.

"And Dexter—he's sweet-natured all right. Just like you told me. But he's ticked off that the rest of the world is still playing football and he isn't. So he's hiding out with a remote control in one hand and a physical therapy manual in the other. Your recovery has become his mission."

"What about me? Why don't you ask about me?"

"Primarily because you wouldn't tell me anything if I did. I know you came here after somebody shot you. Maybe it was a jealous husband. Maybe it was the clerk in the convenience store you were robbing. I don't know. But that happened six years ago, and now you're just sitting around here waiting for the bullet to come out the other side."

He grimaced as if she'd delivered a painful shot of her own. "Sara, some people are just private."

"Fine. So I'll leave you alone—for now. But I want to know about Ryan. I like him. I won't use the information against him, and I won't try to change him. I just want to understand."

Nick studied her face for several moments. He must

have decided that he could trust her, because he finally said, "Okay, here's what happened to Ryan."

FROM THE BEGINNING Nick's story hinted of misplaced trust and unforgivable betrayal. Eliot Ryan had loved racehorses and the thrill of seeing them run. According to Nick, Ryan had been one hell of a jockey. But he'd become a victim of some double-dealing and had been sentenced to jail. And it was this image—Ryan sitting in a cell—that almost brought Sara to tears.

"He suspected one of the trainers he worked for was injecting his horses with a stimulant," Nick explained. "When he called the guy on it, he was told to mind his own business or he wouldn't get a mount in all of Ohio."

"So he kept quiet," Sara deduced.

"Yeah, he did. It happened at a time in his life when his mother was on her deathbed and Ryan was paying some heavy-duty medical bills. His silence bought him a ton of good races and cuts of hefty prize money. But when the story finally broke and the racing commission got wind of the drug use, that same silence cast a whole lot of suspicion on him."

"Is that why he went to jail? For not revealing what he suspected?"

"Nope. He wasn't arrested then. There wasn't enough solid evidence."

"So what happened?" Sara asked.

Nick rubbed the stubble of beard on his chin. "There's a little device that track people know about called the machine."

Machine? A harmless enough name, Sara thought. "What is it?"

"It's a small, battery-powered prod that fits into the palm of a man's hand. About the size and shape of a Bic lighter. And it's highly illegal. With pressure from his thumb, the jockey can turn the device on. Then while he's riding, he can touch the horse anywhere on its body and send a jolt of electricity through that thick horse hide that's strong enough to make the animal run faster."

Sara couldn't imagine Ryan using the machine on any animal. "Did Ryan use the device in one of his races?"

Nick looked at Sara with honest, clear eyes. "I'd bet my entire next month's rent that he didn't."

Sara didn't smile at his attempt to lighten the mood.

"Ryan was framed," he continued, "plain and simple. He won a big race one day, and the jockey who came in second issued a protest, saying he saw Ryan use the machine. The stewards investigated, ran the film dozens of times and finally found a frame that showed Ryan *might* have been using his hand in a way that *might* have indicated the use of a machine. Then the stewards found one of the devices in the dirt—obviously planted. The authorities were called in, there was a short trial, and Ryan didn't see daylight for the next eighteen months. And of course his career was over."

"How did he end up here?" Sara asked.

"Brody used to go to the track a lot before he moved to the island. He knew Ryan, and when he heard about his release from prison, he invited him to Thorne. With his mother buried by then, the poor guy had nowhere else to go."

Now he acts as if he's afraid of his own shadow, Sara thought. And he's definitely more anxious than the others at the thought of strangers coming to the island. "If you ask me—" she began.

Nick put his hand up. "Stop right there, little mother. I didn't tell you this so you'd start conjuring up some scheme to *fix* Ryan."

She leveled her most frustrated glare on him. "No, you told me so you could drive my car. That's a much more noble reason!"

He stuck his hand out, palm up. "That's right, so hand over the keys. A deal's a deal."

Sara wanted to ask more questions, but Dexter's voice boomed from the front porch. "Nick! Sara! Come on. That pontoon boat's coming into the dock, and it's carrying quite a load."

Nick waggled his fingers, his gaze fixed on the keys in Sara's hand. "Remember what you said, Crawford," he warned. "I think your exact words were 'strictest confidence. I won't try to change him.' Does that ring a bell?"

Reluctantly she slid the key ring across the table. "Yes. I won't say anything."

He picked up the keys and started out of the kitchen. He was almost through the door when he whirled around to face her. "That doesn't mean you won't *do* anything, though, does it?"

She answered with a noncommittal grin.

LATER THAT FRIDAY improvements were well under way at the Cozy Cove. By the time he quit for the day, Dexter had painted two bedrooms a cheerful shade of lemon. They only needed floral wallpaper borders around the ceiling moldings and chair rails to complete the decor. Ryan had ripped down old gutters and downspouts to reach damaged fascia boards. Brody had removed outlet covers, cut off the power supply and tested wiring with a strange instrument he carried from room to room. Sara, who knew nothing about electrical work, couldn't gauge his progress, but each time she passed the doorway of a room he was working in, she heard grumbling and complaining.

"Don't know why I'm bothering with this nonsense," he said. "If I have my way, there won't be any people coming to this old inn, anyway. I'm just wasting good fishing time, and for what?"

Sara hadn't seen much of Nick that day, but she determined that he'd had more fun than his companions. The little engine of the Volkswagen had puttered under her window countless times, indicating that Nick probably made twice as many trips as were necessary. And since he never came from the same direction two times in a row, he'd obviously found circuitous routes from the inn to the harbor.

"Way to squeeze six years of driving into one day, Bass," she called out the window during one of his stops. "Remember, when that tank of gasoline is gone, somebody's got to talk Winkie into bringing more from Put-in-Bay—at a cost of twenty bucks!"

The wide grin on his face confirmed that he was having the time of his life. "I wouldn't worry about it, Crawford," he hollered back to her. "Your credit's good with Winkie."

When all the supplies were eventually deposited at

the inn, Sara heard Nick's feet clomping around on the roof and his hammer pounding away at the shingles.

For the next few days Sara decided her best course of action was to stay as far away from the renovations as possible. She split her time between working in the vineyard, giving instructions to Candy on the cell phone and preparing monthly statements and flow sheets on her computer.

It was during these hours of isolation that Sara realized she missed being intimately involved in the refurbishing. She stayed away from the men, but the desire to check on every little detail and the need to celebrate even the smallest improvement was almost overwhelming. The more she stared at numbers on a blue computer screen, the more she wished she was painting and preparing the Cozy Cove.

Sara, who'd always prided herself on her level-headed approach to problems and logical thinking, was now facing a life-altering realization. A big part of her didn't care about the numbers at all. Instead, she rejoiced in watching the old inn come alive. Suddenly Sara Crawford, number cruncher, had become an artistic visionary!

Another discovery she made about herself, and this one was more surprising, was that she actually missed being around the men. Tucked away in her room with only her laptop to keep her company, she listened to their complaints and winced at language that would have been much more appropriate at the Happy Angler. But occasionally she heard a cheerful whistle, a shared laugh or the country twang of Waylon Jennings coming from Nick's turntable, and she knew that deep down she wanted to be part of the community she had inherited.

That was why late the following Saturday afternoon, Sara called Winkleman on her cell phone and made a special request. Since she always read every food label and calculated each gram of fat in her diet, she couldn't believe it was her voice listing the groceries she required.

"Two whole cut-up fryers. A one-pound can of vegetable oil. A large tub of margarine. A pound of cheddar cheese. A bag of flour, and a five-pound bag of potatoes..." By the time she mentioned fresh asparagus and crescent rolls, she could tell Winkleman's mouth was watering.

"Lordy, Sara," he said, "sounds like you'll have enough for a small army."

She smiled into the phone. "If you're fishing for an invitation, Mr. Winkleman, you've got it. Just have the groceries here tomorrow by two o'clock. And you'd better bring a large package of napkins."

"Yes, ma'am."

"And, Winkie," she added, "don't tell the others. I want this to be a surprise."

After hanging up, Sara went into the kitchen to double-check the equipment. Luckily she'd purchased all the necessary utensils on the mainland, including oversize skillets and a large pot for boiling potatoes. She mentally went through the list she'd given Winkie and realized she'd forgotten to mention butter for the rolls.

"No problem," she said to herself. "Surely Brody has butter he can sell me."

She left the inn and walked the short distance to Brody's commissary. When she reached the steps of the cottage, she heard his voice coming from inside. His tone was brisk and authoritarian, almost intimidating, and she stopped before going inside. If Brody was angry about something, she didn't want to be in the path of his tirade. She waited outside but gave in to the temptation to eavesdrop.

"Don't give me any of that horse manure about not being able to deliver," he said. "I know darn well you can."

Sara didn't hear an answering voice and assumed Brody was talking on his phone.

"Hire a boat if you have to," he said. "You'll get your money. I want three hundred feet of your best-grade conduit delivered to Thorne Island as soon as possible. And while you're at it, send me eight new ceiling fans. But don't try to pass off those junky nineteen-ninety-nine specials on me. I want them to be quiet. If one of them even so much as purrs like a cat, I'll have it back in that store before you even know it left."

Brody added other items to his list, including heavy-gauge wire, fuses and some materials Sara had never heard of. Her dwindling bank balance swam before her eyes. What in the world was Brody doing? She couldn't afford to pay for all that. If this was Brody's way of getting rid of her, it might just work.

She bounded up the steps, prepared to confront him. But another sharp retort from Brody stopped her.

"What do you mean, how am I going to pay for all this? Young man, do you have any idea who I am?"

There was a silence during which Sara could practically feel the air crackling around her, and the nervousness of the employee on the other end of that phone.

"Listen to me," Brody commanded. "As soon as we're done with this conversation, you call Vernon Russell, the president of the main branch of First Union Trust Bank of Cleveland. Tell him that Carlton Brody just placed an order at your store and wants him to send payment in full."

Another pause. "No, I don't have his damn number. What do I sound like, a telephone operator? Why don't you earn that big salary of yours and look it up! And I expect to see that order here lickety split!"

Since it was impossible to slam a cell phone with the same vigor one could propel a regular phone to its cradle, Brody must have compensated by pounding his fist on the countertop. Anyway, the loud crack that followed the end of the conversation was proof to Sara that Brody expected his demands to be met.

She turned away from the door. Suddenly aware that she hadn't drawn a normal breath in minutes, she expelled a long whistle of air. Brody's conversation played over in her mind. The man had actually arranged to pay for improvements to the inn!

"Unbelievable!" she said to herself. Like a snake that had just rolled over in the grass, the old grouch had revealed a soft spot.

"What are *you* doing here?"

Sara spun around to stare into Brody's squinting dark eyes. Standing in his doorway, he might have frightened the wits out of her at one time, but not this evening. It was all she could do not to grin.

"How long have you been standing there?" he demanded.

"Ah...not long. A few minutes."

"Long enough to hear a private telephone conversation, I'll warrant."

She shrugged innocently. "Maybe a little of it."

"Just like a sneaky female. Don't read anything into it. I just can't abide shoddy work. And that two-bit junk you ordered wouldn't bring a damn doorbell up to code."

"I didn't realize," she offered weakly. "Brody, I want you to know I appreciate—"

"Never mind that," he said. "Nothing's changed. I still don't want a bunch of beachcombers swarming over my island."

"I know," she said. "I understand your position."

"Good, 'cause I stand firm on it. A little fancy wiring shouldn't put any ideas into your head. Now, what are you doing here, anyway?"

For a moment she couldn't remember. "Oh, yes," she finally said. "Butter. I need to buy two sticks of butter."

He stepped inside his cottage and waved her in behind him. "I'll see if I've got any."

She followed him to the refrigerator. He pulled out a box that had three sticks left in it. "I guess I can let you have two sticks," he said.

"Thank you, Brody."

He lifted his gaze to the ceiling, calculating. "Let's see. A pound of butter is a dollar seventy-nine. You want half of it. That's ninety cents." He slid the sticks out of the box and put them on the counter, waiting until she'd produced the right amount of change.

"I'm not assuming that odd penny," he said. "I do enough around here without throwing money away."

Sara picked up the butter. "You certainly do, and I'm happy to pay the extra penny. Good evening, Brody."

He huffed through his nose, and Sara pictured a bull pawing the dirt in preparation for a charge. Only now she knew his huff was worse than his horns.

CHAPTER TWELVE

ON SUNDAY, a few minutes before two o'clock, Winkie's boat arrived from Put-in-Bay. Dodging questions from Nick about where she was going and why Winkie was there, Sara started the Volkswagen and nudged the gearshift into reverse. "Don't worry, Bass," she called up to him. "We promise not to have any fun without you."

She and Winkie piled the grocery sacks into the car and drove to the back of the inn from where they carried everything inside without being spotted. However, Sara realized it would be much more difficult to keep the men out of the kitchen for the two hours it would take her to prepare the meal.

She assigned Winkie the job of keeping her dinner guests from walking in on the preparations. She gave him a large thermos of lemonade and a cooler of beer. "If they ask for anything other than these drinks, tell them you'll get it," she said.

What proved to be absolutely impossible was masking the aroma coming from the inn kitchen. Once Brody called out to his buddies from a back window, "What's that woman cooking up now? Whatever it is, it doesn't smell half-bad."

"You just wait, Brody," Sara said before taking another sip of a 1990 White Thorne chardonnay. She rolled a chicken breast in flour and put the heavily coated morsel in the fry pan. It sizzled delectably.

At four-thirty, the meal was complete. Sara set six places at the big dining-room table, uncorked another bottle of wine and filled the glasses. Then she went to the bottom of the stairs and called up. ''I want you all to stop what you're doing and come to the dining room. And wash your hands!''

When she returned to the kitchen, Sara had her first panoramic view of the havoc her preparations had caused. The double sinks were piled with dirty pots and pans. The floor and scrub table were dusted with flour and several sticky-looking substances. And the stove she'd scoured and polished days before defied description. Her facial muscles scrunched with distaste as she moved to get a closer look at the crusty brown stains on the porcelain surface.

Resigning herself to having to clean up later, Sara carried bowls and platters to the table and closed the door on the disaster. Aromatic steam rose from a platter of golden fried chicken, mashed potatoes slathered in butter, asparagus dripping with cheese, fresh corn on the cob and milk-thickened chicken gravy.

She had just put a basket of rolls in the center of the table when the men entered the dining room. For an interminably long moment they appeared dumbstruck. Sara decided their stares were appreciative, though, despite the comments that came from their mouths.

''What the hell's all this?'' Brody asked.

''It appears the bean counter can cook,'' Nick answered.

''I think it's nice,'' Ryan said.

Dexter, who had long denied himself such unhealthy fare, didn't say a word. He simply raced Winkie to the nearest chair and attached a napkin to the collar of his paint-blotched knit shirt.

"Dig in, everyone," Sara said. "I hope you like it."

BY THE END OF THE MEAL the one problem Sara didn't have was what to do with leftovers. Every last morsel had been consumed. She allowed the gusto with which the men attacked the food to compensate for the absence of true camaraderie, which she'd hoped might have been a result of all her work. Dinner conversation had centered around the usual—sporting events and fishing.

She passed out slices of cherry pie and stood at the head of the table while the men devoured the last, sweet part of their meal. When Nick noticed her standing there, he said, "Boys, I think we owe Sara our thanks for putting this food on the table."

"I'll agree with that," Dexter said. "I'd forgotten how terrific good food tasted."

"Fit for a king all right," Brody said.

Wiping cherry juice from his chin, Winkie agreed.

Ryan smiled at her. "Thanks, Sara."

She folded her hands at her waist. "You're welcome," she said. "This meal is my way of saying thanks to all of you. I want you to know that I appreciate what you're doing for the Cozy Cove. Each one of you has put in long, hard days, and I'm very pleased with the results. But mostly, it gives me a great deal of satisfaction to know that deep down you really do care about the inn and the island—"

Brody leaned back in his chair, patted his midsection and interrupted her as if she'd never said a word.

"Well, fellas, I guess this just about wraps things up for today. I suggest you all get to bed early. Tomorrow's Monday."

Sara stared at him in disbelief. "Pardon me, Mr. Brody," she said, "but I was talking."

He squinted down the table at her. "You were? Well, you go on talking to these other guys. I'm hitting the hay. Digging Day comes early around here."

"Digging Day? You're not working on the inn tomorrow?"

Brody stared at her as if the chicken wasn't the only thing that had gotten fried in that kitchen. "Now lookie here. Nothing, and I mean *nothing* interferes with Digging Day."

She looked at the other men for support. "But I assumed—"

Dexter stood up and glanced at his watch. "Not only that, but there's an Indians game coming on in a half hour. They're playing in New York tonight. Should be a good game." He nodded toward Ryan. "You coming, little man?"

Ryan rose and gave in to a yawn. "Nope. A meal like this makes me sleepy. I'm turning in." He waved at Sara as he walked toward the lobby. "Thanks again, Sara."

"And I've got to get back while I've still got daylight," Winkie said. "Got a fishing charter in the morning." Brody and Dexter followed him out of the dining room.

Sara slumped into her chair and stared at the mountain of dirty dishes cluttering the table. Out of the corner of her eye she saw Nick put his hand over his mouth. If he was hiding a grin, she didn't think she could stop herself from slapping it off.

"Let me guess," he said after a moment of uncomfortable silence. "You're a little disappointed in their after-dinner etiquette?"

She glared at him.

"Hey, I'm still here."

"It's supposed to make me feel better knowing that you hold yourself up as the epitome of good manners?"

He rested his arm on the back of the chair and stared at her. "I may not be an epitome, but I'm all you've got."

She tossed the napkin she'd been unconsciously shredding onto the table. "Why can't Brody give up that ridiculous Digging Day ritual just once so we can get these projects done? And why do the others have to follow him like sheep?"

He shrugged. "Because we're men. We're inconsiderate clods, as you've pointed out on more than one occasion. Why are you so surprised when we stay in character?"

Sara chewed on her lower lip and nodded. "Bass, when you're right, you're right." She stood up and started around the table, making a stack of dirty plates. When her arms were full, she deposited that load in the kitchen and met Nick at the door. He carried serving bowls and silverware.

"I shouldn't have been surprised," she announced after returning a third time. "I should know what to expect from you men by now." She stuffed soiled napkins into the bowl of a glass and headed for the kitchen again.

"I guess I'm just a slow learner," she said when she and Nick made the last journey into the kitchen. While she scraped food from the plates into the trash bin, he filled the sink with hot water. Sara walked by and squirted a little detergent in. Nick took the plastic bottle from her and added a lot more. Then he slipped the glasses into the water.

Sara took a dishrag and drying towel out of the linen drawer and came up behind him. "I'll do that," she said.

"Never mind. I'm already here."

NICK WASHED the glasses and stacked them on the counter. Sara picked up one and dried it, then dried it some more. She buffed it to a shiny gloss while the other glasses just sat there. Nick moved on to the plates.

He finally looked over his shoulder at her. "Sara, I think you're about to rub the little flower right off the glass."

She turned away from him with an undignified snort and set the glass on the scrub table.

He handed the glass back to her. "Let me wipe off the table."

"I suppose I'm overreacting," she said, watching his movements with a vacant stare. "After all, it is Digging Day, and you've told me how important that is to Brody. It's just that the inn is so important to me..."

"I know."

"And I thought..." She turned away from him. Her voice quivered like sycamore leaves in an island breeze. "It's not so much the Digging Day thing, even though I don't understand why it's so blasted special. I'd hoped..."

Her words stopped, but the quivering didn't. It rippled into her shoulders. She placed one hand flat on the table and covered her mouth with the other.

Nick hadn't heard a woman sob in years, but there was no mistaking the sound when it came from Sara. It was low and mournful. Nick knew she'd had too much to drink. He knew she must be dog-tired. He knew the men had disappointed her. He knew all that, but damned if he could think of a way to comfort her.

So he pleaded to her back. "Oh, jeez, Sara, don't do that."

She hiccupped. "I'm sorry. I don't know why…"

He tossed the dishcloth into the sink and placed his wet hands on her bare arms. "Come on now, nothing's as bad as all that. It was a really great dinner."

"I know that." Her words came out on a sniffling breath.

He turned her around so she was looking at his shirt, instead of the table. Then he couldn't believe the next thing that came out of his mouth. "Look, do you want to talk about it?"

A bigger sob shook her body before she looked into his eyes. "W-with you? What good would that do?"

Thank God! "Well, then, what *do* you want me to do?"

Her luminous moist eyes sucker punched him. She trembled in his arms. Her chest rose and fell against some sort of old-fashioned, lacy cotton thing. Her lips parted as if she wanted to say something, but the only thing that escaped was a soft sigh.

And Nick's breath caught in his throat as a slow burn sizzled inside him. "Damn it, Sara, I don't know what to do to make you feel better. I sure hope this works because I promise it'll do wonders for me."

He kissed her. Her lips were warm and salty, and

sweet with the flavor of White Thorne wine. When he ran the tip of his tongue across the line of her lips, they grew soft and pliant. He had to remind himself that this was a kiss of comfort, not passion.

But the instant he pulled her body to his and pressed his palm against her back, the second his fingers became tangled in her hair, a quick, hot rush of desire shuddered through him.

He felt her dig into the flesh of his shoulders as a sound came from her throat. It wasn't a cry of hurt like the others had been. This was a sensual plea for him to continue. Her lips parted and he plunged his tongue into her mouth. He backed her up a few inches, settled his hands under her bottom, and lifted her to the edge of the table.

His heart raced in anticipation of what was finally going to happen. In another minute she'd be stretched out on that table and he'd be...

Then the damned overdried glass she'd set back down on the table stopped everything.

It tipped over, rolled with a clumsy awkwardness across the surface and fell to the floor with a teeth-rattling crash. Sara flattened her palms against Nick's chest and pushed him away.

"Nick, no. We can't do this."

"Yes, Sara, yes we can."

She moved off the table and stared at him with brilliant blue eyes that swam with passion, not tears. "We agreed not to do this," she said.

Nick clenched his fists, driving super-charged energy to those parts of his body and away from muscles that flexed with wanting to take her in his arms again. "I never should have agreed to that ridiculous condition," he said. "Besides, you were crying, and

I didn't know any other way to make you stop. Aren't you at least going to admit it made you feel better?''

''It made me feel good, but not better. They're two different things.''

''What exactly do you mean, Sara?''

''I don't know. I guess I'd like to be appreciated.''

''You want to be appreciated by us?''

She sniffed loudly. ''Crazy, isn't it?''

''But, Sara, we're fixing up your inn. Isn't that enough?''

She snatched the dish towel and stepped around him to get a plate to dry. ''You have absolutely no idea why I was crying, do you, Nick?''

''I sure as hell know why you stopped!''

There were times when arguing with Sara was challenging and fun. This wasn't one of them. Nick went to the sink and fished in the suds for his rag. ''Never mind,'' he said. ''Let's get this mess cleaned up.''

''No, you go on,'' she said. ''I'll finish.'' When he didn't budge, she added, ''Really, Nick, go! I want you to.''

He swiped carelessly at the chicken platter. ''Why? Because if I stay, you'll be tempted?''

''I don't know. Maybe.''

''And would that be so bad?''

She stopped drying a plate and looked at him for the first time since they'd returned to their chores. ''Yes, Nick. It would be terrible. Now please leave.''

He threw the rag into the water and stormed out of the kitchen. What else was there to do? Though he went to his room, it was still too early to go to bed. Pent-up energy crackled in his body. A burning need clawed at his insides.

He paced, all the while enumerating the many reasons Sara was right. Why it would be terrible if they gave in to the desire that simmered between them. Okay, so they lived in different worlds. Nick knew he wasn't willing to give up his isolated lifestyle to rejoin the mainstream Sara lived in. He was a nonconformist living under an alias, while she was a card-carrying member of the establishment.

So what? Couldn't they put their differences aside and grab a few minutes of pure pleasure?

Nick sat in his chair and plowed his fingers through his hair. He flicked the power button on his computer, and the screen came to life. Okay. He'd put Sara out of his mind for a while. He'd turn his feelings of passion into some of the best writing he'd done since she'd arrived on Thorne Island.

Ivan Banning popped into Nick's head with startling clarity. Nick's fingers flew across the keyboard. Yes! Banning would be the release Nick needed tonight. In this chapter Ivan would meet a sexy, uncomplicated woman and for a few pages the detective would forget about drug deals.

IT WAS WELL PAST DARK when Sara finished cleaning the kitchen. In case Nick turned off the generator, she took a lantern from the parlor and carried it to her room. She was exhausted, and despite her disappointment—or perhaps because of it—she knew she would sleep.

If only she could cleanse her mind of Nick Bass as efficiently as she'd cleaned the kitchen. She glanced down the hallway to his room. His door was open a few inches, letting the glow of his computer screen spill into the hall. She followed the light, stopping just outside his door. She listened to the steady tap of his keyboard. Imagined his fingers gliding smoothly from key to key. Imagined his fingers…

She shook off the far-too-familiar tingle that ribboned down her spine. What *was* he doing in there? she wondered for the hundredth time. What was he writing? Did that computer hold the clues to the man Nick really was?

CHAPTER THIRTEEN

As EXPECTED, Brody's golf cart rumbled to the front of the inn at daybreak Monday morning. Even if the crunch of tires on gravel hadn't wakened Sara, Brody's bellowing would have. Minutes later the front door slammed shut, Nick grumbled something unintelligible at Brody which received an equally gruff response, and the cart set out on its thus far fruitless endeavor to locate a French missionary's fortune.

Sara yanked the bedcovers over her head in an attempt to drown out the noise. But once the cart had left, she realized she was fully awake and might as well use the quiet time to attend to her own chores. She'd work in the vineyard first and attack spreadsheets later.

She dressed, had coffee and decided to check out the newly painted guest rooms. The lemon walls were cheerful and inviting, and once she ordered new linens from the JC Penney catalog she'd brought from Sandusky, the rooms should appeal to anyone staying at the Cozy Cove Inn.

A total of four rooms had been completed. Dexter had only Sara's room to work on before he was done. Nick had made it clear that no one would be entering his sacred domain for any reason, and she'd agreed. After all, his idea to have the men do the work was proving to be a godsend, despite this morning's leave of absence.

Before she reached Nick's closed door, Sara turned around and headed back down the hall. But she'd only walked a few feet when an outrageous idea stopped her midstride. She shook her head to clear her mind. Some ideas should definitely be ignored, and this one was far beneath the conduct of any person who considered herself honorable.

Even so, the glass knob on Nick's door tempted her, and before she could stop herself, she grasped the knob, gave it a quick twist and opened the door. She'd lain awake for hours, wondering what Nick did in this room. She knew the clues to his background lay just across this threshold. If she was ever to discover them, she'd have to take advantage of the opportunity Digging Day presented.

"Sara Louise Crawford, what are you doing?" she chided herself as she stepped into the room. She ought to turn back. She ought to feel guiltier than she did. At that moment, she primarily experienced a jolt of pure adrenaline.

The room was uncharacteristically messy. Clothes were strewn about, the bed had not been made, Nick's empty coffee mug had been left to form a brown ring on top of his dresser. But his desk was meticulous. The computer beckoned her to power it up and learn the innermost secrets of Nick Bass's life.

Sara walked to the desk, her fingers flexing with nervousness at her side. "You know you shouldn't do this," her conscience told her. She paused, waiting for the devil on her shoulder to offer a counterargument. She reached for the power button and jerked her hand back. "No, Sara! You're not a snoop. You have no right to poke your nose into Nick's private life.''

Seconds passed while she debated her course of action. And finally the pesky devil spoke. Was it fair that Nick knew practically everything about her and she knew almost nothing about him? He knew where she was raised, what she did for a living. He'd even eavesdropped on her phone conversation with Candy. Nick, despite all his claims to support a person's right to privacy, wasn't above a little snooping himself!

The devil didn't stop with that argument. If Sara was going to reinvent Thorne Island, didn't she owe it to herself to know as much as possible about the men who, by virtue of a totally unfair stipulation in her aunt's lease agreement, would continue to oppose every suggestion she made?

''There are answers in that hard drive,'' she said. ''Now is your chance to know the real Nick Bass.''

She reached for the power button again. Her finger trembled above it and fell to her side. She couldn't do it. She was about to back away from the desk when she noticed several 9" by 12" postal mailing boxes stacked on the floor. Black printing on the spines caught her eye. *Promise of Fear. Double Dealings. Prospect Murder. Blood Money.* All but the top box had been sealed with clear tape.

''They sound like titles,'' she said. ''Gruesome ones.'' She picked up the top box and turned it over. The heavy contents shifted. Before her conscience could speak again, she opened the box and took out several pages. The same three pieces of information were at the top of each—the words *Dead Last*, a page number and Nick Bass's name.

She recalled her first day on the island, when she'd

gotten a glimpse of Nick's computer screen. She'd thought then that the image looked like manuscript format.

So Nick Bass was a writer! The sealed boxes probably contained finished manuscripts, and Sara was holding the pages of his current project. Nothing could have surprised her more. And nothing could have made her more curious.

"How does a writer, a person who lives in self-imposed isolation, end up with a bullet in his spine?" she asked the empty room. "And why are these novels—" she stopped and counted seven boxes "—sealed in packages and yet appear to have never been mailed?"

"And—" she scanned the titles again "—just exactly what creepy things does Nick Bass write about?"

Sara walked to the window and looked out. A gentle breeze stirred the budding leaves in the trees. She went to the door of Nick's room and opened it all the way so even if she missed the sound of the golf cart, she would hear Nick's heavy footsteps when he arrived back at the inn.

The vines would have to wait. Sara sat cross-legged on the floor, settled the two hundred pages on her lap and began to read.

ONCE SHE WAS well into the manuscript, Sara realized she didn't know a whole lot more about Nick Bass, but she had a clear picture of Ivan Banning. She knew what made the detective stand firm and what made him run. What angered and emboldened him, and what, in his own terms, "scared the shit out of him."

She knew that he had principles, which he ignored

if the situation demanded it, and that he made rash decisions he couldn't afford to regret later. He was sensitive to the problems of the downtrodden but abhorred weakness. At the same time, he felt nothing but contempt for the oppressors no matter what their motives were.

All in all, Ivan Banning was not an especially nice man, yet Sara couldn't help liking him.

So maybe she did know a bit more about Nick Bass, after all.

It was midmorning before Sara stood and stretched her leg muscles. Then she moved to the wicker chair by the side of the door, sat comfortably and resumed reading. As she finished each page, she let it drift to the pile collecting at her feet.

And another hour passed. An hour in which, for Sara, the birds outside ceased to sing, the breeze no longer rustled through the trees, and the waves no longer washed on shore a couple of hundred yards away.

And a man in his stocking feet made no sound entering a silent building.

Sara's heart leaped in her chest when she realized she was not alone. She responded to the intake of a deep breath, looked to her right at the open door and stared into the menacing gray eyes of Nick Bass. He stood as though carved of marble, his shoes dangling from his hands.

Sara followed his gaze from the stack of boxes by his desk to the pile of papers haphazardly strewn on the floor. And then to Sara herself, her face no doubt brilliant with mortification, sitting in his wicker chair with the few remaining pages of his manuscript in her lap.

Sara gulped back a hysterical shriek. "Oh, Nick...I didn't hear... Your shoes..."

He threw his Docksiders onto the floor and they landed with a dull thump. "They're wet," he said. "If you meant them to be your warning device, perhaps the next time you trespass you should equip me with a bell."

Oh God, oh God... Sara pressed the heel of her palm against her forehead and closed her eyes against Nick's accusatory glare. Then she summoned her courage and looked back at him. "Nick, I can explain."

He leaned against the door frame and crossed his arms over his chest. "Go ahead."

What the devil did she mean, she could explain? The situation was obvious. "Well, I could explain, but I don't think what I'd say would put me in a very favorable light. In fact, I can't think of any way for me to come out looking good here."

For an interminably torturous moment, the only part of Nick that moved was a muscle in his jaw. "Then why don't we start with a simple interrogation," he finally said. "What the blazes are you doing in here?" A finger darted out from his crossed arms and aimed at the papers in her lap. "And what are you doing with that?"

She picked up the pages from her lap, wishing they would disappear. "I found these," she said weakly.

"They were lost?"

"No, of course not. I didn't mean it that way. I was standing by your desk and I found the boxes."

"Standing? Snooping? Spying?"

She sucked in her guilt in one long, agonized breath

but didn't speak. His words pretty much summed it up.

Nick pushed himself away from the door frame, came into the room and slammed the door shut with the flat of his hand. Sara jumped to her feet. The rest of the pages fluttered to the floor and fanned around the chair, becoming even more conspicuous.

She backed away from him. His eyes glittered with dark rage.

"You're not going to...hurt me, are you?" she managed to croak out.

His cold voice matched the threat in his eyes. "I haven't decided yet, but it's an option."

An unexpected and uncontrollable giggle bubbled up from her throat. "You're kidding, right? You wouldn't."

His facial expression remained carved of stone. "Why did you pry, Sara? What were you hoping to find?"

A burst of bravado, drawn from some little-known, foolish part of her formed her words. "Oh, I don't know, Nick," she said with false confidence. "A gun maybe? A pair of handcuffs with your initials engraved into them? Something to tell me why a big, strapping guy like you has a bullet in his back and chooses to live like a hermit?"

A sound came from his throat—a roar of disbelief and anger. "It never occurred to you that you don't have the *right* to come into my room, or the *authority* to go through my things, or my *permission* to snoop for evidence about my past?"

"Of course it occurred to me. In fact, I almost didn't do it."

"Wonderful!" He turned away from her and faced

the window. "That's some consolation. Miss Pure-of-Heart *almost* didn't do it! *Almost* didn't violate the sanctity of *my* life!"

Sara took two steps toward him. "Nick, I'm so sorry. Of course you're right—"

His shoulders tensed. His spine straightened. "Don't come any closer, Sara."

She stopped. "Okay, I won't. I'm just trying to tell you that I can't argue with you. I shouldn't have come in here."

He snorted at the obvious concession.

"But if you'll just listen a minute, I have something to say. I think we're missing a very important point here."

He turned back to face her. His features had not gentled. "You mean the point isn't that you are a conniving, sneaky little—"

"Well, yes," she interrupted. "That is one point. And I believe you've made it satisfactorily. But I have a point, also, and it's at least as significant as yours."

His eyes widened with obvious skepticism, but she had his attention. "And that would be?"

She bent down and scooped up a handful of manuscript pages. "That this is good. It's excellent, as a matter of fact." She waved the papers in front of his eyes. "Nick, you are a writer! All morning I've been completely absorbed by this story, even to the point of ignoring my surroundings and not hearing you come in." She pointed to the boxes. "Why haven't you sent these to a publisher?"

The muscle in his jaw worked again. "I think we're

back to *my* point again, Sara. What I do in here is none of your damned business!"

"But it's such a shame…"

He strode to the desk and glared at her. "Don't you get it yet?" He pointed his index finger to the floor and drew an imaginary line across the front of his toes. "There's a line here. Maybe you can't see it, but it's here, believe me. And you can't cross it. Understand that? And don't think for a minute that I'm going to step over that line and bring you to my side so you can get a little peek at the real me, because I'm not."

"Nick, I didn't mean—"

"I know what you meant. You think you can somehow control my actions—that you can turn me into something you believe I am."

"But you *are* a writer!" she exclaimed. "I didn't turn you into one, and—"

He held up a finger. "A couple of days ago we made a deal, Sara. In spite of what happened here, I intend to honor that commitment. We'll get this little dollhouse of yours prettied up so you can go back to Florida where you belong, and I can start packing, if it comes to that!"

The combination of his words and his narrowed eyes made Sara reach behind her for the doorknob.

He wasn't finished. "And for the time this job takes, stay out of my room, Sara, and stay out—"

"Nick! Come down here!"

It was Brody's voice, and for once Sara was glad to hear it. Nick walked around her and flung open the door. "What is it, Brody?"

"It's your father. He's on the phone."

Nick rushed out the door to the stairs without looking back. As she made her escape to her room, Sara saw Nick at the bottom of the stairs reaching for the receiver.

His voice carried up to her. "Dad? What's wrong? Oh, God, I'd forgotten all about it—"

SARA DIDN'T SEE Nick for the rest of that day. When Brody's ceiling fans and conduit arrived, Nick didn't appear to help unload. When Winkie came with groceries and a FedEx package from Candy, Nick was nowhere to be seen. But the captain handed a long, narrow parcel wrapped in plain brown paper with Nick's name on it to Ryan.

Later that afternoon, Sara heard Nick return from wherever he'd been hiding. Ryan met him at the door and gave him the package. Nick's reaction was abrupt and detached. "Just put it on the counter." Then he closeted himself in his room.

When Sara went downstairs later, she passed the mysterious parcel still lying there unopened. She saw Nick's name on the address label, listing the Happy Angler, in care of Otto Winkleman, Put-in-Bay, Ohio, as his address.

But it was the return address that caught Sara's attention. The package had been sent from Johannesburg, South Africa. It bore the stamp of a British insurance company, indicating that the sender valued whatever was enclosed.

Having learned her lesson, Sara walked by the counter without further investigation. "It's none of your business," she told herself, and went to fix a light meal she didn't feel like eating.

She took her plate to the back stoop and ate in the gathering dusk. A few minutes later Ryan came toward her from the vineyard. He smiled when he saw her sitting there.

"How are our grapes tonight?" she asked.

"Doing fine," he said, propping his foot beside her on the first step. "I think the fertilizer is really working."

Though she was curious about Nick's package, Sara held her tongue. Finally Ryan brought up the subject. "I guess I'll go see if Nick ever took that box up to his room. I'm pretty sure what's in it, and even though he can trust everyone on the island, he shouldn't leave it in the lobby."

A fresh jolt of guilt made a bite of sandwich stick in Sara's throat. "I'm not so sure he can trust everyone," she said.

Ryan gave her a puzzled look. Obviously Nick hadn't told the others what she'd done. "It's a present from his mother," Ryan volunteered.

"A present?"

Ryan nodded. "Yeah. Today's Nick's birthday."

Sara remembered the phone call earlier from Nick's father. And now this from his mother. So the man who chose to be a loner wasn't truly alone in the world. There were people who cared about him.

"His birthday?" she said. "I guess you guys don't do much celebrating on these occasions."

"Nah," Ryan answered. "Here on Thorne, one day's pretty much the same as the next."

His statement revealed no bitterness, yet she sensed an underlying despondency. "Good night, Ryan," she said.

He stepped around her and entered the inn. "Night, Sara."

SARA SEARCHED the kitchen cabinets for ingredients she could use. She had no flour or sugar, which made her task nearly impossible. In desperation she took a tub of low-fat chocolate pudding from the refrigerator. It was the one treat she'd ordered for herself from the grocery in Put-in-Bay.

And since it was imperative to have vanilla wafers with pudding, she also had a box of those. She found a small metal pie plate in a cupboard of old utensils and scrubbed it till its surface gleamed. Then she lined the inside of the plate with the wafers and filled the middle with pudding. In the center she stuck an inch-thick utility candle.

It wasn't a very elegant birthday cake, but she hoped it would at least begin to cement the rift between her and Nick. She remembered seeing a sewing box in the parlor and went to retrieve it. Rummaging through scraps and notions, she found a bit of colorful ribbon. She tied it around the handle of a spoon, picked up her "gift," and crept up the stairs. Nick's door was closed, but light seeped from the crack at its base.

Sara placed the pan and spoon on the floor and lit the candle. Then, like a little kid on Halloween, she rapped on Nick's door and scurried down the hall to the next room. She waited inside until she heard his door open then close a moment later.

Her heart racing, Sara peeked into the hallway. With her luck, the candle had fallen over and she'd be responsible for burning the inn to the ground! Or even worse, her pudding cake would still be sitting where she'd left it, only now it would have a gigantic footprint smack in the middle of it.

Fortunately neither of those things happened. The pudding was gone. With a grin, Sara returned to her room. Mission accomplished, she thought, as she closed her door.

CHAPTER FOURTEEN

WHEN HE FIRST AWOKE Tuesday morning, Nick's immediate thoughts were of Sara. His lips curled into a smile, and an indefinable warmth spread to his extremities. Then he forced such reactions from his traitorous body with a sound punch to his pillow.

He wanted to stay mad at Sara. He certainly had a right to. She had totally violated his privacy. He wasn't ready to think about publishing his novels and joining the mainstream again. For now it was enough simply to write. Why hadn't she just left him alone?

After the phone call from his father, Nick had gone back to his room, which looked like an explosion in a paper mill. He'd stacked his manuscript pages into a pile and returned them to the box where they belonged. Order. That was what he needed.

He'd worked hard to establish order in his life. Once he'd mastered the task of walking again with Dexter's help, he'd looked forward to days of plain routine. He didn't need or want complications in his life. He didn't want to remember what Nick Romano had been like before that nice guy Ben Crawford of Brewster Falls called him on the telephone with a story about an old lady who'd been swindled by a big corporation, a story that had been manna to the old Nick, the investigative reporter.

And now his carefully regulated days were being

turned inside out by another Crawford. In less than three weeks, Sara had planted herself on his island, painted and patched up what he'd always considered his nearly perfect life and put her sexy little torch to his long-buried emotions. And if that wasn't bad enough, yesterday she'd pushed her way into his mind and soul. She'd discovered Ivan Banning, the man Nick would never be again.

After the confrontation, he'd gone to the other side of the island, where the waves were hushed and calm. He'd thought about what Sara had done and he'd decided *not* to forgive her.

And then, like a kindergarten kid, she'd rung his doorbell and scurried away, leaving a pudding-and-vanilla-wafer birthday cake on his doorstep. So this morning he faced a whole new battle as he tried without success to tamp his delight at her sweet prank. He'd had to rethink the whole forgiveness idea, and this time, Sara had won. Nick Bass would show mercy.

Her door was still closed when he went downstairs to power up the generator and make coffee. By the time he finished his first cup, he heard the boys come in the front door and head up the stairs. A few minutes later he followed them to one of the guest rooms and discovered Dexter and Brody in a heated argument.

"You can't drill holes now," Dexter declared. "You're going to ruin my paint job."

Brody snorted. "You and your prissy paint! What's more important? You brushing over a few minor holes, or this inn being properly wired?"

"You're doing this job ass-backward," Dexter retorted. "You should have rewired before I painted."

"I didn't know I wanted to then! Besides, who says running a little conduit across the ceiling and replacing a few wires behind the wall is going to ruin the paint? All I need to do is drill so I can get to the old wires."

Dexter waved his brush in Brody's face. "You do that and you can darn well replaster and repaint!"

Brody leaned forward until his nose was inches from Dexter's chest. "Look, you big dummy, I'm bringing this wiring up to code again. I don't care what you say!"

Nick stood in the doorway and marveled at his friends. *Who could have imagined this? A few days ago neither one of these two buzzards wanted to have anything to do with fixing up Sara's house, and now they're hollering at each other over whose contribution is more important.*

He walked into the middle of the fray. Putting a hand on each man's shoulder, he said, "Come on, fellas. Can't we all get along here?"

They both stared at him as if trying to decide who'd take the first swing at his smug face.

"I've got the perfect solution," Nick said, knowing full well his grin had to be irritating the blazes out of them. But this was too good to pass up. "Dex, you help Brody run the conduit to his ceiling fans and pull out the old wiring. And Brody, you help Dex patch up the little damage you're likely to do to his walls."

Brody swatted Nick's hand from his shoulder. "That's just great, Nick. You mind telling us what the hell you'll be doing while we're up here learning to play fair?"

"That's a good question," Dexter said. "Other

than fixing a few shingles and driving that little car all over the place, what *have* you done around here?"

"I've done lots of things," Nick said. "You forget, it was me who came up with this idea."

When that declaration brought scathing looks from the other two men, Nick went on full alert, ready to duck if either one threw a punch. When none came, he added, "Then I supervised and procured, and now I'm mediating. These are tough jobs."

Brody waved a screwdriver around like a dagger. "You've done pitifully little, Nick, and you know it." He jabbed the tool into his carpenter's belt with swashbuckling flair. "Maybe that's a blessing in disguise. You'd have probably messed up anything you'd taken a hand to. Why don't you leave us alone and go find Ryan? Maybe you can help him mess up his job."

Nick gave a mock salute. "I'll just do that." He headed for the door but stopped on the threshold and looked around the room. "I've got to tell you guys. You've done a terrific job. This place is looking good."

A smile started to spread across Dexter's face, but was wiped out when Brody snapped, "Go on, Nick, get the hell out."

"Yeah, go on," Dexter added. "Brody's right. We don't need you here."

Nick chuckled to himself as he went down the stairs. Maybe this day had possibilities, after all.

He found Ryan perched on a ladder by the front porch. With painstaking precision, he was applying dove-gray paint to the fascia board he'd replaced. He looked down when Nick came onto the porch. "How ya doing?" he asked.

"Okay. Brody and Dex have things pretty well under control upstairs, so they sent me down to help you."

"Thanks anyway, but we've only got one ladder. Winkie's bringing the house paint later today, and then you can help."

"You got it," Nick replied, then headed around the side of the inn thinking he'd find a nice shady spot where he could while away a couple of hours pondering what to say to Sara. He had to make her understand that he wasn't letting her off the hook completely.

He wandered through the thicket of brush and ended up at the press house. He was surprised to find the oak door unlocked. Either it had been open since the evening he and Sara had gone inside, or else she'd come back to admire the musty old equipment again. It was something she would do. As he looked around at all the things that had delighted Sara that night, an idea hit him.

He went back to the inn and found Ryan a few feet farther along the eaves than he'd been before. Nick pointed to a pile of discarded lumber on the ground. "Will you be needing any of this?" he asked.

"Nope. I'm finished replacing the wood. Help yourself."

Nick scooped up an armload of lumber and headed back to the press house. He knew what he'd do for Sara.

THREE HOURS LATER Nick stepped into the sunshine of a perfect Ohio spring day and peered over the rolling slopes of the vineyard. He spotted the top of Sara's head above a shallow dip in the ground and headed straight for her. Though his mission was uppermost in his mind, he couldn't help noticing the changes in the vineyard. The grape leaves were broader and greener. Nestled in the foliage, the clusters of fruit, few as they were, appeared larger and rounder. He supposed Sara had a right to feel proud of herself.

She was so intent on shoveling a hole around the base of one of her vines that she didn't hear him approach. And she was a lousy digger. Each time she stuck the blade of the shovel into the earth and stepped on it, she managed to come up with only a pitiful sprinkling of earth and rock.

Nick stopped several feet away from her and waited for her to notice him. When she didn't, he finally said, "What are you doing?"

She screamed and spun around toward him, dropping the shovel. "For heaven's sake, Bass, do you get a kick out of scaring me to death?"

"Not really. I'm sorry."

"Besides," she said, "you don't care what I'm doing."

"Yes, I do."

"I'm digging a hole," she said. "I would think that as a Digging Day participant, you would have known that." She picked up the shovel and leaned on it. "If you're hoping this is going to be my grave, sorry. It's not deep enough."

He scratched his cheek thoughtfully and looked at the pathetic dip in the ground she'd produced. "I don't know. There's not much to you."

"Well, too bad. Now go. I've got too much to do this morning to stand here talking to you." She jabbed at the hole with the shovel. "I'm aerating. This vine needs major drainage help."

He took the shovel from her and scooped up a large layer of dirt. "I'm just glad you aren't digging a grave for me," he said.

"I'll leave that to the next hapless person who dares to suggest you might have talent at something!"

Here she goes again, missing the point about what happened yesterday. He stabbed the blade into the earth hard enough to hear the rend of a root inches below the surface. Now he was in trouble. She snatched the shovel back and glared at him.

He crossed his arms over his chest and glared back. "You know darn well I wasn't mad about what you *said.* In fact, underneath it all, I was kind of flattered."

"Then remind me to run for the hills if I ever offer criticism."

This wasn't going quite as he'd hoped. The words he'd wanted to avoid were popping out of his mouth, anyway. "It was what you *did,* Sara. If you hadn't gone into my room—"

She shook her head in frustration. "Haven't we covered this territory, Bass? I apologized. If you want more than that, I'll send you a postcard when I'm burning in hell."

A smile cracked his composure. "Not necessary. And thanks for the birthday thing."

She picked a strand of silky hair from where it had gotten stuck to her bottom lip and almost smiled back. Her face softened by degrees, while his body temperature spiked. "Consider it a mushy apology—my last one, you understand."

He took the shovel again and leaned it against a

post. Then he offered his hand. "Come with me. I want to show you something."

She made a fist and put it behind her back. "Will it hurt me?"

"Nope. Promise."

"Okay." She motioned for him to lead the way.

Certain she'd just taken a giant leap toward insanity, Sara let Nick guide her to the press house. She'd been back to the old structure several times since going in with Nick, and each time she visited, the comforting atmosphere reminded her why she was working so hard to revitalize the vineyard.

She stepped onto the ancient wood floor and drew a deep breath. Then she whirled around to face Nick. "Okay, we're here," she said.

He retrieved a lantern from a hook on the wall and indicated she should follow him. "Come on."

She walked behind him to the steps leading to the fermenting room, the ones she'd nearly tumbled down. Nick held the lantern over the stairwell so she had a clear view. "Well, what do you think?" he asked.

She bent down and peered into the cellar. What she noticed first was the contrast of wood on the steps. New, light-colored pieces of lumber were interspersed with the old, dark ones. The effect was a checkerboard of natural and aged finishes descending into the near-darkness below.

She straightened and looked at him. "You fixed the stairs."

"Yep." He beamed with pride. "You were so set on going down there that I figured you'd eventually do something stupid. I decided to ward off a calamity by mending the steps and keeping you from breaking your neck.''

She couldn't hold back a smirk. ''Your flattery is exceeded only by your gallantry, Bass.'' Not wanting him to see how touched she was, she added, ''You really think I'd risk my neck to see what you called a worthless bunch of old bottles and kegs?'' she asked.

''Sara, the truth is, I think you'd risk your neck precisely *because* I said that. I think you'd do anything to prove to me that all the old junk down there is a treasure trove.''

He was probably right. She held fast to a stone jutting from the wall and tested the first step, gingerly. When both feet were firmly planted, she glanced back at Nick, who stood behind her with the lantern. ''Are you absolutely certain these stairs are safe?''

''I fixed them, didn't I?''

''That's not an answer. Are you absolutely certain they're safe?''

He sighed with exasperation, grabbed her arm and hauled her back to the top. With the lantern swinging from his hand, he stomped down the steps as fast as his limp would allow. In a few seconds he was at the bottom smiling up at her. ''Satisfied?''

''I think I've got the hang of it,'' she responded. ''You have to go down so fast that the rotten wood doesn't have a chance to crack.''

He held his hand up to her. ''Just trust me, Sara.''

She descended into a small, rectangular room with walls of cream-colored limestone. It was at least twenty degrees cooler down in the cellar. Sara shivered. ''Is it always like this, do you suppose?'' she asked.

"I guess so. Must be the limestone," Nick said. "And the lack of natural light. But you're the wine maker. Isn't it meant to be cold?"

"For white wines especially," she said. "This should be perfect for a good chardonnay."

He stepped into the center of the room and hung the lantern from a hook in the ceiling. Light spread out around them, illuminating numerous barrels perched on wood block frames. They were of several sizes, up to probably fifty gallons, made of sturdy oak and stamped with names of French barrel makers. Their dark brown color showed striations of deeper hues, evidence of natural aging. Sara wandered among the barrels, touching the smooth, worn slats held together with iron staves.

The walls of the basement were lined with racks of bottles and corks and syphoning tubes. Some of the corks crumbled to dust when Sara held them in her hand.

When she'd made a cursory inspection of the room, Sara returned to Nick. He stood next to the lantern, his arms folded, his gaze intent on her face.

"This is where it happened, Nick," she said. "This is where the Krauses made wine for more than a hundred years."

He screwed his face into a grimace. "In the same barrels?"

She laughed. "Probably. I don't doubt that the wine in Aunt Millie's cellar came from these very barrels. As long as you refill a barrel right after it's emptied, dangerous microorganisms don't have a chance to grow."

"And if you don't refill?"

She wrinkled her nose. "Then the barrels can get pretty nasty."

"So, ah…Crawford…" He rubbed his chin while scrutinizing the kegs. "When those little pellets of yours hanging outside are full grown, you're not considering putting their juice in these things, are you?"

She went to one of the smaller barrels and pulled out the wooden bung. When she smelled the interior, she jerked her head back. "Whew! I can't use these barrels. I'll have to order new ones when the time comes to harvest."

"That's a relief."

She stepped back and regarded the barrels with the eye of an artist. "They would make charming planters for the front of the inn, though."

"You refuse to give up on anything, don't you, Crawford," Nick said. "I'll bet you always look for a new use for something that's old and tired."

She almost laughed out loud. "Funny you should say that, Bass, since that theory didn't work on you at all."

He scratched the back of his neck and conceded her point. "Chalk one up for the bean counter."

Suddenly her teeth began to chatter. "One freezing bean counter, you mean. Let's go back upstairs."

He caught her arm as she walked by. "I can think of a couple of benefits to this cold temperature, Sara."

She arched her eyebrows. "Oh, really? Name one."

He pulled her to him and enclosed her in his arms. "You'll like this one. It's probably described in one of those homemaker magazines you've got in the bathroom. I call it natural heating. I believe they relied on it in the old days."

Against her better judgment, she let him hold her. Surely she could allow herself to bask in his warmth and yet not fall victim to his questionable charms. Confident, she snuggled in closer. "The difference is, Bass," she said, "the people you're talking about must have actually *liked* each other."

He reacted with a slight flinch, and then tightened his hold. "What do you mean? I like you."

She smiled against his faded shirtfront, her lips against the little green alligator symbol.

He ran the palm of his hand down her hair. "And I figure that deep down you like me. You wouldn't be trying so hard to change me if you didn't."

"I'm giving up on that quest, Bass. I've got a hard head, but you finally pounded some sense into it."

He leaned back and placed a hand on each side of her face. Then he grinned with boyish mischief. "What? This little head? I wouldn't think of pounding on this beautiful noggin. My mind's too full of other, more interesting uses for this tangle of gold hair." He combed through the strands with his fingers and returned his hand to her face.

"And this adorable nose." He pressed his lips on the tip and moved to her earlobe. "And these ears..." He nipped playfully. His tongue twirled the small emerald stud of her earring. His breath was warm on her skin.

She made a weak attempt to pull away. "Don't do this, Bass."

His thumb roamed over her lips. "And these," he said. "They were made for kissing." He smiled at her. "They do talk a lot, but they were made for kissing, and lately I find myself lying awake at night just thinking about them."

His mouth touched hers, gently, sweetly. He nibbled on her lower lip, traced the outline of her mouth with his tongue and covered the territory from corner to corner with teasing hints of what his lips were capable of doing. She rose on her toes to meet his subtle yet sexy demands, and the game became all too real.

When his mouth devoured hers, she answered with a passion as great as his own. She melted into the circle of his arms and opened her mouth to draw his tongue inside. He explored with hunger and greed. His breath came in harsh, ragged pants. Hers came out on a low, throaty groan.

His lips moved to her neck, leaving a trail of moist warmth to her collarbone. She arched her head back, an invitation for him to move to her chest. He pressed urgent kisses everywhere her skin was exposed. He parted the lapels of her blouse and his mouth sought the crest of one breast.

"Bass, why do we do this?" she rasped on a soft rush of air.

"I don't know, sweetheart," he mumbled against her skin. "Probably because it feels so good."

His hands dropped to her waist, and he lifted her off her feet. Her back came in contact with one of the barrels, and he pressed her against it. She felt his erection straining against his shorts.

Swiftly he unbuttoned her shirt. His hand slid over her skin to cup her breast over her bra. Her nipple hardened instantly. His mouth fed on hers again, sucking, teasing, tantalizing until her bones felt as though they were melting.

Nimble fingers found the front closure of her bra. It snapped free, and he worked a thumb and forefinger over her nipple, bringing it to an aching peak. God, she wanted this man. She shouldn't, but every nerve in her body cried out for the pleasures only he seemed able to provide.

He cupped one breast from below and rubbed his thumb over the puckered tip, gently, teasingly while he returned his mouth to her swollen lips. When he'd kissed her to a state of near-oblivion, his mouth moved to her ear again. "Sara," he croaked, "we can't go on like this. If I don't make love to you soon, I'll go crazy. But not here."

She answered back on a throaty breath. "When? How?"

"Tonight. We're going out."

He kept a hand lightly on her arm and slowly backed away, letting her find her equilibrium again. "We're going out?" she said. "You mean a date? You're going to leave Thorne Island?"

"Well, no. We're not leaving. We'll have the date here."

With trembling fingers, she fastened her bra and the buttons of her blouse. "Here? Dinner and a movie on the island?"

"There are all kinds of dates, Sara."

"Okay." She would have agreed to practically anything.

"Good. I'll work it out. I'll pick you up at your room at seven." He reached for the lantern to lead their way back upstairs. Before going up, he leaned over and kissed her with a hunger that promised much more. He smiled at her when he drew away. "Is it okay if we use your car, though?"

CHAPTER FIFTEEN

WINKIE ARRIVED in the early afternoon with cans of white paint for Ryan and a thick Bosch-and-Lindstrom envelope of work for Sara. By two o'clock she was in her room staring at numbers and columns on her laptop. It was almost impossible to maintain the level of concentration necessary to keep earning the salary she needed to cover the small fortune she was spending on her inheritance.

If the sounds of progress at the Cozy Cove weren't enough to distract her, there was the fact that she had accepted a *date* with Nick for tonight. She wanted to convince herself that she had no idea why on earth she'd accepted his invitation. But she knew precisely why she'd said yes. She could no longer deny the powerful chemistry between her and Bass. She certainly didn't understand the attraction. In fact, it scared the hell out of her.

Sara chewed the end of her pencil and allowed her thoughts to wander back a couple of hours to those moments alone with Nick in the press house. If they'd stayed there any longer, they'd have ended up on the floor of the fermenting room. And now all she could think about was the chance to complete what they'd started.

"Get a grip, Crawford," she said. "Even if you have one night of unforgettable passion, what will it mean to your future? You can't afford to indulge your fantasy of living on the island forever. You have to make a living. It will be a long time before the inn shows enough profit to pay back even a portion of what you've spent so far."

And Nick Bass had no plans to leave the island. He'd practically cringed when she mentioned their date might mean a trip off Thorne. So where did that leave them? With entirely opposite goals, conflicting personalities and homes at opposite ends of a very large country.

"It's for the best, Sara," she said. "You wouldn't be happy with Bass. You snipe at each other constantly. Just think how it would be if you lived side by side on these skimpy forty acres for a lifetime." She sighed. *Yes, just think...*

Her cell phone rang, scattering her thoughts, and she pressed the green connect button. "Hello."

"Hi, Sara. It's me."

A voice from the real world. "Hi, Candy."

"I've got some things to tell you."

"Okay. Go ahead."

Sara made notes as Candy listed items of immediate concern at the firm. Yes, she would have Mickelson's Tool and Die accounts ready on Thursday. Yes, she'd test a new software program designed for Warren Klingman's chain of dry-cleaning establishments. Yes, yes, she'd do everything.

"Oh, and Sara, there's one more thing." An ominous tone had crept into Candy's normally chirpy voice.

"Yes?"

"Mr. Bosch asked me this morning when you were coming back. He said your one-week vacation was turning into a marathon. I think he really wants an answer.''

Of course he did. And he had a right to one. Sara gave Candy a date that left one week to complete all the projects on the island. She had to supervise the remaining renovations, place an ad in the Sandusky paper for a manager to run the inn in her absence, design a brochure to leave with Ohio travel agencies and order new linens for the guest rooms. She also had to find time to go over the details of the wine harvest with Ryan so he'd know how to proceed. How was she going to get everything done without help?

"Sara? Sara, are you there?"

Candy's persistent voice brought Sara back to the present and gave her an idea. She fumbled in her purse and pulled out her credit card. "Yes, Candy, I'm here. Remember when you said you might like to come to Cleveland?"

"Yeah."

"Write down my credit-card number and call my travel agent. Book yourself a round-trip ticket to Cleveland from Friday afternoon to Monday night. I'll call you later with directions to the island."

Sara jerked her ear away from the phone at Candy's squeal. "You mean I'm coming there?"

"Yes. I can really use your help. And I'll want you to make one stop on your way here."

"No problem. This is so exciting."

"Okay. See you Friday. Bye."

Sara leaned back in her chair and smiled. With her date still ahead of her, she couldn't begin to relax, but at least her work schedule had been addressed.

THE MINUTES on Sara's travel alarm ticked slowly toward seven o'clock. She'd showered, applied a minimal amount of makeup and brushed her hair into semiobedient waves. Deciding what to wear was more difficult. What does one wear on a date that has no apparent destination? She finally stepped into her best pair of sandals and slipped a gauzy flowered skirt over her hips. A white elastic top matched the splashes of gardenias in the print, and a short-sleeved green overblouse picked up the color of the leaves. It was the best she could do.

She stood in front of her mirror and filled her lungs with the fresh air coming through her window. It promised to be a beautiful evening, but even so, a severe case of nerves fluttered like a hundred moths in the pit of her stomach.

At twenty-nine Sara was no naive schoolgirl suffering through her first crush. She knew exactly where tonight's date would lead, and instead of feeling any reservation, she was filled with a heady anticipation that made her body warm instantly. In a few hours she would be locked in the most passionate way with Nick Bass—sexy, handsome, challenging Nick Bass. When Sara left Thorne Island next week, she would take more than blisters on her fingers and a depleted checking account. A lot more. She would take the memory of Nick and tonight.

"Sara, you ready?"

His voice rumbled low and mellow through her door, and she felt its power in every nerve ending. She opened the door to face the man who would make tonight magical. He wore navy chinos and a white knit shirt with navy pinstripes—the first shirt she'd seen on him that didn't look as though it had been worn three times a week for the past six years. And in his hand was a small bouquet of wildflowers. Sara was overwhelmed, and the date had hardly begun.

NICK RESISTED the temptation to toss the pitiful collection of flowers over the second-story railing and hope Sara hadn't seen them. Nick Romano wasn't a flower picker. The scraggly bunch of blossoms he'd gathered an hour before paled next to Sara. But it was too late. From the smile on her face when she reached for them, you'd have thought he'd brought her orchids.

"These are lovely," she said, placing the flowers in a glass of water on her nightstand.

Nick started at Sara's hair and let his eyes roam slowly down her slim body to the delicate white sandals and pink toenails. It was hard to remember they were going *out*. He clenched his hands into fists to keep from grabbing her right there and then. How did she manage to create the illusion of wide-eyed innocence in the body of a fully grown, tempting woman?

His tongue felt thick. "You look sensational," he finally said.

"Thanks. You do, too."

He glanced down at his shirt. "My dad sent me this for my birthday. It's not really my taste, but maybe after I wear it a couple of hundred times, I'll have it broken into the Bass lifestyle."

"What a bright future that shirt has to look forward to," she said. "By the way, if I'm not being too nosy…"

"You? Nosy?"

She gave him a smirk. "Can I ask what your mother sent you? Ryan told me the long package was from her."

"You can ask, but I haven't opened it yet."

"How can you not open a present?"

"Easy. *I'm* not nosy." He pretended to duck. "But since you are, I'll let you open it later."

"Bass, you're impossible." She rummaged through her purse until she found her car keys. "Do we really need these?"

He smiled. "Considering I've lived here six years without them, probably not." He took them from her, anyway. "But a guy needs his fantasies."

"Then we are driving somewhere?"

"Yes, we are."

She walked by him, a faint scent of flowers lingering in her wake. It smelled like something from his childhood. Hyacinths? Violets? Hell, he didn't know, but if he ever smelled it again, he'd recognize it as his favorite flower.

Once in the car, he navigated the narrow gravel pathway that curved around to the other side of the island. He cut the engine when the path ended at the wide stretch of beach where he'd retreated to the day before. It was his favorite spot on the island. Knee-high waving grass, stately paper birches and a few renegade pines protected this area from rough weather. He walked around to help Sara out of the car and removed a wicker basket he'd left in the back seat.

"It's nice here," she said, walking away from him to the shore. The wind lifted her hair from her shoulders, revealing her slender white neck. Her skirt billowed out from her legs, and Nick caught a glimpse of smooth, suntanned calves. He'd seen her legs lots of times, of course, but never seductively peeking out from a confection of wind-rippled silk.

He swallowed hard. "I like it. It's restful." As if he felt like resting!

She walked back and watched him spread a plaid blanket on the ground. "What's in the basket?" she asked.

"A little date-christening gift from your Aunt Millie," he said, removing a bottle of wine.

"Ah. White Thorne chardonnay."

He took two crystal goblets and a corkscrew from the basket. When he'd opened the bottle, he filled Sara's glass and handed it to her. Then he filled his own.

"What should we toast?" she asked.

He thought for a moment, then raised his glass. "How about continuing my fantasy?" he said. "To a nearly deserted island and the two people who were lucky enough to find it."

She clinked her glass softly against his. "Funny. I was just thinking of that as *my* fantasy."

He leaned over and brushed his lips over hers. "I suppose it's okay if we share it." He took more things from the basket. "I've got crackers and a cheese spread, I guess. I'm not sure."

"Aha. I thought I heard Winkie's boat before we left."

"Yeah, and pretty soon I'll have him delivering pizzas."

She laughed and started to sit down, but he stopped her. "Wait, I haven't shown you our biggest tourist attraction."

"You mean besides Brody's hat?"

"Yeah, but this one's not as revered."

He took her to a slight dip in the land, a sandy spot surrounded by reeds and cattails. There, embedded in the ground was a bronze plaque with printing on it. Unfortunately time, wind and water had eroded many of the words.

She bent down to read it. He'd known she would. She loved old stuff. "What is it?" she asked. "I can make out the words *Commodore Oliver Perry*."

"Right. Have you seen the tall monument to him? The one on South Bass Island?"

"Sure. You can't miss it."

"Well, here is his other monument, slightly less impressive. It's dedicated to Perry's role in the 1812 Battle of Lake Erie. He had a lookout here where his men watched for the British advancing from the eastern half of the lake and southern Canada."

She rubbed her fingers over the lettering. "I can see it now. The date and part of the message." She looked up at Nick and gave him a sly grin. "What I can't understand is why this plaque is still here."

"What do you mean?"

"I would have thought you guys would have dug this up on Digging Day."

He chuckled. "We did. A couple of times. We've turned this old thing upside down and sideways. The fortune's not buried here."

He took her elbow, helping her to stand. "So about that fortune, Bass," she said, "do you think there's a chance it really exists?"

He hid a little smile behind his hand as he led her to the blanket. "Wouldn't it be something if it did?"

He knew she had a hundred questions, but he tipped her glass toward her mouth. "Drink up, sweetheart. Dinner should be ready back at the Cozy Cove in about a half hour."

THEY ARRIVED at the inn just after dark. Nick parked the Volkswagen and followed Sara inside. She noted that the pocket doors separating the lobby from the dining room were shut tight. She hadn't noticed that when they'd left.

Nick bolted around her and ripped down a sign that had been taped to one of the doors. "Guess we don't need this any longer."

The words *Sara Keep Out* made her smile.

"Well, we're here, so we might as well eat." Nick slid back the door and Sara stepped into the dining room, only it didn't look like the same room where she'd served fried chicken. Tacked along the walls were strings of old-fashioned Christmas bulbs.

Sara clasped her hands over her mouth to hold in a gasp of pure delight. "Where on earth did you find those?" She next saw wire reindeer, each one outlined in flickering white lights. "And those?" Two-tiered topiaries lit with the same lights stood in each corner of the room. "And those?"

Nick rocked back on his heels and grinned. "So you like the decor? Actually it appears that Mrs. Kraus was a fanatic about Christmas. I found all this stuff in the attic a while back. I never figured I'd have a use for it."

Sara walked slowly around the room, stopping, touching. "It's wonderful. Like a fairyland. How did you know I love Christmas lights?"

He answered with a meaningful grin that made a verbal response unnecessary.

"That obvious, huh?"

Now she admired the dining-room table. "And the dishes. They're beautiful." Both place settings consisted of five pieces of bone china. Each piece was different from the others, but each one displayed painstakingly hand-painted floral decorations. "Mrs. Kraus, also?"

"She must have been a collector."

Sara waited until Nick came up behind her and pulled out her chair. As she sat down, she said, "You know something, Nick? This is going to have to be one terrific meal to measure up to the ambiance."

"No problem." He uncorked another bottle of wine that had been left chilling in a silver ice bucket and filled both their glasses. "I intend to show you that I have talents you've never even dreamed of."

A flush of heat crept into Sara's face. *You're wrong there, Bass. I've dreamed of them many times.* "I'm already impressed, Nick. I would be even if tonight's meal was hot dogs and beans."

"Then hang on to your socks. Because I'm about to knock them off."

He disappeared into the kitchen and returned ten minutes later with a golden-brown ham covered in pineapple glaze, and a bowl of roasted potatoes. Second and third trips produced a medley of fresh-steamed vegetables, hot cinnamon apples, Caesar salad and warm rolls.

When all the dishes were in place, he sat down. "Dig in. Doesn't stay hot forever."

Sara was dumbfounded. Nick Bass, salami eater, had suddenly become Wolfgang Puck. She narrowed her eyes at him. "How did you do all this?"

He passed her the potatoes. "Prepared ahead, that's all."

"You made all this food and kept it warm in the oven all this time?" She took a big helping of vegetables.

"Sure. It was easy." He shook his fork at her as he made his point. "I keep telling you and Dex and Brody I'm a planner. It's what I do."

She allowed a hint of a smile to convey her suspicions. "I'm going to buy that explanation, Bass, though I know I shouldn't. I'm not wasting another minute wondering how you conjured up this amazing meal."

He reached over and covered her hand with his. His teasing eyes caught the reflection of dancing flames from candles in an old silver candelabra. His smile was warm and overwhelmingly sexy. "Sara, if you like this, just wait. I plan on conjuring up one hell of a dessert."

Oh, God, she didn't doubt it. In fact, she could already taste it.

WHEN THEY WERE FINISHED eating, Sara offered to carry the dishes into the kitchen.

"Okay," Nick said. "And while you're doing that, I'll see if I can get a fire going in the parlor." He watched her stack the plates. "But no washing. I'll do it in the morning."

"Deal." She blew out the candles and took the dishes to the sink. As she ran hot water over them, she let her mind wander. It had been a perfect evening. Nick had truly given her a date to remember. Sight-seeing, fine dining in a dazzling setting, a charming companion—what more could a girl ask for? A future maybe? Sara knew that wasn't in the stars for her and Nick. But tonight, for this one enchanted night, she wouldn't think about that. She wouldn't think about the differences between her and

Nick, either. For tonight she would just live a memory she'd never forget.

A rustling in the backyard drew Sara to the screen door. The night was cool, the breeze refreshing. A fire would be nice, she decided as she scanned the outside for the source of the noise.

Squinting into the darkness, she saw a large red-and-white paper sack a few yards from the back porch. An animal was rummaging through it.

Thinking it a raccoon or possum, Sara whispered loudly, "Scat! Go away."

Her command was answered by a loud meow. A gray cat backed out of the sack, freeing the thing to roll in the wind until it hit the porch steps and stopped. That was when Sara saw the words on the side. A grin spread across her face. "I knew there had to be a logical explanation. So that's what you meant by planning, Bass. Delivery from the Boston Market."

A tremor of delight rippled through her. The man was sinfully clever, devilishly dishonest. She absolutely couldn't be falling in love with him, could she?

Sara walked away from the screen door. She wouldn't tell him she'd discovered his secret.

"Sara, you coming?" he hollered from the parlor.

"On my way," she called back. "By the way, how long have we had a cat?"

His voice grew louder as she approached the parlor. "Oh, so you've finally seen End Run. He belongs to Dexter. Stowed away in Winkie's boat one time. Dex wouldn't let Winkie take the cat off the island. He thought Winkie'd make a cement collar for him and toss him in the lake."

She entered the parlor and watched as Nick poked

a flaming newspaper roll under the logs. He looked up at her as she came close. "Dex is something, isn't he? Steel on the outside, but cotton on the inside. Some men are funny that way. You just can't tell about them."

"Yes," she said, smiling down at him. "Some men are full of surprises."

CHAPTER SIXTEEN

NICK DROPPED the newspaper into the fire and sat back to watch the flames curl around the glowing stack of logs. "Now that's a fine blaze," he boasted as though he'd just invented fire, instead of coaxing it to life in the Cozy Cove hearth.

Sara sat beside him. "Do you use the fireplace often?"

He picked up the tongs and turned one of the logs so it would catch faster. "Maybe a couple dozen times in the six years I've been here."

She hugged her knees to her chest. "I love it. During the winters in Brewster Falls, Dad always lit the logs first thing when he came in from work. That's something I miss living in Florida."

Nick leaned back on his elbows and stretched his legs in front of him on the thick hearth rug. His shoulder touched Sara's. "Yeah, they're nice. Always seemed kind of silly, though, to light one when it was just me down here—me and all those sheets I kept over everything."

Sheets Sara had washed and put away in the linen cupboard. She gazed around the room at all the things she'd dusted and polished. A feeling of such contentment washed over her that she hesitated to speak for fear of breaking the spell cast by the crackling flames and the beauty of the old furnishings. She couldn't remember when she'd ever known such peace, or such anticipation. "It was a shame to hide all this grace and elegance under sheets," she said after several minutes had passed.

"Not if you wanted to keep it graceful and elegant, it wasn't."

Sara tipped her head until her cheek rested against Nick's shoulder. "Speaking of elegance…"

He turned his face toward her. "Yeah?"

"You did it, Nick."

"Did what?"

"You actually made a date happen on Thorne Island, even when both of us know just about every inch of it and thought we'd seen it all. I've cleaned off years of its dust, brought sunshine into its dreary rooms, buried my hands in tons of its soil…"

"And I've dug holes in all the places you missed."

She laughed softly. "That's right. And still you created something new and exciting. It was as fine a date as I've ever had, and I feel like going upstairs and pressing those flowers you brought me into a big, thick book so I'll always remember it."

He snickered. "I can guarantee you this, Sara. There aren't many women out there who've ever had flowers from Nick Bass to press in a book."

"Then I'm honored."

He slipped his arm around her, and Sara nestled deeper against him. "Are you tired?" he asked.

"A little. But mostly just content."

He reached to the wing chair beside them and pulled down a fringed, velvet pillow. Then he bent one leg and tucked his foot under his body. Laying the pillow on his bended knee, he coaxed Sara to lay her head on it. She sighed deeply.

"I don't want you *too* content," he said.

She wrapped her hand around his arm. "Too late. I feel like hot syrup and you're the pancake."

"I can live with that image."

And so could Sara. She knew what was going to happen. She wanted it almost desperately. But a slow burn could be more satisfying than a quick sizzle. "Nick, tell me about your parents," she said after a moment.

He tensed slightly. "What's to tell? Mom went her way and Dad went his."

"Nick...that *is* something to tell."

He paused, obviously considering whether to take her into his confidence. "Okay. Did you ever hear of the Westerling family?"

Like lights on a marquee, the famous name flashed in Sara's mind. She arched her neck to see into Nick's eyes. "The giants of the tire industry?"

"The very ones."

"They live on that huge estate in Akron. The one with gates so high you can't see over them."

He nodded. "My mother was Vivian Westerling. Raised in wealth, schooled in the arts and destined for social prominence."

"I'm impressed. And your father?"

"Carlo...the Italian gardener who trimmed their hedges."

"No kidding?" Sara was immediately intrigued. "They fell in love despite their social differences?"

"It was more like they fell in lust." He leaned over her and she could see his eyes twinkling in the firelight. "In case you haven't noticed, Italian males are hot-blooded, passionate people. Most women can't resist their charms."

"Yes, I've noticed," she answered.

"That's how it was for my mother. As I understand it, there were a few clandestine meetings in the greenhouse, followed by illicit rendezvous in my mother's lavender boudoir. And as fortune would have it, a determined little seed was planted in my mother's blue-blooded belly."

"I see."

"Yes, and so did Grandmama after the first trimester. A family meeting took place, during which a suitable mate for Mother was discussed, and appropriate financial rewards for the groom suggested."

Sara leaned up on one elbow. "You mean they were going to *buy* a husband for your mother?"

"They tried, but she wouldn't have it. She wanted her Carlo, so she married the gardener in a private ceremony in the drawing room. She had the baby, and all was well—for the year they stayed together."

"But if they were so in love, why did they break up?"

"Very simple. My mother found out she couldn't buy Gucci purses on a gardener's salary. And my father discovered that in all the fine lineage of the Westerling clan, not a female among them could make a good marinara sauce."

"That's so sad," Sara said.

Nick took her shoulders and guided her back to the pillow. "Not so sad really. My mother travels the world and enjoys her wealth and privilege. And my father lives in Euclid with the same lady friend he's had for twenty-five years. Her ravioli is out of this galaxy, by the way."

Sara thought of the phone call from Nick's father

and the package from his mother. "They both care about you." she said.

"Ah, yes, the stubborn, reclusive son is the burden they both must bear."

"Do you ever see them?"

"That is the burden *I* must bear. They come to visit—at different times of course—at least twice a year."

"Really?" For some reason the information both surprised and pleased Sara. "I'm glad."

He laughed softly, twirling a strand of her hair around his finger. "I figured you'd like that part. I told you once that you care too much."

"And I told you—"

"I know, I know. I also said you were trying to change me." He smoothed the hair from her brow, repeating the gesture several times until finally he said, "And it half scares me to think that perhaps you have."

She smiled. "Nick Bass, admitting to being scared?"

"Half-scared, Sara. I said half."

She stilled his hand by clasping it with hers. "Nick, a person cannot change anyone who does not wish to be changed."

His lips curved upward, but in the dim light, she couldn't tell what the smile meant. Was it contentment? Or a mask to hide his fear at the realization that she'd become important to him?

"Sara Crawford," he said softly, "when I'm alone and I think of you, and believe me, I *do* think of you, I don't know what I wish. But when I'm with you, like now, I know damn well what I want. Every inch of my body coils into one tight spring ready to pounce.''

She released his hand, and his palm came to rest on her cheek. ''Then for once, Nick, we want the same thing.''

He stroked her cheek with his thumb. ''You realize that we've been on a course to this point since the first day you arrived on the island. I know you tried to fight it, but I must admit, I didn't try very hard.'' He traced the bow of her lip with his index finger. ''Hell, Sara, I didn't try at all.''

She watched his lips form the words that confessed he'd wanted her from the beginning, just as she'd wanted him. They'd been playing a game for days. Cat and mouse. Attack and withdraw. And now the game was over.

''Nick?''

''Hmm?''

''Now who's talking too much?''

His gave her a heart-stopping grin. ''I guess that would be me.''

''Yes, it would.''

He stretched out beside her. His shadowy gaze wandered slowly over every inch of her face as if he could read her desire there. Sara wrapped her hand around his neck at the same time their mouths joined. There was no hesitation in that first hungry kiss. With his tongue he let her know what he wanted, and she gave it freely. The kiss lasted for an exquisite eternity as Nick's head moved over hers.

He outlined her jaw with his finger, following the journey with soft, teasing nips from his mouth. Her eyelids trembled when he kissed her there. He swept the hair away from her ears and continued his assault with his mouth. She sighed his name, and it seemed her own voice floated somewhere above and beyond their bodies.

"Sara, you taste wonderful." He breathed the words into her ear. When he leaned up on his elbow and looked at her, his eyes seemed veiled by a fine, damp mist. Surely what he saw in her eyes was the same impassioned glaze of a woman whose mind has gone numb to all but the most primeval urges of the body.

"I'm going to love every minute of loving you, Sara," he said. His fingers curled around the band of her elastic top. The heel of his palm pressed against the swell of her breast. Sara covered his hand with hers, brazenly coaxing him to pull the fabric down her chest. At that moment nothing seemed more vital to her existence than to have his hand on her bare flesh. He slipped the top to her waist and cupped her. Sara drew in a sharp breath.

She heard the soft rasp of a zipper before the waistband of her skirt fell against her hip. His mouth captured hers again for a brief, shattering kiss before his voice came low and intimate in her ear. "I don't know about you, Crawford, but I've about had it with all these clothes."

He worked the silky material down her legs. A flip of his wrist sent the garment fluttering beside the hearth. With equally eager hands, Sara pulled his shirt from the waistband of his trousers and slipped it over his head. She put her hands on his shoulders, massaging bunched muscles that flexed at her touch.

After quickly untying the knot at her waist and sending her blouse to join the skirt, he slid her panties down her legs and she kicked them free.

Her breath hitched in her lungs and her body tensed with expectation. When she lay naked to his gaze, he spread his hands on her hips and moved his fingers to find her most intimate part. That one tingling speck in the universe sent spirals of warmth through Sara's body. She raked her fingers over his back. His muscles rippled against her palm. Ribbons of pleasure coursed through her as he entered her, driving her upward until her body shuddered and she cried his name.

LATER, DESPITE LYING in the shelter of Nick's arm, Sara shivered in the breeze coming through an open window. He stopped the lazy pathway his thumb was making down her arm. "You're cold," he said.

"A little."

He reached for a quilted throw lying over the arm of the wing chair. He covered them, then slid his hand under it to trail his fingers softly over her breast. She nestled more closely against him. "Mmm, this is much better," she whispered.

Nick would have remained locked with Sara in front of a cozy fire forever. He liked feeling her steady heartbeat against his hand and listening to her soft murmurs of contentment. Unfortunately most of his body had other ideas. For several minutes his lower back had been sending signals of distress to his shoulders and neck. The calves of his legs reminded him that he'd only been walking without a cane for a few months.

He shifted to his side, felt another stabbing pain and couldn't stop a hiss of discomfort from whistling through his teeth. "Sorry, sweetheart," he said, rotating his shoulders. "Just gotta move a little."

Sara sat up, taking a corner of the blanket with her. "Oh, Nick, I'm sorry. I should have thought about your injury. Of course it isn't good for you to lie on a hard floor."

He grinned up at her, though it took some effort to do so. "I thought a soft body would make up for it."

She grabbed her skirt, stood up and slipped it on. He wished she hadn't. "I have an idea," he said. "Let's exchange this cold, hard floor for a nice, soft mattress."

She gathered the rest of her clothes in her arms. "Are you sure you're up to it?"

He grinned wickedly and lifted the blanket. "Do you need proof?"

"Okay, I believe you."

"Good. Then you go ahead of me, and I'll just grab a couple of sodas and meet you upstairs."

She ran up to her room and threw on an oversized shirt that covered her hips. She only fastened the three middle buttons in anticipation of Nick removing it. "Sara Crawford, what has come over you?" she asked the rosy-cheeked woman in her mirror.

Nick's door was partly open when she went down the hall. Still, she knocked.

"Come on in," he said.

He was sitting on the side of his bed popping the top on a can of diet soda. A pair of boxer shorts covered his lower half.

She took the soda he offered and noticed the long, narrow package from South Africa leaning against his footboard. She stared at it.

Nick settled back into his pillows and was silent for a few moments. Finally he said, "Go ahead, open it."

Sara's face flushed. "*You* should open it, Nick."

"I already know what it is. So if you want to know, you open it. It's not like it can stay in that box forever."

She was only human, after all. Who wouldn't want to know what an extremely wealthy, well-traveled woman had sent her only son for his birthday? She took two steps closer to the package. "You sure you don't mind?"

"For God's sake, Sara…"

"Okay, okay." She tore off the outside packaging to reveal a colorfully designed box with a ribbon around it. She looked to Nick for approval before going on. He just rolled his eyes.

Sara untied the ribbon and opened the box. The next barrier was a layer of tissue paper. She parted it and uncovered a magnificent walking cane, unlike anything she'd ever seen. The stick was made of intricately carved ebony. The handle was a shiny metal tiger's head with sparkling stones for its eyes. Reverently Sara lifted the cane from the box. She studied its components in the light from Nick's desk lamp. The metal couldn't be…could it?

"Hey, it's a nice one," Nick said blandly.

"Nick, this tiger—it's not… I mean it's too large, so it couldn't be…"

"Gold?" he finished for her. "Mother would never send anything less."

"And the eyes?"

He took the cane and examined the glittering jewels. "Let's see, she's in South Africa. They're diamonds."

Sara slumped into a chair. "Oh, my God, diamonds. I've never even seen rhinestones that huge!"

Nick slid off the bed and carried the cane to his closet. "Yep, it's pretty sweet."

"That's all you can say, 'It's pretty sweet'?"

"I don't know that it's my favorite." He opened the closet door, and hanging from hooks on the inside were four other equally grand walking sticks. "All of these are sweet," he said.

Sara could only stare. Outside of a museum, she'd never seen such magnificence. Each cane was unique in design and obviously exorbitant in quality and value. She looked at the newest offering as he hung it next to its companions. "I can't believe you left this lying on the counter downstairs. These pieces should be in a vault."

He gave her a look that she found extremely smug. "Why? Who's going to steal them? It's not like anybody knows they're here—except the guys and now you." He leaned over and kissed her forehead. "And I'm beginning to trust you."

"You know what I mean, Bass. These are priceless treasures from your mother."

"Yes, and I appreciate the thought, but the truth is, she sends me these canes because she can't think of anything else to give me." He turned away from Sara and walked across the room. "My mother has always had a hard time dealing with my injury. She had a hard time accepting the occupation that resulted in it, too."

"I can't imagine why," Sara countered. "What an insensitive woman not to support the son who robs banks for a living."

He smiled, but offered no rebuttal. "The point is, these expensive gifts are her way of saying she's sorry about what happened, but she really can't deal with it. I understand that. Last year I told her I didn't need any more canes. I was okay. But—'' he ran his hand down the shaft of the latest addition ''—I don't think my mother knows me well enough these days to come up with a different idea. And that's really my fault, not hers.''

''I think that's sad,'' Sara said. She walked back to the packaging to pick up the discarded paper. An envelope fell out of the box. ''There's something else. A card.''

''Oh, yeah, she always sends a card. Go ahead, open it.''

Sara thrust it at him. ''I am *not* going to open your card. It's much too personal.''

He shook his head. ''It's not personal, I guarantee you. Besides, are you the same woman who snuck into my room and went through my most private possessions? And now you won't even open an envelope when I give you permission.''

The man had a point. ''Fine, I'll open it,'' she said grudgingly.

When she pulled the card out, a credit card slipped to the bed. It was a Platinum Visa in Nick's name.

Nick grabbed it up quickly. ''Oh, yeah, I forgot. My yearly credit card.'' He reached into his nightstand drawer, pulled out a pair of scissors and snipped the card in two. Then he jerked his thumb at the greeting card in Sara's hand. ''Read what she says. Read it aloud.''

Sara had to remind herself that nothing Nick did should surprise her. '' 'Darling,' '' she began when she found her voice, '' 'please use this to buy a plane ticket to Paris. I'll be there the last week of May and would love to show you the sights. You know what they say about Paris in the spring. Who knows? Maybe you'll fall in love.'''

Sara looked up at Nick and found his expression flat. "She signs it, 'Kisses, Mom.'''

He threw the pieces of plastic into the wastebasket. "Nice invitation, but I think I'll pass."

Nick's decision made Sara more curious about his past than ever. That, and the fact that she'd just made passionate love with the man, made her blurt out her next words. "Nick, have you ever been in love?"

He chuckled. "Oh, sure, dozens of times. Sometimes with more than one woman at a time."

Sara gasped. That was his answer? How could he say such a thing to her after what they'd just done on the floor of the parlor? Hadn't it meant anything to him?

He lay back on his bed and grinned at her. "You know, Sara, I'm feeling pretty darn good right now. No aches, no pains, and a fully charged battery. And you look so damn sexy standing there…"

She threw the greeting card at him. "That's great, Nick. But think about this. We almost got it right tonight. Almost. But I'm feeling a pain myself right now. If you want to know where it is, just watch my backside as I walk out the door!"

CHAPTER SEVENTEEN

AFTER A FITFUL night's sleep, Nick awoke to utter silence. No hammering. No sawing. No bickering. Obviously no repairs in progress. Something was wrong on Thorne Island, and Nick figured he'd have to face the island's problems, as well as the big one he'd created for himself the night before.

He'd made a serious blunder with Sara. He'd been joking of course, but Sara had taken him seriously. Now he wondered if all the charm he could muster would get him out of it. Plus, his leftover pains—reminders of the wildly passionate encounter on the parlor floor—only made the situation worse. Sitting up in bed, he had to smile. Hell, the pain was a small price to pay. He'd meet Sara on the floor again in a minute. If she was speaking to him.

He limped to the bathroom and noticed Sara's door was closed. She probably wasn't up yet. Just the thought of her slim, silky body nestled between the sheets sent waves of desire through his protesting body. Some time ago, because he liked the idea, he'd convinced himself that she slept naked. Yes, he'd have to make things right with her pretty quickly. He couldn't accept any off-limits restrictions now that he'd made love to her. He couldn't imagine not touching her again. In one night, Sara had made him feel like more of a man than he'd felt in years.

When he came out of the bathroom, he considered starting the reconciliation right away. He could open her door, slip inside and watch the first light of day shimmer over her sleeping form. He could bend over and kiss her awake, and then her arms would reach out for him and draw him under the covers for an unforgettable hour of make-up sex.

Or she could strike out with a fist and shove him on his keester.

Remembering the way Sara had been last night, the way she'd sashayed out the door in a huff, Nick decided the odds might not be in his favor. "Better take things slow, Romano," he told himself as he proceeded to the kitchen unsatisfied. "You've got some serious kissing *up* to do before you can do some serious kissing."

With a cup of coffee in his hand, Nick set off to find his buddies. Sara's mood wasn't going to improve any if the boys had suddenly called a strike and weren't working today. It was to his advantage to get them back on the job. He met Ryan on the way to Brody's cottage.

"I was just coming to get you," Ryan said. "Brody wants to have a meeting."

"Oh, Lord, I was afraid of that," Nick said. "He's in a mood, is he?"

"Yeah, I think so."

Brody was behind the bulwark of his counter when Nick and Ryan arrived. He glared at Nick. "I'm surprised you could get up this morning," he barked.

"It wasn't easy," Nick said.

"You want to tell us about that little scene over at the inn last night?" Brody's words dripped with venom.

"What little scene would that be, Brody?"

"The one that included all the fancy lights in the fancy dining room, and a special delivery from Put-in-Bay. Winkie won't leave the Happy Angler for a week because of all the money he made yesterday!"

Nick wondered just how much of the "scene" Brody had witnessed, but he dismissed his concern quickly. Even Brody wouldn't get his kicks out of watching someone else's fun through a parlor window. "Not that it's any of your business, Brody, but I arranged a little dinner for Sara last night. That's all there was to it."

"The hell it was! I can imagine where your little wine and dine led—probably upstairs for some mattress high jinks!"

Mattress high jinks? It was all Nick could do to remain serious in the face of Brody's wrath.

"But the worst part is," Brody continued, "you're consorting with the enemy, entertaining her like she was queen of Thorne Island, for Pete's sake, instead of the conniving Mata Hari she is. You've got some explaining to do, Nick. Me and the guys don't appreciate you being a turncoat."

Nick exploded. "Cut the crap, Brody! This isn't a war with enemies and turncoats. Sara's been plenty fair with us. Hell, she could have hired a lawyer and tossed our butts off this island the first day if she'd wanted to. But she didn't. She went along with our plan to let us repair the inn ourselves. She fixed a big dinner to say thanks.

"Look around you. Until Sara got here, we were stuck in boring ruts. The seasons came and went and we stayed mired in our own complacency. Now we're

actually talking, working together and accomplishing
something for the first time in years.''

Nick realized he'd jumped on a soapbox, but he
couldn't stop now. Sara *had* made a difference in their
lives, a big difference. And she deserved to be treated
with a little respect.

"Look at Ryan. He's happier than he's been for
ages now that he has those vines to look after. And
you and Dexter are arguing over whose contributions
to the island are more important, and that's because
you suddenly have pride in the outcome. That's what
we've been missing around here. Pride. And purpose.
And Sara's given them both back to us.''

Dexter and Ryan nodded their heads slowly in
agreement, but Brody continued to glare at Nick.
"Yeah, and I bet she's given you a whole lot more
than that!''

Nick pounded his fist on the counter, sending
Brody jumping back a few steps. "That's none of
your business, and I'll be damned if I'll defend myself
to you!''

Brody shook his fist in the air, though he stayed
far behind the counter. "Yeah, well you're a traitor,
Nick, plain and simple. You sold yourself to the first
tight—''

Something in Nick's expression must have made
Brody cut short his tirade because he stopped midsentence. It was a good thing, too, because Nick's fist
had coiled into a weapon at his side, and he was very
close to using it.

"You know what you are, Brody?'' Nick said.
"You're a miserable old coot who hasn't had a happy
day since you made your first million. You've clung
to your bank balance like a lifeline, never spending

any of it, never sharing it. You've alienated your kid and everyone in your life, and for what? To sell groceries and dig for treasure you're not even sure exists.''

Nick laughed bitterly. ''You want to know what's funny? You call that business you started Good Company Hygiene Products. That's quite a name for a guy who doesn't know what it means to *be* good company.'' Nick looked at all three men one at a time, then returned his gaze to Brody. ''But life's full of little ironies, isn't it, boys?''

He headed for the door. ''I'm going to work. Alone or with the rest of you. Have it your way.''

As he went down the walkway, he heard Brody shout after him. ''I paid for those ceiling fans with my money!''

Nick just shook his head. He was really close to giving up on Brody. But maybe he could try one more thing. It was time for one of his phone calls to Junior.

NICK LOOKED UP at Sara's window as he approached the inn. The shutters were open. She was up.

He walked around to the rear of the building, figuring she'd be in the kitchen. ''As long as you're on a roll, why stop now?'' he said to himself, abandoning his previous plan to go slowly where Sara was concerned.

When he reached the bottom of the porch steps, he looked through the screen door. There she was, her back to him, pouring herself a cup of coffee. ''Facing Brody was easy,'' he said, squaring his shoulders. ''Now let's see what you're really made of, Romano.''

He opened the screen door just a few inches so it

wouldn't make any noise and squeezed his body inside. Then, glad he'd worn his old moccasins, he tiptoed over to Sara. He knew she hated to be scared, but he couldn't give her time to stockpile any more ammunition against him than she probably already had.

He stopped a couple of feet behind her. Her hair was piled on top of her head, leaving strands trailing down her neck. Short cutoffs provided a tempting view of her gorgeous legs. He reached for her with both hands, thinking to circle her waist over her yellow knit top.

She raised a butter knife in the air. "Touch me and I'll gut you, Bass."

He pulled his hands away and clasped them behind his back. "Good morning, Sara," he chirped. Then he stepped around, leaned on the counter and looked at her. "I see we haven't exactly decided to let bygones be bygones, have we?"

She picked up her coffee and pivoted away from him. "No, *we* haven't."

She went outside and he followed. She sat on the bottom porch step and he sat beside her. She inched away from him and he inched closer. She stared at the trees. He stared at her profile.

"So how long?" he asked.

"How long what?"

"Until I can touch you again."

Finally she looked at him. It was a start.

"You know, Bass, it is absolutely astounding to me that a guy with as much nerve as you have could live as a hermit on this island. I would think you'd be just dying to show the world your incredible charms."

He grinned like a little boy. At least he hoped it looked innocent. "I only care about showing you my charms, Sara."

Sardonic laughter sputtered from her mouth. "Oh, I've seen. I've seen. What about all those dozens of women you've been in love with? Why deprive them?"

He raised his hands, palms up. "It was a joke, Sara!"

She nodded her head slightly, a gesture that said she wasn't buying it. "I see. Maybe I would have found it funny at some time, Nick. But right after making love to you, it just didn't seem that humorous."

"All right. I'm an insensitive clod."

She blew a breath between her lips as if to say he'd get no argument from her.

"Look, I know it's not a news flash," he said. "I blurt things out without thinking how they're going to sound. I'm sorry. I really am." He inched a little closer. "Can I lay my hand on your knee? I promise I won't go any higher."

Her lips pulled down in a sort of frown, but she raised her coffee mug to her mouth, removing her elbow from the requested knee. He quickly claimed it before she changed her mind.

"Last night was wonderful, Sara," he said.

She flashed him a squinty-eyed glare.

"Don't do that! I'm being serious. I can't get you out of my mind. You don't know what it took for me to stay in my room last night. I wanted to break down your door and come in and plant little apology kisses all over your face and write little I'm-sorry messages all over your beautiful naked body with my fingers, and—''

''Why would you have broken down my door?'' she asked.

''Huh?''

She set down her mug and stared at the trees again. ''It wasn't locked, you idiot.''

His fingers walked slowly up her thigh to sneak under the ragged fringe of her shorts. When she turned her head to look at him, his mouth was waiting.

WHY FIGHT IT, SARA? she asked herself as his lips teased hers. She had less than a week left on Thorne Island, and despite the risk to her heart, she wanted to take as many memories of Nick Bass with her as possible. He made her senses spiral to new heights while her mind abandoned every notion of self-preservation it had ever had. *He's a man who speaks without thinking and thinks without logic.* But she couldn't stay mad at him because she couldn't stay away from him.

His mouth moved up her neck to tantalize her earlobe. ''I'd like nothing more than to keep doing this,'' he said. ''But I told the boys I'd be working on the inn.''

She pressed her finger against the basketball on his Cavaliers T-shirt and pushed him away. ''Don't let me keep you.''

He grinned wickedly and jerked his thumb toward the door. ''We could go inside. I'll say I suddenly got this pain in my leg…''

She gave him one of the reprimanding looks he'd gotten used to. ''No, Bass.''

He stood up and reached for the screen door. "Okay, you're one of those business-before-pleasure types. That's all right. I have all day to think about the pleasure, and all night to see if expectations live up to it."

She waved him away with pretended impatience.

He snapped his fingers. "Oh, by the way, speaking of business, I decided to do something right today."

"Must have been a stretch for you."

"No, really. I'm going to call Brody's son and invite him here."

Almost nothing could have surprised her more. For some reason she'd imagined Brody growing up with wolves. She couldn't visualize him fathering a child. "Brody has family?"

"He doesn't have a wife anymore, for obvious reasons. But he does have a son."

An image of a short, pudgy curmudgeon the spitting image of his father sprang to Sara's mind. "Where is he?"

"Pennsylvania. Brody disowned him after the kid borrowed money and didn't pay it back."

Sara snickered. "Hardly Father-of-the-Year material, is he? How do you know how to reach the son?"

"I made Brody give me Junior's number one time when the old man got so worked up over something his face turned beet-red. I thought he was having a heart attack. He wasn't. It was just his natural coloring. Anyhow, I told him I needed someone to contact to remove his body just in case. He finally gave me the information but made me swear I wouldn't call the kid."

"But you did, anyway."

"Of course. He turned out okay, but Brody won't

give him a break. He's got a good job. He's responsible, but Brody's too stubborn to notice. I call Junior several times a year. And Junior really cares about the old guy. Anyway, if I can use your cell phone later, I'll give him a call and tell him to get over here. It's time.''

So Nick, who'd accused Sara of interfering and wanting to change things, was about to violate one of the sacred trusts of Thorne Island manhood. ''So, will Brody be happy about this?''

''Happy? He'll be madder than hell. Probably try to run me over with the golf cart. But he pretty much wants to do that today, anyway. I think he'll get used to the idea once Carl gets here. He'll finally see that Junior isn't after his money.''

''A bold move, Commander.''

He smiled and started to go inside, but Sara stopped him. ''Wait a minute. As long as we're on this subject, what about Dexter and his situation?''

Nick's brows furrowed. ''What situation? He's happy.''

''How can you say that? He's miserable. Until the inn project came up, he spent all his time watching television. I've seen the notebook he carries around—the one with all the x's and o's on it. He's obsessed with football plays. And watch his eyes. A fighting instinct lies beneath that teddy-bear exterior. He looks like he wants to ram his shoulder into someone's solar plexus. He wants football, Nick. He needs it.''

Nick rubbed his chin. Sara could almost see the ideas churning in his mind. ''Yeah, I suppose you're right,'' he said. ''Okay. I'll make one phone call on Dexter's behalf—only one, though, Sara. If it doesn't pan out, that's it. I like having Dex around here. I don't want him to leave unless he really wants to.''

"Fair enough.'' *And what would it take to make you leave, Nick?*

"Next I suppose you'll tell me to send Ryan back to the racetrack,'' he said, scattering her thoughts.

"No, I won't, but I wish there was something we could do for him.'' She hushed his response with a finger to her lips. "Here they come.''

All three men approached from the direction of Brody's cottage. Brody was obviously still angry. He stomped to the back porch and put his fists on his hips. "Well, come on, Nick,'' he said. "This is your party. Let's get working.'' Then with a snide glance at Sara, he added, "And speaking of parties, why don't you and the little woman here start by taking down all those friggin' love lights in the dining room?''

Sara's jaw dropped. Nick swore. And Brody, ignoring the reaction, continued into the inn, followed by Ryan and Dexter, who had the decency to hide their embarrassment by clearing their throats loudly.

Once the men were inside, Sara whirled on Nick. "You told!''

"No, I didn't. Brody doesn't know anything. He saw the lights, yeah, but he doesn't know what we were doing. He just wants us to take the lights down because he hates to waste fuel.''

Sara put her head in her hands and moaned. Brody may not have known what happened between them, but he definitely suspected.

Nick patted the top of her head. "Relax, Sara. We don't have to worry about fuel. We don't need those lights. We can generate enough electricity in the dark

with our body heat. Now tell me where your phone
is so I can make those calls."

"It's on the kitchen table," she said.

Nick went inside and Sara listened to the soft pad
of his shoes across the kitchen floor. How was it possible for such an obviously bright man to so completely miss the point?

CARL JUNIOR'S NUMBER was one of the few Nick had
committed to memory. Nick announced his name to
Junior's wife when she answered, and he immediately
came to the phone. "Hey, what's up, Nick? Did
something happen to the old man?"

"No. But I think it's time something did."

Junior chuckled. "Now, Nickie, you're not going
to kill him, are you?"

"It might be the other way around. I want you to
come here, Carl."

"Did he tell you to call me?" The suspicion in
Carl's voice was obvious.

"No, but it's time."

"Why now?"

"He's mellowing, Carl. I think he really wants to
make amends." Nick winced at the obvious lie.
Maybe hell wouldn't be such a bad place. "When can
you come?"

There was a pause while Junior considered the invitation. Finally he said, "I'll talk to my wife. How
can I get back to you?"

Nick looked at the number Sara had written on a
piece of paper. "Use this cell number. If a woman
answers, don't hang up. Believe it or not, she's part
of this picture."

Next Nick dialed information to get the number of the manager of the Cleveland Browns football organization.

WHILE THE MEN WORKED in the Cozy Cove, Sara called the newspaper office in Sandusky. She placed an ad for a manager for the inn knowing she'd have to tell applicants that the position depended on whether the Cozy Cove passed inspection and whether they received any reservations.

Then she called the JCPenney catalog store. She ordered coordinating comforter sets, pillows and curtains for each of the finished guest rooms. Giving in to a last-minute impulse, she added colorful throw rugs to the list, rugs she'd scatter around the floors to warm a guest's bare feet on chilly mornings.

Finally she called Candy in Florida.

"Hi, Sara," Candy said. "I get to Cleveland at one-thirty Friday afternoon."

"That's great, Candy. I need you to do a favor for me when you get to Sandusky."

"Sure. What?"

"Pick up an order at Penney's. The store is near the ferry dock, so it won't be much out of the way."

"Okay."

"And Candy, rent a car with a good-size trunk. The things I've ordered aren't particularly heavy, but they'll take up a lot of room. You'll arrive in plenty of time to get the last ferry to Put-in-Bay."

"Okay."

"A man named Winkie will be at the ferry to meet you and bring you to the island. He wears a weird little naval cap, and he probably won't have shaved for a couple of days. But he's basically a nice man and will get you here unharmed."

"Okay. See ya."

Candy's amazing, Sara thought as she ended the connection. She lives in a world of chaos and yet remains totally unflappable. It was definitely a quality to be envied.

During the next two days Dexter and Brody finished all the renovations to the interior of the inn and were now busy with the porch roof and a sign for the front gate. Ryan and Nick painted the exterior of the Cozy Cove and hosed down the mossy stone walls of the press house. When Sara called the code-enforcement office to request a visit by officials for Monday morning, she felt confident Thorne Island would pass inspection.

But how would its residents feel if guests were permitted to stay on the island? That remained the big question. Sara kept her eyes open for any last-minute sabotage by Brody, but so far she hadn't noticed any sneaky behavior.

Still, she couldn't shake a general melancholy that had come over her. Her stay on Thorne Island was coming to a close. She'd made her flight reservation to Fort Lauderdale for Tuesday evening. She hadn't told Nick. Perhaps deep down, she feared his reaction would be an indifferent shrug. Maybe he wouldn't care. Sara could almost feel the stab to her heart when she considered that possibility.

Nick certainly hadn't been indifferent to *her* in the past couple of days. He'd come to her room both nights after the island settled into darkness. He was a wonderful, sensitive lover. He caressed and courted Sara with fervent words and passionate embraces. He mixed humor with desire and could just as easily send her into fits of laughter as inflame her with flights of absolute ecstasy. Nick was sexy beyond belief and he was fun.

And on Friday afternoon, just four days before Sara would leave for Florida—just three weeks since she'd arrived on Thorne Island, one question kept invading her thoughts. Had she fallen in love with him?

She'd told him about Candy coming to Thorne Island to help her. He joked about having to share her attention with the "pizza-eating secretary." It seemed, however, that underneath all the teasing he was really worried, because at four o'clock on Friday, he came to her room with sandwiches, and a bottle of wine and a grin wide enough to melt Sara's heart.

For the next two hours they feasted on delicacies of both the soul and the body. Deliriously exhausted, they lay in each other's arms on Sara's bed until the sounds of Winkie's boat broke the sweet, contented bliss.

Sara jumped up and scrambled around for her clothes. "Candy's here!" she said.

Nick crossed his arms under his head, stretched back against a pillow and watched her with amusement dancing in his eyes. "So it seems."

She threw his shirt at him, and it landed on his face. "Well, don't just lie there. Get dressed."

He did as he was told. "Okay, okay. We wouldn't want Candy to think there was anything other than number-crunching going on in here."

They left the room together and went to the stairs. Candy's giggles floated through the front screen door several seconds before she actually appeared. Nick and Sara had only descended a couple of steps when the door was yanked open by a hand that glittered with a half-dozen bangle bracelets.

"There's so much stuff," Candy said, sliding a large JCPenney bag over the threshold. She followed it inside, looked up the stairs and flashed a huge grin. "Hi, Sara. I made it."

"Hi, Candy. I hope the packages weren't too much—"

The next words stuck in Sara's throat. Carrying a similar bag under each arm, an extra-large sack in each hand and a leather duffel over his shoulder, her father stepped into the Cozy Cove lobby.

"Dad!" Sara cried.

Ben Crawford set down his bags and smiled up at her. "Hi, Sarabelle."

At the same time from behind her, she distinctly heard Nick mumble, "Damn."

Ben's eyes grew round as hubcaps. He snapped his fingers several times as if to kickstart his memory. "I know you," he said, pointing at Nick. "Romano. You're that reporter from the *Plain Dealer*. I wondered what happened to you."

Nick cleared his throat. "How ya doing, Ben?"

Romano? Reporter? Sara sank to the bottom step and stared at her father. Then she cast a quick glance over her shoulder at the man who'd shared her bed and somehow managed to turn her sensible world upside down. Who was this impostor who faced her now with dark, glittering eyes and a guilty grin?

CHAPTER EIGHTEEN

BEN CRAWFORD walked over to Sara, took her hand and pulled her up from the stairs. He studied her features and frowned. "What's the matter with you, Sara? You look like you've seen a ghost."

"Not me, Dad," she said, using every ounce of willpower to keep her voice from trembling. "I think you're the one who's seen the ghost."

Ben chuckled. "Oh, you mean Romano here? I'm surprised to see him I must admit. It's been a few years." He looked at Nick who'd descended the remaining steps to stand beside Sara. "What're you doing on Millicent Thorne's island?"

Sara gave Nick a fake smile. "Yes, Mr. *Romano,* what *are* you doing on Aunt Millie's island? We're all dying to know."

"It's a long story," he said. "Mostly, Ben, I've just been hanging around here recuperating."

"You ought to be hanging from a noose," Sara said in a voice only Nick could hear. Then to her father, she said, "What are you doing here, Dad?"

"I just got curious about what was happening on this island and decided to check things out." He crooked his thumb at Candy. "Imagine seeing your secretary at the ferry and then finding Romano here. Sure is a small world."

Since his broad grin was aimed at Nick, Ben

seemed more interested in Thorne Island's apparent celebrity than he did his daughter. He stuck out his hand to his old acquaintance. The two men shook, and Ben started firing questions.

Fuming on the inside with anger and, almost worse, a desperate curiosity for more details of her father and Nick's shared past, Sara tried to listen to what they were saying. Candy, unaware of these developments and her boss's emotional turmoil, talked incessantly, blocking out their words.

"You picked the nicest colors for the bed linens, Sara."

Sara mumbled a quick thank-you and stepped closer to her father.

"No kidding," Ben said. "Those rotten bastards from Golden Isles had you shot?"

"Yeah, well, it was a long time ago," Nick answered. "Just a bad memory now."

Sara glared at him, and he responded with a sheepish look that said he knew he was in trouble. Sara looked at her father. So Nick was the one who'd brought down the Golden Isles Development Corporation. And for some reason during the last three weeks, he had chosen not to mention this detail. How could he have done this to her? How could he have kept a secret that was so interwoven with her own life?

Candy's voice forced Sara's attention back to the mound of JCPenney sacks in the lobby. "So what do you want me to do with all this stuff?"

All at once bed linens didn't seem important. "The bags belong on the second floor," Sara answered. "I'll help you carry them up in a minute."

Candy dragged one sack to the stairs and started up. "No problem. I'll get them up there."

Ben picked up two more and followed her.

Needing to put space between her and Nick, Sara went to the kitchen. She looked for something to do—a dish to wash. A spill to wipe up. Nothing needed doing. Her efforts had been too thorough to provide her with an outlet for her anger and frustration now. With no other options, she paced, nearly running into Nick when he threw open the door and came into the room.

"I know, I know," he said, trailing after her when she spun away from him. "I've got some explaining to do. But right now I'm just getting your father a beer."

She would have blasted him right then, but he held up his hand and pointed to the back door. "Oh, hi, Ryan."

Sara caught a glimpse of Ryan's timid face before he retreated back down the steps. The little guy had a knack for sensing tense situations.

Nick hurried to the door and held it open. "Ryan, buddy. Don't go. Come in." Desperation was written all over Nick's features, the coward!

Trapped by the invitation, Ryan cautiously stepped inside. He looked from Sara to Nick. "Who's here?"

Having to concede that Nick was spared her revenge at least for the moment, Sara managed to give Ryan what she hoped was a reassuring smile. "There are some people I want you to meet in the lobby, Ryan. Follow me. I'll introduce you."

Ben and Candy had returned from carting the bags upstairs when Nick, Sara and Ryan entered the lobby. Nick strolled by Sara as casually as if he was in the vineyard, instead of the mine field she imagined for him. He handed Ben the can of beer. Then patting his stomach, he said, "Should have gotten myself one while I was there. I'll be back in a minute."

Sara followed his progress out of the lobby with her eyes. "Meet me in the press house in half an hour," she said to his back.

He made a pretense of checking his watch. "I think I can make that appointment."

"Thirty minutes, *Romano*."

Once Nick left, the other three people in the lobby stared at Sara with expressions that clearly indicated their confusion. And no wonder. There was enough emotional electricity sizzling in the Cozy Cove to eliminate the need for the generator.

Sara made the introductions. Then despite the thoughts tumbling wildly in her head about her own concerns, she noticed an undeniable interest in Ryan's eyes when his gaze passed quickly from her father to settle on Candy. She shouldn't have been surprised, since Candy had never looked more outrageous, but still, this was timid Ryan whose eyes were popping out of his head.

Red hair poked out from a red felt hat with the brim rolled up to reveal Candy's perfectly penciled eyebrows. Her magenta lips flashed an exuberant smile. She wore a red and purple print top tucked into purple lycra pants. Red sandals with impossibly thin straps completed the outfit. The two-inch heels made Candy only that much taller than Ryan. In her bare feet, she would meet him nose to nose.

Sara couldn't help smiling. She'd been hoping something good would happen in Ryan's life, but she'd never suspected it would come breezing through the door of the Cozy Cove in the effervescent form of her assistant. But there was no denying the attraction. Ryan was mesmerized.

He rubbed the toe of one canvas-clad foot against the back of his other leg and shoved his hands in the pockets of his denim shorts. But for once, he didn't look as though he wanted to bolt. His eyes were glued to Candy's mouth, which moved at its customary speed.

"It's so nice to meet you, Eliot," she said. "I love this island already. And this inn. It's so quaint. It's like Mr. and Mrs. America live here." Her hand fluttered out to touch Ryan's arm. He jerked slightly, but if she noticed, she didn't react. "You're so lucky to live here. I'll bet you hear birds sing all day long."

He nodded, took a couple of steps toward the door and pointed to the porch. His lips quivered with the first tentative efforts toward speech. "Do...do you like the flowers?"

Candy pranced around him, stepped outside and looked at the hanging baskets. "I *love* flowers. These are beautiful."

He followed her. "I take care of them."

"My goodness. I wish I could make things grow, but heavens, if I touch a plant, it just withers. You really have a talent."

"I could teach you," he offered. "You want to see the vineyard?"

Sara looked out the door as Candy and Ryan walked around the inn to the vineyard. "Well, if that doesn't beat everything," she said. "I guess it's true that there really is someone for everybody. You just have to be in the right place at the right time."

A low, teasing voice rumbled from behind her and

sent ripples of tingling familiarity down her spine. "I'll bet you planned this whole thing," Nick said.

She turned around, momentarily letting her anger subside in favor of a strange delight. "Did not. But I'd be quite proud of myself right now if I had."

Nick consulted his watch. "Oh, look at the time. Gotta go. I've got an important appointment in a few minutes."

"Do you know who that fella is, Sara?" Ben asked after Nick had gone.

Sara just shook her head. Yes, she now knew his name and that he was the reporter who'd come to her Aunt Millie's aid. But she also knew he wasn't Nick Bass, the man she'd naively taken into her bed and into her heart.

MINUTES LATER Sara crossed the backyard of the inn and cut through the shrubs separating it from the vineyard. She stopped within a few feet of the press house and took a deep breath. The door was open, indicating Nick was probably inside. Clenching her hands, she stepped through the door and into the cool, shadowy dimness.

In the moment it took for her eyes to adjust to the rose-gold hues of dusk, she was drawn to the vague, gray shapes of the crushing vat and the press baskets. She was furious at Nick, yet she couldn't ignore the peace this room and its symbols of tradition instilled in her.

"Over here, Sara," Nick said from the center of the room. He was seated on the top step of the short stairs that led from the floor to the edge of the crushing vat. His voice was soft and soothing, perfect for the atmosphere of ages-old craftsmanship, yet entirely wrong in the context of his deceit. He lifted his hand and held it out to her. She approached him but ignored his gesture.

Dropping his hand, Nick slid over on the step, making room for Sara to sit beside him.

"I guess you're mad," he said when she remained standing.

"Why did you lie to me?"

"I never lied to you."

"Not telling me is the same as lying."

He rubbed his thumb and forefinger across his brow. "No, Sara, it isn't. I told you all you needed to know. That I was living cheaply on Thorne Island as repayment for a kindness I'd done for Millicent Thorne. That is entirely true."

"You just failed to mention that this kindness was part of your job as an investigative reporter. You failed to mention that Thorne Island was saved from corrupt developers because of your story. You failed to mention that my aunt lived the rest of her years in financial comfort because of your efforts."

He looked up at her, his gaze searching every detail of her features. Her eyes had adjusted to the light now, and she was able to read the bewilderment in his expression.

"Pardon me for saying so, Sara," he said, "but this list of charges against me reads more like a commendation than a condemnation."

"Oh, it is, Nick. You were brave and noble in your dealings with my aunt. A seeker of truth and justice."

He opened his mouth, and his question came out slowly. "But...you're still angry with me."

"I am as angry right now as I can ever remember being in my life."

He shook his head, confusion still clouding his normally clear eyes.

"Don't look so perplexed, Nick. It's simple. I don't like games. Especially between two people who, I *thought,* had come to mean something to each other."

He reached for her hand, but she jerked it away. "Come on, Sara. You mean a lot to me. You know that."

"No, I don't. Shortly after meeting you, I told you who I was, who my father was, why I was here, what I did for a living. You told me almost nothing about yourself. You were a blank tape, Nick. As time passed I told you even more. I told you my expectations for Thorne Island. I told you about my job, my childhood…"

"Yeah, well, you're just not as private a person as I am. I told you I don't like to talk about myself."

Sara pinned him with a stark glare. "You could have given me something, Nick. You knew practically everything there was to know about me. And what did I know about you? Zero! Oh, I'd heard a bit about your parents, and I'd begun to fantasize all sorts of things…"

Apparently liking the sound of that, his eyes brightened, and he reached for her again. "Yeah? What things?"

Sara slapped his hand. "Grope at me again, Ba… *Romano,* and your hand will know how a grape feels in the press basket."

He dangled his hands between his knees. "Well said, Crawford. Point taken."

Determined to make him understand, she turned away from his penetrating gaze and the threat of a mesmerizing grin that had clouded her judgment on more than one occasion. She stared at the ceiling. "I knew that you'd been shot but I never knew why. You wouldn't talk about it. I slept with a man who could have been a criminal, a mobster or even an idiot who didn't know how to handle his own gun."

As usual he had a quick response. "It wouldn't have been that last one. I was shot in the back, remember? There's no way I could have…"

She heard a rustle and knew he was twisting around trying to prove he couldn't have aimed a pistol at his back. This childish ploy to get her attention was the last straw. She whirled on him, pushed at his chest while he was off balance and watched him tumble into the crushing vat.

"Sara!" His cry sounded hollow coming from the cavernous old tub.

She grasped the side of the vat and leaned over. Her voice quivered with rage. "Don't you even know how to be serious? Do you have to make a joke of every honest emotion you're faced with in life?"

He grabbed for his lower back. "Oh, I'm damn serious right now. You knocked the sense of humor right out of me, woman. I may never crack a smile again."

"Good. Then just lie there and listen because I have a question for you. At what point, if any, were you going to tell the woman you'd been sleeping with who the hell you are? If my father hadn't shown up today, were you maybe going to tell me tomorrow? How about Sunday? Or maybe you were going to wait until Tuesday afternoon when I carried my suitcases out the front door. Or maybe you were never going to tell me at all."

He pushed himself up to a sitting position and stared at her. "You're leaving on Tuesday?"

"Yes, I am. Now answer the question."

He set his elbows on his raised knees and let his hands hang. After appearing to consider his answer carefully, he finally said, "Truthfully, I probably never would have told you."

His admission, though it did nothing to mend the hole in her heart, was strangely gratifying. At least Sara knew he was telling the truth. "Why not, Nick? Am I so hard to trust?"

"I wouldn't have told you because it doesn't matter. It has nothing to do with what happened between us."

"It does matter, Nick. Why can't you see that? Don't you think I care how or why you got shot? For God's sake, I was fall... I was beginning to have feelings for you, despite the fact that you are the most difficult man I've ever known."

He lifted his hands, then let them fall again, obviously still weighing his words. "Look, Sara, over the years I've gotten used to not telling anyone my troubles. As time went on, I realized there were three reasons for that. The first one is that I needed to protect everyone around me. The less people knew, the less danger they'd be in."

She stared at his profile, noting the lines of anxiety at the corners of his eyes. "What do you mean, Nick? Was someone besides you hurt by the men from Golden Isles?"

"No, thank God. But I received threats against my family while I was in the hospital. When the plan to bump me off didn't work, the boys at Golden Isles had to stop me from testifying somehow. Their threats came in all sorts of disguises—letters, packages, even notes on flowers. But they were clear, and they were aimed at my mother and father.

"I sent my parents into hiding until the trial was over because I knew I was going to testify. And I did. On closed-circuit TV with armed guards posted at the door of my hospital room."

Sara's stomach churned at the image. What would she have done if someone had threatened her father? Would she have followed her conscience and testified? She only knew one thing for certain—she would have been scared out of her wits. And she was scared now, for Nick, just thinking about it. "How awful for you," she said. "For your family."

"It's over. Forget it. I don't want your sympathy, Sara." He arched his back and frowned. "What I want is to get out of this vat. It stinks in here, despite what you think of all this romantic old crap." He stood up. "I'm talking, just like you want, so promise me you won't dump me back in here."

She took his hand to steady his climb to the outside. "I won't throw you in again."

When he was safely on the floor, he said, "You're sorry, then?"

"No."

A semblance of a grin lifted one corner of his mouth. "Didn't think so." He sat on the steps again.

"And reason number two for keeping all this to yourself?" she reminded him.

"Self-preservation. Even when those guys were convicted of everything from grand larceny to attempted murder, even after they went to jail, I was still scared to death."

He looked at her and shrugged one shoulder, almost as if he was relieved to have admitted it. "You happy now? How's that for honesty? A big guy like me confessing that the idea of facing another bullet was enough to turn my insides to mush."

He raised his thumb and index finger and held them an inch apart. "That little piece of steel only this long, that bullet, has taught me not to trust anybody unless I know them almost as well as I know myself. And that's a hard habit to break—" he stared intently into her eyes "—even with someone you grow to care about a whole lot. So I figured that keeping my mouth shut about my past for, say, the rest of my life, and assuming an alias wasn't such a bad plan. And once you start living a lie, Sara, it's no easy thing to start living the truth again, even when you begin to trust."

Sara's anger became almost a liquid thing as it slowly ebbed from her body. In its place was hurt and sorrow for both of them. And the sad realization that Nick might never again experience the confidence the bullet had taken from him. But there was still one little detail that didn't make sense, and she had to ask him about it. "Nick, you're living *here,* on the island that started this whole mess. Didn't you think the Golden Isles guys would look for you here? Didn't you think they'd want revenge?"

"Yeah, I thought about it. But this place is like Alcatraz. Nobody gets on or off without us knowing it. And Winkie wouldn't bring anybody he didn't trust." He flashed her a bona fide grin. "You should feel good. For some reason Winkie trusted you right off. That's never happened before."

She allowed herself a slight smile. "And the third reason you've never told anyone your story?"

"That's simple. Nobody likes a whiner. And believe me, for years that's what I was. Ask Brody. He had to pay a nurse a fortune to keep coming here day after day to put up with me—and him. The days when it was too cold and Winkie couldn't cut through the ice, Brody, and eventually Dexter, played nurse-maid.''

Sara nodded. She was beginning to understand the men of Thorne Island and the bond that held them together. ''That explains a lot, especially about your connection to Brody.''

''Yeah. I owe him.''

She went to the steps and patted Nick's side. He took the hint and slid over to make room for her. ''I guess I can see why it was hard for you to tell me the truth,'' she said. ''And why you've stayed here so long. But what happens now? It's been six long years, Nick. What are you going to do?''

He looked at her as if those questions had never occurred to him. ''Why do I have to do anything?'' he finally asked. ''I like it here. I'll probably never hear from anyone associated with Golden Isles. But there's no need to change the way I live.''

That simple, direct assessment of Nick's future knocked Sara right off her shaky axis. ''So even if you're not afraid anymore, you'll still stay on Thorne Island?''

''It's my home, as long as you let me live here. If a few visitors traipse over here once in a while, I guess I'll just have to put up with them. I can still write my books.''

''But what about...'' She almost said ''us'' but stopped in time. What she couldn't stop were the tears burning behind her eyes. She looked away from him.

''What about what?'' he asked.

258 THE MEN OF THORNE ISLAND

She swallowed, searching for something safe to say. "The books. What will you do with them?"

"I don't know. Keep writing them, I guess."

"And storing them in boxes?"

He shrugged and put a hand on her arm. His touched ripped through her and settled as a violent trembling in her abdomen.

"Were you serious?" he asked. "Are you really leaving Tuesday?"

She nodded.

"I hadn't thought about that. I knew that some-day...but Tuesday. That's soon."

The first fat, sloppy tear rolled down Sara's cheek. She quickly brushed it away, thankful for the deepening darkness enveloping them. And thankful, too, for the voice she heard coming from the back of the inn.

"Sara! Sara, where are you?"

"That's my dad," she said. "I have to go." She slipped her arm from Nick's hand and stood up.

"Wait a minute," he said.

"No." She ran from the press house and didn't look back. What would have been the point? He wasn't coming after her, anyway.

CHAPTER NINETEEN

NICK LOOKED AROUND for something to bust. Unfortunately the logical breakables—the bottles—were in the fermenting room downstairs, and after his tumble into the vat, he didn't think his protesting muscles could take the steps. He could bash a press basket or two against the wood floor, but as angry as he was, he couldn't bring himself to destroy one of Sara's precious artifacts.

Damn! What did the woman expect of him? She'd wanted him to talk, and by golly, he had. She'd wanted honesty, and he'd given it to her. And what did she do? Just when he had this communication thing down pat, when he was about to rattle on about the most important issue yet, the two of them, she'd left him sitting here feeling like an idiot.

He leaned back against the vat and stared at the ceiling. "So much for honesty," he said, knowing only the ghosts of the Krauses were listening to him. "People are basically just a big stinkin' disappointment. If they don't shoot you, they expect too much."

Sara had expected miracles from him since the day she arrived. She'd poked around until she'd gotten him to spill his guts. And for what? So she could run off just when he wanted *her* to utter a few meaningful syllables.

Enough was enough. And Nick Romano had had,

enough emotional turmoil in the past few years to last him a lifetime. When you spend nearly half a decade just learning to put one foot in front of the other, you can't very well cater to the demands of everyone you meet. Let Sara Crawford go back to her calculators and sharp pencils and men who probably weren't fit to cork her wine bottles. Nick would go back to the way things were, the way they ought to be.

He stood up and headed for the door, cursing the muscles and joints that creaked like old bedsprings, reminding him that he wasn't the man he wanted to be. He walked into the gray dusk and shook his head. If he was so sure of himself and so ready to let Sara go, why did he feel so damn awful?

SARA TRIED not to think about Nick through the weekend, but that was as impossible as believing he would change. He would never give an inch. She knew that now, and there was nothing for her to do but go back to Florida. She should have anticipated this outcome from the beginning. All the clues had been there, and if she was suffering a broken heart, she had no one to blame but herself. But that didn't make it any easier to bear.

She kept busy working on the guest rooms with Candy. They replaced bed linens and curtains, and fluffed and primped little details into cozy perfection. She made certain the kitchen was in order and the pots and pans gleamed.

Ryan was a constant companion to the two women. Most of the time, he and Candy hardly seemed to know Sara was in the room. A thousand "Find Your Perfect Mate" magazine quizzes couldn't have produced a more ideal pairing.

By Saturday afternoon Sara had received two phone calls in response to her advertisement in the Sandusky paper. They came from pleasant-sounding Put-in-Bay women who seemed eager to manage Sara's little empire, didn't mind the daily ride with Winkie and weren't opposed to light housekeeping and cooking. She took their phone numbers but postponed the decision to hire one of them knowing that the most obvious manager for the Cozy Cove Inn was right now falling for Eliot Ryan. Candy would fly back to Fort Lauderdale on Monday, but Sara believed it was only a matter of time before she returned to Thorne Island.

Ben Crawford added his own personal touches to the island. Using lumber scraps left over from repairs to the roof and porch, he mended the dilapidated dock and painted it the same dove-gray as the house. He drilled huge holes in the pilings and strung bright yellow mooring rope from one end to the other, fashioning a cheerful handrail. Nick helped him, probably because the harbor was far enough away from the inn that he wouldn't have to see Sara.

When the men came for meals, Nick took his sandwich and beer outside. At dusk he retreated to his room. That was when Sara went to the harbor and saw for herself the remarkable improvements. And in spite of the deepening ache in her heart, she experienced a quiver of delight. Thorne Island was finally beginning to resemble the image she'd had ever since she'd first heard about her inheritance.

And soon, Sara would have to leave it all behind.

Then it was Sunday, the day Carlton Brody Junior announced he would come to Thorne Island. And

Nick and Sara spoke to each other again because in the midst of a tempest, even wounded souls come together.

WHEN HE SAW Winkie's boat carrying Junior approach the island, Nick suggested that Ben wait at the dock to meet them. Then he jumped into the bee and raced down the pathway to the inn. Scrambling up the porch steps, he hollered in the front door of the Cozy Cove. "Sara! Sara, where are you?"

No answer. He hurried through the inn and down the back steps as fast as old hurts and current panic would let him. He spotted Sara a hundred yards beyond the back shrubs in the midst of a row of grapevines. When he called her name, she looked up, interpreted the wild flailing of his arms and ran to meet him.

"He's here?" she asked breathlessly. For a moment Nick wished the anticipation in her eyes was for him. It had been once.

"Yep."

The corners of her mouth showed fine lines of anxiety. "Brody still doesn't know?"

Nick shook his head. "I wonder now if we should have warned him. When a volcano is about to blow, at least you see the smoke first."

Sara smiled, and Nick realized how much he'd missed the sight of it.

"Too late now. There he goes." She pointed toward Brody's cottage where he'd just come out the front door. "I've never known him not to hurry down to the dock when Winkie pulls in, unless he's fishing or digging."

Nick nodded. Everything Brody did was regulated by the comings and goings of Winkie's boat. "Yeah.

You'd think the old geezer was expecting more than a bag of groceries and his latest bank statement!''

With the flat of her hand, Sara nudged Nick ahead of her. It was a casual touch, yet Nick felt it deep inside.

"Let's go," she said. "We've got to circle around him so we get there first. Dad can't handle two Brodys."

Nick reached around and grabbed her hand. She let him thread his fingers through hers. It felt as natural as the moon rising over Thorne Island. Her fingers were slightly gritty from vineyard dirt and warm from the sun. Suddenly Nick didn't want to go anywhere. But he had no choice. Thanks to him, a life was possibly at stake. They cut around the side of the inn, pierced a thicket of trees and reached the dock just as Brody appeared at the end of the pathway.

"Now who the hell's here?" Brody grumbled. "We might as well be on Coney Island for the crowds we get lately!"

Nick strode down the dock and took the line Winkie tossed to him. Sara stayed on shore with Brody, monitoring his reaction to the unexpected arrival.

Nick had only seen Junior a couple of times at the racetrack where Nick and Brody used to meet. But because of his phone calls to him over the years, he knew that Junior was a nice kid. Kid, heck. He was only eight years younger than Nick. The man who stepped out of the boat and extended his hand was a familiar, yet polished version of the boy Nick remembered from the track. "It's been a long time, Nick," Junior said. "I *think* I'm glad you invited me here."

Nick shook his hand. "How ya doing, Carl?"

"Okay, I guess." He glanced at the shore where

Brody was squinting into the sun. "So there he is," Carl said matter-of-factly. "Why doesn't he come down here? Did he send you to test the waters?"

Nick rubbed the back of his neck. "Truth is, Carl, I didn't tell the old man you were coming."

Carl's hands shot to his chest in a defensive gesture. "You didn't tell him? That's just great." He turned back to the boat. "Fire up the engine, Winkleman. I'm outta here."

Footsteps pounded like a jackhammer on the dock. "Damn it to hell, Carl, is that you?"

Nick and Carl stood rooted to the dock, gazes riveted on the menacing presence coming toward them. Short and squat and churning like a Sherman tank, Brody came closer. Nick grasped Carl's upper arm and leaned in to him. "There, you see, Carl? I think your dad's glad to see you."

"Yeah. I expect him to put on a party hat any minute."

Carl's shoulders sagged as he faced the approaching figure. "Yes, Dad, it's me."

Brody stopped within a few feet of his son and planted his fists on his hips. "What the hell are you doing here?"

Nick stepped between the two men. "I called Junior, Brody, so if you've got the urge to kill somebody, it'll have to be me." For a minute Nick thought he might.

"Why would you do something so—"

"Lay off Nick, Dad," Junior said. "Yes, he called me, but I agreed with him that it was about time I came. I've known about this place for years."

Brody's eyes became narrow slits. "So Nick told you where I was?"

"Not just Nick," Junior said. "Vernon Russell at the bank told me, too. I kept the information just in case you ever wanted to see me. And then Nick said you'd had a change of heart, so I came."

Brody uttered a few indecipherable mutters.

"I was wrong," Nick said. "Your father's heart can't change, unless it's just to grow blacker."

Brody directed his anger at Nick. "If my heart's black, it's turncoats like you that made it that way." Jerking his thumb at Carl, he added, "And a greedy son who never amounted to a hill of beans and only saw his father as a dollar sign he could tap in to whenever he needed a few thousand."

Carl shoved at Brody's shoulder, forcing his father to face him. "You pulled that dollar sign out from under me quick enough, *Dad*. And I guess I should thank you, though it's hard to get past the resentment to say the words. But I sure as hell don't need your money now."

Brody sneered. "You marry rich, Carl?"

"No, sir. I married right."

Sara advanced down the dock. Nick waved her back, trying to spare her the unpleasantness, but she walked right into the fray. "All right," she said with forced cheerfulness. "I see this is going well. You're talking."

Here she goes with that talking-is-the-cure-for-everything baloney.

"Why don't we all go up to the inn and have some iced tea?" she said. "Winkie, you come, too. And Dad."

Winkie and Ben had been watching from a safe distance, but at Sara's urging they joined the group. Most everyone meandered down the dock toward shore. Most, but not all. Brody planted his feet and glared at Sara. "This is all *your* fault, you know," he said, shaking his finger at her nose.

"Yes, I do know that," she said sweetly. "That's why I offered to make the iced tea."

Moments passed while Sara and Brody remained locked in a staring contest. Nick waited and watched, not knowing which one he'd put a dollar on if he could find someone to bet with. It was Brody who finally caved in. He pounded a fist into his palm, turned on his heel and clomped away from her. "Damn it to hell," he said, and followed the others toward the inn.

Sara walked behind him, passed Nick and said with a beatific smile, "I love family reunions."

Nick caught up and fell into step beside her. "I guess we're going to live through round one. Now we just have to see how Dexter does tomorrow."

Because Nick and Sara hadn't talked since the meeting in the press house, she hadn't heard the result of Nick's call to the Cleveland Browns organization. "Someone else is coming?" she asked.

"Yeah, someone's coming all right. Two some-ones. The owner and the manager. When I mentioned Dexter Sweet's name, you'd have thought I'd brought Vince Lombardi back from the dead."

Sara giggled like a kid who'd just gotten her wildest birthday wish granted. "They're going to offer him a position. I just know it."

"I'd say that's pretty obvious," Nick grumbled. "Things are changing, Sara, whether I want them to or not. Ryan's been walking around gaga-eyed ever since that dizzy assistant of yours showed up. And now we might be turning Brody into a creature resembling a human being.''

Sara gave him a sly smile. "Just don't blame it all on me, Nick. I wasn't the one who called Carl Junior."

"Only because you didn't know he existed."

She touched his arm, a gesture that seemed to make all his problems disappear into the minuscule compartments where they belonged. Except for his biggest problem of all—Sara was leaving in two days. That one weighed him down like a pair of cement galoshes.

She walked ahead of him up the steps of the Cozy Cove veranda. "It's a test, Nick," she said over her shoulder. "To see if you can rejoice in someone else's happiness. I think you're up to the challenge."

Nick wasn't sure. He watched her go into the hotel to brew the tea she'd promised to serve at the Brody peace talks. There was no denying there was a lot of fierce determination in her. The woman who swore from day one that she wasn't going to change anything had succeeded in changing just about everything.

But it wasn't Sara's iced tea that produced the peace between Brody and Junior. It was Nick's mediating skills—and a bottle of Kentucky bourbon. By Sunday night Carl had admitted that at one time in his life, he'd been an irresponsible son who'd expected his father to pay for his mistakes. And Brody had confessed that his military and corporate background might have made him a judgmental parent who never tried to understand his only son.

The two men still had a long journey toward forgiveness and acceptance, but when Carl agreed to stay over Sunday night in the Cozy Cove, Nick knew they'd at least made the first steps. And he was more confident of a permanent reconciliation Monday morning when Brody canceled Digging Day so he could take Junior fishing.

Yes, things were changing on Thorne. So did Nick wish Sara Crawford had never come to the island? Did he wish he'd never seen the first strand of silky hair blow across her cheek, or heard the first moan of sexual satisfaction from her pink mouth, or felt the first tremors of passionate anticipation in the parts of her body he'd come to know so well?

Despite feeling absolutely miserable, Nick knew the answer without even thinking about it.

Hell, no.

THE MANAGER of the Cleveland Browns called Sara on her cell phone Monday afternoon as she waited for the building-code inspectors to finish their tour of the Cozy Cove, which had been going on for three hours. Winkie had dropped off the inspectors, picked up Ben, Candy and Carl Junior, and headed back to Put-in-Bay.

"Yes, sir," Sara said into her phone. "I certainly do know what this call is about."

"We're on our way now to meet up with that boat captain you told us would bring us to the island. I assume Dexter is there."

Yes, yes! He's been here for years waiting for you. Where else would he be today? "He's here. We'll see you soon."

She ended the call and hurried to the other end of the hall to tell Nick.

He turned off his computer, stood up and took a

deep breath. "Operation Dexter is under way," he said.

She crossed her fingers for good luck and watched him head toward the stairs. When he'd left the inn, she let the forced smile fade from her lips. "Oh, Dad," she said to herself. "If only things were as simple as you make them sound."

Her last conversation with her father kept replaying in her mind. "I don't know, Sarabelle," he'd said that morning in the kitchen. "If I were you, I'd forget all about going back to Florida and I'd set my cap for Nick. He's made of stern stuff, and he's smart, too. I've grown to like that young man while I've been here."

She'd only grinned at him over the rim of her coffee cup. "I'll be sure and let him know how you feel, Dad."

He'd fielded her grin with unexpected seriousness. "You'd do better to let him know how *you* feel."

"There's nothing between us, Dad," she'd lied.

Now, as she closed the door to Nick's room and walked down the hall to pack her bags, she wished she'd told her father the truth. "It wouldn't make any difference," she said to the empty hallway. "I'm out of money, out of time and out of arguments. And there just isn't any elastic left in my heart."

NICK WATCHED a couple of innings of the baseball game to give Winkie time to bring the Browns execs across the lake. When he heard the sputter of the boat engine, he walked to the television and turned off the power. Dexter stared first at Nick's hand, which had just interfered with his Monday afternoon, and then at the blank screen where he'd been watching the top of the seventh at Jacob's Field. "What'd you do that for?"

"Because you're done watching baseball for to-day," Nick said.

Dexter sat up straight and wrapped his big hands around his knees. "Don't tell me Brody has called another meeting?"

"No. I did. Did you hear Winkie's boat?"

"Yeah, but I figured if it was a grocery order, you guys could handle it. The game was on."

"It's not a grocery order. I want you to come with me."

Grumbling, Dexter stood up from his well-worn leather love seat and ambled toward the door.

"Aren't you going to put some shoes on?" Nick asked.

"What kind of a meeting on Thorne Island requires shoes?"

Nick tossed a pair of size-thirteen sneakers at Dex. "This one."

THEY REACHED the side of the inn and stopped when voices floated out to them from an open parlor window. "Maybe you'd better look inside and prepare yourself," Nick suggested. "I have this picture in my head of you putting on the same goofy expression you have when you see a photo of Tyra Banks."

Dexter grinned. "Heck, there's nobody in the world who affects me like she does." He leaned forward and peeked inside. He stared a few seconds and then spun around and slammed his back against the outside wall. "Do you know who those men are?" he managed to gasp.

"I ought to. I invited them. That's the general manager and the owner of the new Cleveland Browns. I thought you'd recognize them from the fan posters on your walls.''

"I don't have any fan posters.''

"It's a joke, Dex.'' Nick rolled his eyes. "Jeez, why doesn't anybody ever get my jokes?''

Dexter pushed himself away from the wall. "What are they doing here?''

"They came to see you, of course.'' When he read the look of total confusion on Dexter's face, he added, "No joke. They came quite readily, I must admit. Even risked a ride on Winkie's tub.''

"Why?''

"I don't know. For the thrill of it.'' Sensing another attempt at a joke had failed, Nick added more seriously, "Look Dex, I don't know what they're going to say to you. But I have a hunch they might be going to make you an offer you can't possibly refuse.''

"You mean they're recruiting losers now?''

Nick wasn't falling for Dexter's sympathy bid. "Apparently. But there's one sure way to find out.''

Nick half pushed, half pulled Dexter to the front door of the Cozy Cove. But once the big man stepped into the parlor, an immediate display of manly rituals took over and confidence bloomed in every feature of his face.

The general manager, who'd worked with Dexter during his playing days, punched Dex on the shoulder, though it looked like it was all he could do not to hug his former teammate. "So this is where you've been hiding, you big ox,'' the man said.

The owner of the new Cleveland Browns faked a punch to Dexter's abdomen. "It's about time we tracked you down, Sweet. You've been harder to find than a pigskin in a pen of hogs.''

Virtually ignored in a room filled with scrapbook reminiscences and fiercely pumping testosterone, Nick backed into the lobby. ''Good luck, old buddy,'' he whispered. He headed for the stairs and the comfort of his keyboard. God, he needed Sara right now. Part of him resented the hell out of her since she was responsible for all the changes on Thorne Island. But the part of him that he'd nearly forgotten about, the part that had helped an old lady who was being cheated out of her retirement by a big corporation— that part realized the men of Thorne Island owed Sara a debt of gratitude.

But of course the biggest part of him, the chunk that missed Sara almost every minute of the day, involved the crazy interaction of every nerve, every sense, every emotion he'd kept buried for more than six years. That part just wanted to hold her and feel her next to him and believe that she wasn't going away.

He stopped at the entrance to a guest room at the top of the stairs. Before Sara arrived, all the doors to the rooms on the second floor were kept closed. There was no reason to ever look inside any of them. Now the doors were open, beckoning a visitor to enjoy the cheerful atmosphere of polished wood furniture, yellow and blue walls, bright fabrics and slowly turning brass ceiling fans.

Nick entered the room and crossed to the window. The freshly painted white shutters were open, the dainty floral curtains tied back with velvet cord. Sara liked the windows that way, open to let in the sunshine. He looked over the vineyard and spotted her strolling among the grapevines.

Giving them a last, loving dose of Sara-care, he figured. Baby-talking them into warming up to Ryan, coaxing them to thrive in spite of her absence. In a little over twenty-four hours she would be gone. Unless he did something to stop her.

Every time Nick walked across the yard or climbed the stairs, he was reminded of the hardest battle he'd ever fought in his life, the prize he'd figured was the most worth winning of any that would ever come his way—the ability to walk again. Now he wasn't so sure. Now he figured keeping Sara on Thorne Island was the prize he'd been born to win.

CHAPTER TWENTY

NICK ACCEPTED Brody's offer to split a frozen pizza and once again discovered that Brody wasn't much of a cook. The man didn't even wait for the cheese to melt on top of the pizza before taking it out of the oven. He wasn't much of a gourmet, either. He gobbled down the lukewarm pie and declared it fit for a king. But that was Brody—the new and improved, slightly more optimistic Brody. And since Nick didn't feel much like eating anyway, the state of the pizza didn't really matter.

There were two reasons for Brody's emerging good humor. He had opened the door to communication with his son, and despite a softening of his attitude toward Sara, he would soon be saying farewell to the woman who'd upset his life. Never mind that if Sara Crawford hadn't shown up on Thorne Island, Junior probably wouldn't have come either.

Ironically Brody's good fortune was Nick's reason for despair.

At dusk Nick left Brody's and walked around the back of the inn, thinking he might find Sara in the kitchen. He didn't, but the porch light was on, prompting him to go toward the vineyard. He saw her next to the press house at the point where rows of thick, twisting trunks began their orderly march up and down the gentle slopes of Thorne Island. She was a silvery statue in the last gray light of day. Nick walked toward her with the clearest of intentions, but with a dubious arsenal of words to accomplish it.

Sara stood with her arms folded across her chest. She didn't hear Nick approach, or if she did, she didn't respond.

Nick thought about calling her name, but decided against it. If he was going to sneak up on her one last time, he would risk her anger to satisfy his desire to feel the softness of her skin first. Stepping behind her, he slid his hands along her arms and clasped her fingers with his. She breathed a contented sigh and leaned against him. It was not the reaction he'd expected, but it was the one he relished.

Encouraged, he pulled her close to his chest and studied her profile. "Is that a smile I see? And should I hope you were thinking about me?"

She dropped her head back to his shoulder. "It was a smile," she said, "but it wasn't for you. The Cozy Cove passed all inspections today. We need another bathroom, but the inspector said he'd let it slide for a while under the grandfather rule."

"Congratulations, Madam Innkeeper. You should be proud of yourself."

"I'm proud of all of us," she said.

"So when can we expect our first visitors?"

"Since I hear that note of dread in your voice, I know the answer will make you happy. Not until after the grapes ripen. About four months, I think. Plus, I need to find someone to handle guest relations—someone civil, accommodating and perhaps even cheerful."

He repeated the qualifications with exaggerated

thoughtfulness. "Civil, accommodating and cheerful. I'll need a dictionary to understand those words."

She chuckled softly. "And to think you once accused me of changing things around here. There's the proof that I haven't accomplished much as far as you're concerned."

He turned her in his arms. "Here's the proof that you have." He captured her mouth in a slow, building kiss.

She melted against him and breathed her own life into the joining of their mouths. Until she realized it was not what they should be doing. She flattened her palms on his chest and pushed him away. "No, Nick. We can't do this."

"I think we do it better than any two people on the planet."

She frowned. "And you don't see that as a problem?"

He tucked a strand of hair behind her ear. "No. I see it as a gift."

She stepped away from him and faced the vineyard again. "Unfortunately I can't take any gifts with me when I leave tomorrow."

"There you go, Crawford. Spoiling the moment." He reached for her hand and twined her fingers through his. "Let's take a walk and look at these miraculous grapes of yours."

She fell into step beside him even though she argued that it would be dark soon. "We won't see much of anything."

"That's all right. I don't really care about looking at grapes, anyway. I just suggested it because when you're in the vineyard, you tend to forget how ticked off you are at me."

They moved down one row of vines as rays of the golden-rose dusk spilled over broad grape leaves and trunk spurs supported by Sara's carefully mended guide wires. Somewhere, tucked into their protective leafy houses, Sara's grapes grew, coaxed by her gentle touch and unflagging determination.

"So what are we going to do about this problem we have?" Nick finally said.

SARA PRESSED her fingers against her lips to hold in a groan of frustration. What answers was he looking for? What solution could there be for a man who wouldn't leave and a woman who couldn't stay? There wasn't one. Time had run out for her and Nick.

She disentangled her hand from his and stared up at him. His eyes, the color of cinders, were unreadable. Did he feel some of the hurt she experienced? "There's no problem, Nick. I stopped thinking of you that way in the press house on Friday," she said.

"Oh, no," he countered. "You can't dismiss me so easily."

She started walking.

He followed. "A minute ago you kissed me as if I *was* a problem."

"Not a problem. A mistake. One I was bidding a long-overdue farewell."

He stepped in front of her and flattened his hand against his chest. "That hurts, Sara. Really hurts."

His little-boy innocence wasn't going to work this time. "Look, Nick, what exactly do you want from me? For that matter, what do any of you want from me? I'm leaving. You'll have your precious island all to yourselves again. As I see it, you've only benefited from my being here. Brody's talking to his son. Dexter's going to join the Browns organization. Ryan's in love. And that's not even taking into account that you men no longer live in squalor!''

Nick's eyes widened in a reasonable imitation of shock. ''Squalor? Just because we didn't live with tablecloths and throw rugs doesn't mean we lived in squalor.''

''Whatever.'' She tried to walk around him, but he prevented her from getting away.

''And what about me?'' he challenged. ''Sure, all those good things have happened for the other guys, but once you go away, what will I be left with?''

''Status quo, Nick. What you've always wanted. Total and complete noninterference.''

He grabbed her arms, locking her in front of him. ''That's not what I want anymore. Now I want you to interfere. Any time you want.''

Sara closed her eyes, blocking out the familiar gleam in his eyes. When she opened them again, she met his gaze head-on. ''For how long, Nick?''

''What?''

''How long do you want me to interfere with your life? Another week? A month or two? How long?''

This time the shock in his eyes was real. ''I...I don't know. I want you to stay here for as long as you want to. Who's marking time on a calendar, anyway?''

''I am. And I'm already days behind schedule.''

''Oh, that's right. You're the bean counter, and I'm hearing accountant-speak again.''

''No. Reality-speak.'' She wrenched herself free of his hold and glared at him. ''You want me to stay?'' The words came out as a dare.

''Yes, I want you to stay.''

"Well, guess what, Nick? I'm broke. And if I don't get my tail back to Fort Lauderdale, I'll be jobless, too."

He flung a hand in the general direction of the inn. "At least you won't be homeless."

Frustrated rage boiled through Sara's bloodstream. Was he totally oblivious to her anger and hurt? Didn't he understand the futility of their situation? Maybe he did because he backed up a step. Knowing that more words would only lead to more argument and ultimately no solution, Sara executed a quick little jig and maneuvered around him. "Good night, Nick."

He caught her arm and spun her back around. The blistering fire in the look she leveled on him should have made him let go. It didn't.

"Oh, no, you don't," he said. "We're going to talk this thing out. You're not going to run."

Unfortunately for him, his command only fanned her smoldering anger and sent it sizzling to every cell in her body. "Run?" she snapped back. "You want to talk about running? Fine. You want to be with me so badly, Nick, why don't you come to Fort Lauderdale? You want me to admit I care about you? Okay, I will. I care. Now if *you* care, get on that plane tomorrow and come with me."

The vein at his temple throbbed. Obviously he was working up a good anger of his own. Undaunted, Sara poked him in the chest. "I'm not the one running, Nick. You are! Isn't it about time you realized that no one's chasing you? You've been running from the world more than six years now. Don't you think it's time you came back into it?"

His jaw muscles clenched. His breathing was raspy.

He was truly, completely furious. "I don't have to prove anything to you," he ground out.

"No, that's right, you don't have to prove anything to me. You don't have to sell your manuscripts. You can hide behind the mask of Ivan Banning forever, since he's the man you don't have the courage to be. You don't have to leave this island ever, unless it's in a pine box. But I can't stay here warming your bed and soothing your ego. I've got to go, Nick."

Her words had a physical effect. If ever a man looked beaten, Nick did, and she hadn't so much as swung a punch. The vanquished look on his face was nearly Sara's undoing. Her eyes stung with tears. She did so love this man.

She clamped her lips together, forcing back a sob. And she waited. *Say something, Nick. By God, if you care at all, say something.* He merely stared at her with wounded eyes. She turned away from him and said, "And God knows, if I'm leaving, it's got to be tomorrow."

TUESDAY MORNING while Sara had her coffee in the sparkling kitchen of the Cozy Cove Inn, Ryan came in the back door. "The grapes are looking fine this morning," he said.

"That's great, Ryan. I know you'll take care of them." She slid her cell phone across the table toward him. "I'm leaving this so you can call me whenever you want. Let me know when you think the grapes are ready to harvest."

He picked up the phone and dropped it into his shirt pocket. "I will." Then he grinned. "Is it okay if I use it to call Candy sometimes?"

"Sure. I expected you would."

He sat across from her at the table covered in its cheerful, blue floral cloth. "Will you come back for the harvest, Sara?"

She wouldn't. "I don't know," she said. "Maybe. If not, you can keep me informed every step of the way."

"Sure thing."

The sound of someone clearing his throat drew their attention to the back door. Brody peered through the screen like a kid waiting for an invitation. "Can I come in?"

Sara waved him inside. "Did you come to make sure my bags were all packed?" Even though she said it with a smile, she suspected it was true.

He grunted. It almost sounded like a chuckle. "I can see where you might think that. But no. I came to say goodbye. And to tell you that there might have been a time or two when I let my manners slip where you're concerned."

Sara rolled her eyes at the ceiling. "Oh, gee, let me think if I can remember you doing that."

"It's not that I didn't like you. It's just that this has always been our place—"

Sara pushed back her chair and stood up. "Do you want some coffee, Brody?"

"I could drink a cup."

After she handed him a steaming mug, she said, "Look, Brody, I'm leaving today. We don't need to rehash all the reasons our relationship wasn't made in heaven. We both know them all, anyway."

He took a sip. "S'pose so. My son pointed out that I can be difficult. I just wanted to tell you that I'll try to be a little friendlier when you start renting out the rooms here, or at least make myself scarce. Besides,

I plan on leaving here once in a while to check up on Carl and see if that woman he married is really as wonderful as he says.''

Sara felt a stab of pity for the extraordinary Mrs. Carl Brody Junior. ''I'm sure you'll like her,'' she said. ''Just as much as she'll like you.''

He set the cup down on the counter, half-empty. ''Well, I've said what I've come to say. Good luck to you, Miss Crawford. And by the way, you did a good job with this place.''

''Thanks.''

WINKIE ARRIVED at noon in the pontoon boat to take Sara and the beetle to the mainland ferry. At the sound of his engine, Sara grabbed her bags and left her room. She glanced at the door at the other end of the hall. It was closed. She didn't hear any sound coming from the other side. She descended the stairs, left the inn and loaded her suitcases into the Volkswagen.

As she drove away from the Cozy Cove, Sara looked in the rearview mirror to get a last glimpse of the inn. It was even more charming than she'd believed possible when she'd begun her renovations. She'd put more of herself into this project than anything she'd ever done in her life, and she was proud of the results.

She envisioned the Cozy Cove as it would look in the different seasons. In a couple of weeks the trees would have their full dressing of leaves and would drape the house in cooling shade. The wildflowers in back would be a riot of color, and the tulips Ryan had planted by the front porch would sway in the summer breeze.

In the fall the house would be framed in gold and russet. The pathway to the harbor would be carpeted in crisp, fallen leaves by October. Sara could almost hear their cheerful crackle underfoot.

But it was winter she could picture most clearly. Living in Florida, she missed the clean, white flakes of snow that covered everything. With smoke curling from her chimneys and warm lights coming from the parlor, the Cozy Cove would surely be the perfect image of its name.

Maybe Sara would come back in winter. Maybe by then she'd be able to.

Besides Winkie, one man waited at the dock for her. It wasn't Nick.

Dexter attached the ramps to the pontoon boat and helped guide Sara as she drove the bee onto the deck. When they finished, he climbed on board and gave her an awkward hug. "You promise you'll watch the games, Sara? If you have to buy a special pass for your satellite dish so you can get the Browns games, I'll pay for it."

"You won't have to, Dex. I'll want to see every game, and I'll be looking for you on the sidelines with the other coaches."

Winkie revved the engine. "Let's get moving, Sara, or you'll miss your plane."

Dexter jumped onto the dock and pushed the cumbersome boat into the blue-green water of Lake Erie. Winkie adjusted the throttle and turned the chugging craft around to face Put-in-Bay. Sara walked to the stern and held on to the railing. She searched the shoreline for the one person who hadn't said goodbye. Nick was nowhere in sight. Maybe it was better this way. There was nothing more they could say to each other, no way to bring their different worlds together. But still, she wished she'd see him just one more time.

She blinked hard to prevent a flow of tears. "Stop it, Sara. You're going home," she said to herself. "You have to do this. You couldn't go on forever living like Goldilocks with four grumpy bears. You have to go back where you belong. And financially you have no choice."

But all the logic and rational thinking in the world couldn't convince her. As she watched the newly patched roof of the Cozy Cove disappear among the tops of the trees, she realized she wasn't going home at all. She was leaving it.

CHAPTER TWENTY-ONE

SARA ENTERED the reception area of her office and breathed a sigh of relief. Emily Marshall wasn't at her desk so Sara wouldn't have to deal with her new assistant's flawless attention to detail. In the two months since Emily had taken Candy's place, Sara hadn't once caught the middle-aged dynamo in a mistake. She also hadn't seen the woman smile.

It wasn't like Emily to miss Sara's arrival in the mornings. What if something had happened to her? Sara's fears were put to rest when she entered her office. Coffee simmered in the spotless glass pot. Lethally sharp pencils sat in a perfect row on her blotter. Her computer screen displayed appointments for September sixth with irritating clarity. Emily was fine.

Just then—ignoring Sara's repeated requests to enter without knocking—Emily rapped sharply three times before squeezing through the narrow space left by her stingy opening of the door. "I'm sorry I wasn't here when you came in, Miss Crawford," she said. "I try to schedule my trips to the ladies' room at times when you have least need of my services." She blushed under her pale makeup. "Unfortunately Mother Nature had her own agenda this morning."

"It's quite all right, Emily," Sara said, wondering just how Mother Nature toyed with a woman whose demeanor and personal time clock hadn't altered in any noticeable way since Sara had met her.

"I hope the coffee is to your liking," the woman said. "I thought it was strong yesterday, so I adjusted the numerical setting to four instead of five."

No, please, Sara thought. I need at least an eight! Forcing a smile, she said, "How does the schedule look for today?"

Emily clucked her disapproval. "You know how people are. It's September, and quarter three paperwork is due. I'm sure we'll have some Johnny-come-latelies today with last minute questions."

Sara rubbed her forehead in anticipation of the headache she'd have by five o'clock.

Emily set a cup of coffee on Sara's desk. "I have the hard copy list of your morning clients. We should be able to meet with all of them by lunch if we keep our noses to the grindstone."

Sara pinched the bridge of her nose to offset the headache she'd just gotten and thought of Candy who probably didn't even know what a grindstone was. She, along with her menagerie of pets, now lived on Thorne Island with Eliot Ryan in his cottage near the north shore paper birches. Candy had agreed to be manager of the Cozy Cove Inn. The first visitors would arrive in a week.

Emily left the office, and Sara rotated her chair so she could see out the window. All that met her gaze was a smattering of clouds reflected in the glass facades of even taller buildings than the one that housed Bosch and Lindstrom. There wasn't a real tree or bird in sight. And the ocean, while only a mile away, was hidden by the monoliths of Fort Lauderdale's downtown banking complex.

Sara was happy for Candy, and she reminded herself of that even as she longed to see Ryan's hanging baskets and the sloping terrain of the vineyard. She was happy that Candy had found the one man who could appreciate her idiosyncracies and help manage her chaotic life. Sara's mind wandered, as it often did, to the man who, for almost four weeks, had identified the holes in her life and unintentionally and unexpectedly filled them. But Sara's story lacked the happy ending because he was also a man whose own life was apparently complete without Sara in it.

And today the holes were bigger than ever. She missed it all—the inn, the vineyard, the men...the man. She especially missed that other Sara Crawford who'd inherited an island and discovered her soul. She missed them with a deep-down ache she was beginning to believe would never go away. Now there were only debits and credits and balances on paper, which left Sara feeling that her life was desperately, incurably out of balance.

Another tap on the door interrupted Sara's thoughts. "Come in, Emily," she called.

The assistant poked her head into the office. "I'm so sorry, Miss Crawford, but there is the strangest man outside. He's *Eye*-talian if you know what I mean, and he insists on seeing you."

Italian? Sara's heart leaped. It couldn't be. Not when she was just thinking of him. Miraculous coincidences didn't happen to logical women like her. Happiness just didn't drop out of the sky for sensible women. Still, stubborn hope flickered inside her. "Did you say Italian, Emily?"

"Yes." She stuck her arm inside as if trying to keep the appendage as far from her face as possible.

Her fingers curled around the top of a brown paper bag with grease stains on the bottom. "He says his records are in here. And he's carrying a pizza, which he says is for you."

Disappointment heavy as a stone sat in the pit of Sara's stomach. "It's all right, Emily. That's just Mr. Papalardo. Show him in."

An anchovy pizza was the last thing Sara wanted at nine o'clock in the morning, but Mr. Papalardo dropped it on her desk with a flourish. "For you, Miss Sara," he said. "'Cause I know my records, they are not what you like to see."

She smiled at him, genuinely pleased to see his mustachioed grin. He was a cheerful, if annoying, reminder of that other life, the one that had satisfied her before she'd known she could be much happier in another place. "Don't worry about it, Mr. Papalardo. I'll straighten it all out."

"I know you will. You are a smart lady."

If I'm so smart, then why am I so miserable?

Pointing to the steaming box on her desk, he added, "And I know you like anchovies."

Sara waited for Mr. Papalardo to leave her office before moving the pizza to the top of a file cabinet. She dumped his records on her desk. In thirty minutes she had the papers sorted into manageable piles. Later she'd call Candy to tell her their favorite client had come in. And to ask after the grapes, and the inn, and Dexter's new job with the Cleveland Browns, and Brody's son, Carl.

She never asked about Nick, but when Candy mentioned him, Sara drank in the information as if it were the sustenance that kept her alive. Nick was still tapping away at his computer, digging with Brody on

Mondays and fishing. Although some days he did putter around the press house. And he'd gotten his own
cell phone and used it on occasion. Some days he
even asked about her.

While Sara prepared for her first scheduled appointment, Emily Marshall fielded phone calls and elimi-
nated interruptions. After two hours Sara longed for
a diversion. She even admitted to an unexpected surge
of relief when there was a knock at her door. "Come
in."

This time her assistant insinuated a mere three-
quarters of her slim body through the opening. "I'm
sorry to intrude, Miss Crawford, but this seems to be
our morning for strange visitors."

Sara sighed. "Who is it now?"

"There's a man outside who insists on seeing you.
He's even more overbearing than Mr. Papalardo. He's
in quite a state and won't take no for an answer. He
says he hasn't filed personal income tax for years, and
he needs a good tax accountant to keep him out of
prison."

Emily pinched her lips together before adding in a
coarse whisper, "He used the word *prison.*"

This change-of-pace problem might be an interesting diversion. "Tell him I'll see him tomorrow and
give him an appointment for the afternoon," Sara
said.

Emily Marshall grew more agitated. She tugged at
the silk bow on her blouse. "I don't think that will
satisfy him," she said. "He's quite demanding.
Frankly, he frightens me."

Despite the fact that almost all men frightened her
assistant, Sara had heard enough. She picked up the
phone to call security. She had only punched in two

of the four digits when Emily was propelled the rest of the way into the office. Sara stopped dialing and put the phone back on the receiver.

Precariously balanced on Emily's left hand was a silver platter. "Now the man insists I show you this."

Sara held on to the edge of her desk and stood. Disbelief made her dizzy, while hope made her heart race. She approached the shining platter and blinked hard to bring the familiar objects into clear focus. There, surrounded by a band of sparkling silver, lay a cluster of plump, oval, magnificent green grapes.

Sara reached out and grasped one between her thumb and forefinger. It was cool and firm and separated from its tiny twig with a succulent snap. She held it up in front of her eyes and covered her mouth with trembling fingers. Still, a gasp of profound awe escaped her lips and filled the office. It was followed by a spurt of joyous laughter. "They're mine, Emily! These grapes are mine!"

"What nonsense…"

Sara popped the grape into her mouth and bit down. "Wonderful," she said around the sweet, sloppy juice teasing her tastebuds. She grabbed her assistant's arms, ignoring the look of terror on the woman's face. "Where is he? The man who brought these—where is he?"

"He's crazy," Emily proclaimed. "Another crazy *Eye*-talian."

The door opened all the way, revealing Nick leaning against the frame, his arms crossed over his chest. "That's just great," he said. "This woman's only known me ten minutes, and she's already got me pegged."

Sara's heart seemed to stop beating altogether before returning with a vengeance to hammer against her ribs. Not taking her eyes off Nick, she absently removed the platter from her assistant's hand and set it on the desk. Emily scurried toward the door and flattened herself against the frame—to avoid contact with Nick—while she made her escape.

He came all the way into the office and closed the door. "You busy?"

Giddiness left Sara weak and exhilarated at the same time. Nick looked spectacular. Tall, strong, ruddy with Thorne Island sunshine. No one had a right to look that good. He brushed his hair off his forehead, for a moment appearing almost shy.

"She's right, you know," Sara said. "You are crazy."

He nodded. "But I'm getting better. Some people need help from a good therapist. I just need a sexy accountant."

Sara flattened her hand against her stomach, trying to quell the trembling radiating from there to all her extremities. If it reached her knees, she knew she'd buckle. "Do you know where to find one?" she asked.

He stepped closer. "Oh, I've found one, if she'll just give me an appointment. I'm not sure I deserve it, but I'm hoping she'll take pity on me."

Sara's gaze dropped from the dusky pewter of Nick's eyes to his chest, where a three-inch band of colorful fish swam all the way around the light blue background of his shirt. "Where did you get that?" she asked.

"At the Fort Lauderdale airport. As long as I'm in Florida, I should look like a Floridian."

"I don't know about that," she said, suppressing

her laughter. "But it does make me take pity on you."

He put his arms around her and pulled her flat against the fish. "Good. I'll take your pity and any other emotion you care to throw in."

"How long do you plan to stay?"

"Well, that depends on you."

"Really?"

She raised her face to accept his kiss. He slipped his finger under her chin and lowered his mouth. The kiss started slowly, a plea to forget the mistakes of the past. Sara answered with a building passion that soon fired the kiss into a hard, hungry demand to make up for lost time.

When it ended, she drew back and looked into familiar eyes that mirrored her own happiness. "Was it hard, Nick?" she asked. "Was it hard for you to leave the island and come here?"

"Every damn thing I've done in the last four months has been hard, Sara. Some of them even impossible—like trying to get you out of my mind. Only, right now none of them seems as impossible as trying to keep my hands off you and remembering this is a place of business." He slipped his hand under her suit jacket and massaged her back over her blouse. "God, I've missed you."

She nestled her cheek against his neck. "You don't know how many times I've wanted to tell Candy to give you the phone just so I could hear your voice."

He kissed the top of her head. "We could have worked this out," he said. "The more I thought about it, the more I realized that one of us was just too stubborn to give an inch."

Sara threaded her fingers into the hair covering

Nick's collar. The coarse, dark curls twined around her nails. The style was different. Longer. Maybe he hadn't even seen Gina since she'd been gone. "I agree with you," she said, "only don't tell me which one of us you think was the stubborn one. I don't want to spoil this moment."

He laughed softly in her ear. The rich, throaty sound hummed through every part of her, confirming that even the sound of his laughter fired her passion for him. She pulled his head down and met his mouth for another shattering kiss. "We've got to make this work, Romano," she said. "Come floods or pestilence or bankruptcy…"

"Not bankruptcy," he announced. "Money's not a problem."

She stepped away from him and smiled at his typically cocky expression. "I accused you once of robbing banks. Have you taken up the profession for real?"

"No, nothing like that."

She studied his features more closely and realized he was being perfectly serious. He truly wasn't worried about money. And then it hit her. "Don't tell me you found the missionary's treaure."

"Well, yes, I did, but…"

Grasping his hand, Sara exclaimed, "Where was it?"

"I was working with Ryan in the fermenting room to get things ready for the grape harvest, and behind a crumbling section of the limestone wall, I discovered a leather pouch with Father Bertrand's initials." He chuckled. "Funny, after all the Digging Days I suffered through, I find out the coins weren't buried at all." He reached into his pants pocket, pulled out a gold medallion and handed it to Sara. "Here's a souvenir. Unfortunately someone got to the pouch before I did. There were only a few coins left.''

She studied the faded likeness of a human face surrounded by a wreath of flowers. ''Did you tell Brody you found it?''

''No. I got him down in the cellar on false pretenses and let him discover the pouch himself. After all, the treasure hunt was his idea from the beginning.''

Sara pictured Brody's excitement. ''What did he do? Immediately transfer the coins to his safety deposit box?''

Nick smiled. ''Actually, he didn't. He put the pouch back behind the wall and let Carl Junior find it when he came for his first official Digging Day.''

''Oh, wow. How unselfish of him.'' Sara rubbed her thumb over the coin. ''Fatherhood has given Brody a new heart.''

''Something like that, I guess.''

Sara put the coin on her desk. ''So, if there wasn't a great fortune, what did you mean when you said money wasn't a problem? It is for me. I'm still paying off my Home Depot charges.''

He peered over her shoulder at the tray of grapes. ''Didn't you notice what the grapes were lying on?''

''The platter?''

''No. The paper.''

Sara stared down at the tray. With care, she slid a leaflet of papers from under the fruit and held it up with both hands.

''Oh, my God, Nick!'' She spun around to face him. ''It's a publishing contract!''

He grinned broadly. ''A three-book deal. You might want to look at page two, at the part about the advance. I know it starts with a one, but there are a few zeros following it.''

The room spun, and the weakness that had been threatening Sara's knees attacked with alarming ferocity. She leaned against the desk and concentrated on breathing. ''I knew the books were wonderful.'' She let a smile express her awe and the sudden realization that Nick had changed. ''Nick, you're making money.''

A lopsided grin communicated his embarrassment. ''I guess making money's not such a terrible thing.''

She looked at the contract again. ''And you're using your real name.''

''Yeah, but just so you don't start commending me on my bravery, I should tell you that I checked up on the Golden Isles boys. They're likely to remain locked up for quite some time. And since I'm using my real name, I've agreed to write a weekly column for the *Plain Dealer*, too. Looks like I'll be going into Cleveland every week or so.'' A wickedly innocent smile curled his lips. ''Which brings me to my real reason for coming here today.''

Sara affected a suspicious frown. ''Oh? I thought your real reason was to see me.''

''That, too. But if I'm going to Cleveland, I need a car. I thought maybe you'd let me use yours.''

He dodged the grape she hurled at him. ''My car doesn't go anywhere without me.''

''Then I'll just have to marry you and take you with me. I need a car that much.''

She had raised her hand to fling another grape, but it never left her fingers. Instead, she just stared at the face waiting expectantly for her reaction. After several seconds Nick said, "I guess that wasn't very romantic."

A very unladylike whoop hovered just at the back of Sara's throat. It was all she could do to keep it from erupting in joyous discord from her mouth. "No, it wasn't," she said. "Do better."

He took the grape from her hand and entwined his fingers with hers. "Sara Crawford, would you do me the honor of becoming my wife and making a life with me on Thorne Island? And will you have babies and crush grapes and make wine for our table?"

She started to speak, but he popped the grape into her mouth. "And if you say yes, I promise to abandon my life as a recluse and travel with you wherever you want to go. Our world can be a cozy inn or the four corners of the globe. I only know that my world is with you."

Sara reached for him. He stepped into her arms and held her close. "How many ways are there to say yes?" she whispered.

"Only one matters, sweetheart."

"Yes, yes, yes!"

He gently pulled her arms from around his neck. "Before you get too enthusiastic, I should tell you that what your assistant said is true. I haven't filed income tax in a long time. I really do need a good tax accountant."

Sara rummaged through the papers on her desk. When she found the document she needed, she gave it to Nick. "Consult Chart A, Romano. In this country, if you are under sixty-five, you only need to file if you earned more than $8,800 dollars in one year." She chuckled at the light that came on in his eyes. "I may not know everything about you, darling, but I could swear on the steps of the Treasury building that you fit the parameters of an IRS exemption from filing responsibilities. But thanks to your publishing windfall, you are indeed now a computer entry.''

He grinned down at her. ''God, Sara, I love it when you talk dirty.'' He'd just crushed his lips to hers when the office door swung open and Emily Marshall marched in with a security officer behind her.

''Good heavens!'' the woman exclaimed.

Ending the kiss, but still holding Sara close, Nick whispered in her ear, ''Jeez, Sara, doesn't that woman know how to knock?''

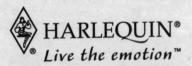

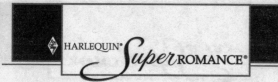

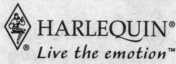

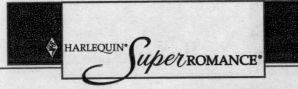

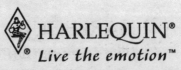

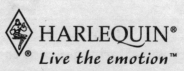

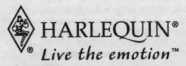